The epic *Harbinger of Blood, Fire, and Thorn* in the series.

When the black elf king comes calling,
Hide your children and your gold,
When dead men hunger, outside, the bitter
cold,
When trolls venture down from mountain
peak,
Hold tightly your bones, for them they seek.
Beware they who thirst on island bleak,
The Regent to come and scourge your keep,
The Black Hand will stalk you, their ranks
ever deep,
And Thetan will be there, of his wrath you
will weep,
The Harbinger of Doom, your soul to reap.

BOOKS BY GLENN G. THATER

THE HARBINGER OF DOOM SAGA
GATEWAY TO NIFLEHEIM
THE FALLEN ANGLE
KNIGHT ETERNAL
DWELLERS OF THE DEEP
BLOOD, FIRE, AND THORN
GODS OF THE SWORD
THE SHAMBLING DEAD
MASTER OF THE DEAD
SHADOW OF DOOM
WIZARD'S TOLL
VOLUME 11+ (forthcoming)

HARBINGER OF DOOM
(Combines *Gateway to Nifleheim* and *The Fallen Angle* into a single volume)

THE HERO AND THE FIEND
(A novelette set in the Harbinger of Doom universe)

THE GATEWAY
(A novella length version of *Gateway to Nifleheim*)

THE DEMON KING OF BERGHER
(A short story set in the Harbinger of Doom universe)

To be notified about my new book releases and any special offers or discounts regarding my books, please join my mailing list here: http://eepurl.com/vwubH

GLENN G. THATER

BLOOD

FIRE

AND

THORN

A TALE FROM THE
HARBINGER OF DOOM SAGA

TABLE OF CONTENTS

I
WHAT HAS COME BEFORE

Lomion was never a peaceful country. Not by the choice of the Lomerians, but rather by that of their unruly neighbors, the whims of nature, and the beasts of the wild.

Vast mountain ranges loomed north of Lomion's borders. Large portions of those ranges were so remote, and so inaccessible, that no man knew their ways, or had even seen most of their sights. Inhospitable swamps and bogs of all manners and types dominated the lands to Lomion's east, endless deserts beyond. To the west, lay more mountains and hills, and forests aplenty. To the south, seemingly endless woodland, some of it dark, and much of it dangerous.

Lomion's borderlands were the buffer between civilization and the wild. And nowhere was wilder than the northern marches at the foothills of the Kronar Mountains. In the shadow of the great peaks stood Dor Eotrus, a fortress of great size and sophistication. It guarded not only the borderlands, but also the road that connected the great northern cities of Kern and Lomion City.

For centuries, northern knights, led by the nobles of House Eotrus, held back the wild and all the challenges and horrors that all too often spewed from it. Sometimes their labors were easy, sometimes hard, and at other times, Eotrus blood soaked the ground, towns and villages burned, and the kingdom itself was threatened.

But nothing the Eotrus experienced down through the centuries quite matched what happened one winter in the Vermion Forest, short miles from the great fortress itself. In secret, in the forest's gloomy depths, fanatical wizards of The League of Light (called The Shadow League by their detractors) wrenched open a mystical gateway to another world – a magical passage to the realm of Nifleheim, a paradise to those who worshipped Azathoth and the Nifleheim Lords that called him master, but the very hell of myth and legend to most others. The wizards' purpose, to bring Azathoth, their long-lost god, home to Midgaard – to restore his rule over the world of man.

Opening of that gateway was outside the realm of reason, beyond knowledge and history. It was something unknown, alien, and nigh unfathomable. Yet it was real. It happened. The gateway opened. And beasts of the nether realms came through, or so the Eotrus said. Monsters, they marked them. The stuff of nightmares. And with them came three of their great lords: Lord Gallis Korrgonn, the son of Azathoth; Lord Mortach; and Lord Bhaal.

The Eotrus stood against them. Hard men. Tall, strong northern warriors, born and bred. Veterans of more wars and skirmishes than any armed force in Lomion.

But they were accustomed to battling mortal men and the beasts of the wild lands. They knew not how to fight monsters out of myth and legend. Despite all their skills and boundless courage, what came through the gateway took the lives of Lord Aradon Eotrus, the Patriarch of

8

House Eotrus (father to Claradon, Jude, Ector, and Malcolm); Sir Gabriel Garn, peerless weapons master and true hero; the famed wizard, Par Talbon of Montrose; the legendary ranger, Stern of Doriath Forest, and nearly all those who took to the field with them.

In the end, it fell to a mysterious foreign knight called Angle Theta, a stranger to Lomion, to close the portal before Azathoth could come through. Theta succeeded, and in so doing, banished Bhaal back to Nifleheim, but Korrgonn and Mortach escaped into the world.

In a dark corner of Lomion City, Theta and Mortach met, and dueled to the death, Theta victorious. How a man, however skilled at arms, could defeat a veritable god, none could say. But some said that Theta was no man at all. Some said that he was the legendary and infamous Harbinger of Doom – a creature of pure evil that haunted Midgaard since time immemorial, having been cast out from the heavens for crimes against the gods.

Meanwhile, Korrgonn, aided by the League of Light, and the Sithian Mercenary Company in their employ (and with Jude Eotrus as their captive), boarded a ship called *The White Rose*, and set out for the land of Jutenheim where resided an ancient temple where Korrgonn believed they could open another mystical portal and bring forth their god.

Then began a hunt the like of which Midgaard had rarely seen. Theta, supported by the Eotrus and their allies, set out aboard *The Black Falcon*, their purpose, to stop Korrgonn. To kill him and the cultists with him, and thereby, prevent

Azathoth's return, then and forever.

But Claradon Eotrus and Theta were being hunted too. The ship called *The Gray Talon* stalked their heels. Aboard, Milton DeBoors, a legendary sword master and bounty hunter (employed by Chancellor Barusa of Alder), and a contingent of soldiers from House Alder, the Eotrus's most bitter enemies. Their attacks left Claradon severely wounded and near death.

Along the way south toward Jutenheim, each of the ships' crews suffered terrible casualties, at the hands of each other, from traitors in their midst, from foul weather, waves of supernatural creatures, and monsters of the deep. The weeks and months stretched on as they traversed the vast Azure Sea, moving inexorably toward Jutenheim and a confrontation that would decide the fate of all Midgaard.

II
BLOOD, FIRE, AND THORN

Par Glus Thorn the sorcerer stood tall, broad, and stately at Black Rock Tower's high window. He gazed out and down across the snowy, forested landscape, contemplating esoteric mysteries beyond the ken of the goodly men of Midgaard.

He was clad, as he always was, in a harsh black cassock that brushed the floor, black buttons down the front. No one had ever seen him wear anything else. His face was austere, bespeckled, and haunting, with a pallor near as white as his close-cropped hair, which matched the snow-covered hills. His chiseled features were rugged and lined, though, in their way, strangely ageless.

The window before him stood open to the wintry air, as usual, for it never grew cold in the laboratory, what with any number of braziers ever afire, fueling the endless array of experiments that he and old Lasifer cooked up, not to mention the healthy fire that sputtered and crackled in the big brick hearth in the corner.

Thorn turned back to the equipment: contraptions, geared and wired, spinning and smoking; glass and ceramic vessels of every shape and size, filled to varying levels with liquids of every color — some heating, others chilled with ice. The scent, a strange mixture of soot, sulfur, and exotic oils. Books, small and large, worn, torn, singed or moldy, leather bound and engraved, written on paper, thick or thin, the oldest on skins; scrolls crafted of this exotic material and that, and myriad rolled-up parchments of every conceivable diameter, lined shelves that covered the walls, floor to ceiling, corner to corner – the envy of even the great libraries of the world. The wood floor, stained and splattered and scorched; the ceiling, once whitewashed, now sullied of soot and ash, cobwebs in the high corners.

Par Lasifer, Thorn's ancient, though rather nondescript, gnome apprentice, stood atop a tall stool and carefully poured yellow liquid from a glass jar into a bubbling decanter of brown goo suspended above a hot brazier.

Curious sentinels cloaked in black, with hooded cowls that entirely obscured their faces, stood on either side of the large circular chamber's two doors. Each held a thick wooden staff capped with white bone. Their hands (their only flesh exposed to the room's light) were thin, almost snow-white in color, even paler than Thorn's; their height, modest; their posture somewhat stooped. These were the stowron — they who've dwelt for ages unknown in lightless caverns deep beneath the roots of the Kronar Mountains. Each all but blind, their noses and oversized ears highly sensitive to compensate for their feeble vision.

Lasifer shook his head and scowled as he stirred the contents of a glass jar.

"Another failure?" said Thorn, his deep voice, powerful and imposing despite being marred by a slight lisp.

"I fear so, master," said Lasifer. "The reaction

stopped prematurely. Judging by the speed at which it's congealing, I don't think we can get it to restart: it's ruined."

"Have we tried a larger quantity of phosphorous infused with essence of alambic?" said Thorn.

"I tried several variations of that last night while you slept, master. None had the desired effect."

"Then phosphorous is a dead end too."

"I fear so, master."

"Sulfur, selenium, carbon, salt, chalk, lime, gypsum, and now phosphorous — all failures. We're running out of natural elements."

"And young Eotrus is running out of blood."

"It renews with rest and nourishment, and he's getting plenty of both. Time is our enemy in this, not lack of blood. *The White Rose* grows closer to Jutenheim each day. If we delay, the Harbinger will catch the ship. He may disrupt the ritual. I can't allow that, as this may be our last chance to open a portal to Nifleheim and bring through the lord."

"Indeed, master. We may never find another orb, rare things that they are. Rarer than most anything. Could some base metal hold the key, do you think?"

"Our thoughts drift together, my apprentice. There is iron in blood. There is copper in it too. Mayhap upon metals we should refocus our efforts. We must identify what is unique in the line of kings before we reach the temple or all our efforts may be for naught. One way or another, the secret of the blood of kings must be ours."

A strangely muffled knocking from one of the

doors turned Thorn about, a surprised expression on his face.

"What's this?" he said. "Something must be awry. They would not dare interrupt otherwise."

Lasifer merely grunted in acknowledgment. The stowron reacted not at all.

"Nord," said Thorn to the stowron closest to the door. "See to that."

Nord shambled to the door in the odd, apelike gait characteristic of stowron. He pulled on the door handle, but although the door was not locked, it resisted his efforts, as if it were held fast by some unseen force. After a few moments of effort, the door swung open; a rush of cold air from outside blew through the room and was sucked through the open door. The strange breeze dissipated as quickly as it came. The open door revealed a curious sight; beyond it, no caller stood, and the adjoining space was not a hallway or stair or even another laboratory as one might expect. At first glance, it appeared a tiny, well-decorated chamber, no larger than a generous closet, but on closer inspection it was no normal room at all. It had the size, shape, and accouterments of the inside of a nobleman's coach, richly-appointed with cushioned benches to either side, polished mahogany panels lined the walls, spanned the low ceiling, and finished the floor. On the far side of the coach room was a second door with a large window, shuttered and draped. It was from beyond that door that the knocking originated, though no hail of greeting or other sounds accompanied it.

Nord entered the coach room and closed the door behind him. Thorn remained at the window, waiting, a hint of annoyance on his face. He had no time or patience for unnecessary interruptions. Lasifer continued his fiddlings, mixing, pouring, and stirring the contents of various jars, decanters, and tubes.

After a short time, Nord re-entered the laboratory trailed by one Par Keld of Kirth, a middle-aged wizard, stocky, balding, and nervous. His face was pale and expressionless, but fear seeped from his very pores. "Greetings, Master Thorn. I need of minute of your time."

Thorn stared at the wizard expectantly but offered no reply or courtesy.

Par Keld's mouth opened and closed several times but no more words ventured out.

"Step forward," said Thorn as he pointed to a spot on the floor just in front of where he stood.

Keld walked to the spot, sheepishly, beads of sweat trailing down his forehead. He looked very small as he stood before Thorn, though in truth he was not much shorter than the average volsung.

"You need my time, you say?" said Thorn as he placed a gentle hand on Keld's shoulder, as if to comfort and counterbalance any harshness his words might convey. "No one is permitted to interrupt my experiments."

"My apologies, Master Thorn," said Keld. "I'm keenly aware of that; everyone is. I just need to talk to you. It will be quick."

"You need?" said Thorn raising an eyebrow. "You need?"

Keld looked confused and grew paler by the moment. "It's just that I have information that you must know."

15

Thorn smiled. "Of course you do. You would never have interrupted me otherwise."

"Yes, exactly," said Keld. "You know that I wouldn't. I never have. It's not my way. I'm very respectful; much more so than most of my brethren, not that I'm saying anything against anyone of course."

"Yet interrupt you did, and now you waste more of my time, babbling away, yet unable to spit this essential information from betwixt your lips. That is a violation. One that I will not tolerate." Thorn's comforting hand whipped across Keld's face, slapping him, hard. He turned his palm and slapped him again as he brought his hand back. Keld winced from the blows, shock upon his face. Then Thorn slapped him again, and again – no fewer than eight times before he was done. Through the ordeal, Keld lowered his chin and turned this way and that, though he dared not bring up a hand to block the blows or to defend himself in any way. Tears streamed down his cheeks, now fiery red, and a slight trickle of blood dripped from his nose.

"Now Par Keld," said Thorn in a soft, almost soothing voice, "you will tell me this important information. But I caution you to speak quickly. I've no more time to waste on you."

Keld took a deep breath to compose himself before he spoke. "I don't know how they got on board," he said, his eyes focused on the floor, his breathing heavy and strained, one hand rubbing his cheeks, "but that elf and his golem were on watch. Maybe they got distracted or fell asleep; I don't know. Those two don't seem reliable to me, they never have, but I wasn't there, so I don't know."

"Who got on board?" said Thorn.

"The island was supposed to be deserted. We weren't told to expect anything like this."

Thorn clenched his jaw and his voice grew louder and sterner. He put his hand back on Keld's shoulder; his thumb planted against the base of his throat. "Who got on board?"

Keld hesitated and struggled for words as the pressure against his throat grew and Thorn's eyes bore into him. It wasn't the pain that stopped him, for it was slight, especially compared to that of his cheeks, which still badly stung; it was the fear of what that pain could become. He knew what Thorn was capable of. With that one hand, Thorn had the strength to crush his throat and end his life, or at least, Keld believed so. He shifted from foot to foot; his eyes darted from exit to exit. "I don't know who they are; what they are," said Keld. "If you or Lord Korrgonn had warned us, I would've stood the watch myself. I assure you we would have been ready for this. We—"

"Ready for what?" said Thorn, raising his voice further and clamping down on Keld's throat. "What has happened? Stop your babbling and spit it out or I'll put you right on the floor."

Keld paled at the threat, whatever it meant. "I don't know," he said, gasping. As he spoke, Thorn's grip softened so as not to stifle his words. "I don't know. I don't want to tell you the wrong thing. You should have a look for yourself before it's too late."

Thorn shoved Keld with a slight, almost effortless motion; Keld stumbled back, and fell hard on his rump. Then Thorn moved toward the coach room door with unexpected speed, his face in a sneer. Lasifer followed on his heels, having at some point climbed down from his stool. As was his fashion, Thorn seemed more to glide across the room than walk, for his head didn't bob as he walked, as men's are wont to do. His feet were obscured by his long cassock, which widened toward the ankle, such that no one could say for certain whether he walked as any other man, or moved by some arcane locomotion practiced only by the sorcerers of his esoteric order. He did wear shoes though — large, black, and polished, which were sometimes visible when he sat.

Par Keld pulled himself to his feet and followed after Thorn. Keld lowered his voice to a whisper and spoke in conspiratorial fashion when he caught up to Thorn. "I really don't know what's going on. I'm just doing my job, what I'm supposed to do. That's all. You know that."

Thorn ignored him. A stowron opened the door to the coach room and Thorn looked inside.

"I have no idea, really," said Par Keld as sweat beaded on his brow. "The elf was on watch. I only now just heard. Not wise to trust elves, they're only out for themselves, and that's the truth, widely known. Not like me. They don't see the big picture, the greater good. That's what's wrong with people."

Thorn's voice was deadly sharp. "You had orders to inform me at once if there was any sign of trouble."

Keld looked taken aback. "I — I just did. That's why I'm here, to report everything, as is my duty. I always do my duty, unfailingly. You know that; no one is more loyal than I am. I just don't know anything about what happened; I wasn't there, but Par Oris was, I'm sure. He was on deck; maybe he knows. He ought to know. He's always at his post; very reliable even though he's old and slowing."

"Stowron attend me," said Thorn.

Two stowron moved past Thorn and crouched before the far door of the coach room. Another prepared to enter behind Thorn, Keld, and Lasifer.

"Open it," said Thorn, who then muttered some arcane words so silently that no one heard them.

One of the stowron turned the handle of the coach room's far door. It responded by emitting various clicks, pings, and other strange mechanical sounds. After a few moments, it swung open of its own accord to reveal a noisy, chaotic scene — a scene that but for the ancient magics harnessed and tamed by Thorn's steady hand should not have been there at all. For before them, the way opened into the main hold of the ship called *The White Rose*, far at sea, far from Thorn's tower, far from any land other than a strange island of death and doom where lurked a dark god of the gelid depths named Dagon, and his murderous children, the dwellers of the deep.

The central storage hold thronged with seamen and soldiers, many broken and bleeding. Cries of pain, wails of agony, and the pleading and praying of dying men assailed the newcomers' ears. The sounds were akin to a battlefield after a skirmish — sounds all too familiar to men like Glus Thorn.

Men shouted back and forth, barking orders, securing doors, assembling barricades — a clumsy and ramshackle line of defense formed not far back from the hold's main door.

Crewmen worked to weigh down the hold's large ceiling hatch with loaded crates hung from a heavy chain they had fastened to the hatch's frame. Apparently, they sought to prevent someone or some thing on deck from opening the hatch and gaining entry to the hold from above. Most of the room's tension though was focused on the knot of men that stood braced and battle ready — swords, axes, and crossbows in hand — at the door that led out to the storage deck's main corridor. Some of those men were wounded, though for the moment they paid their hurts little heed.

"You see, it's just like I said," said Par Keld. "They've lost control; they wouldn't listen to me. They've lost the ship. They're incompetent, all of them."

One by one, as quick as they could, the group climbed out of the coach and stepped down to the hold's deck. The door they had just passed through was indeed attached to a large, ornate coach. There it sat, toward the side of the hold. Seemingly, it was a working coach, normal in all respects, though unhorsed at the moment. Looking back and around the coach, there was no sign of the great tower from which they had lately come.

Sounds of battle, swordplay and explosions (magical discharges no doubt), were close at hand, and drawing closer — soon to reach the main corridor that led to the hold. And with those sounds came yells and screams: some human, some not.

Smoke wafted through the hold's door, and with it, a strange scent of burning flesh akin to rotting fish tossed on a fire.

Several panicked men, seamen mostly, and one lugron, dashed into the hold. The battle drew nearer.

"Look here! What's happening?" shouted Thorn, though no one seemed to notice him or those with him. Thorn reached out and grabbed the nearest seaman in a viselike grip, nearly pulling him from his feet. "Who is attacking us? Who are we fighting? Speak, man, or I'll put you right on the floor."

"Sea devils," said the seaman, breathless and wide-eyed, his face pleading for release from Thorn's iron grasp. "Giant things, ten or twelve feet tall with faces like fish – devil fish. They've taken the ship, your wizardship; we're the only ones left. All our men are dead; they're all dead. And now they're coming for us!"

"Sea devils?" said Thorn. "What foolishness is this? Are you mad?"

"It's true, your wizardship," said the seaman.

"It's true," said Par Keld.

"A last line of defense," said Lasifer from Thorn's side. "This battle has gone on for some time."

Thorn shot Par Keld a look that would have killed him, if it could have.

The sounds of battle grew louder, progressing into the corridor just outside the hold.

Par Keld dashed towards the hold's door.

"Close that door, now," he boomed.

Rascelon, *The White Rose*'s captain, brawny with black and white hair and beard, stood beside the door, sword and main gauche in hand, blood dripping from his brow. "We've men still fighting out there," he said. "Including some of yours."

Par Keld bristled, but tried to sound reasonable. "If we don't barricade that door, they will get in and kill us all."

"It stays open until our men come through," the captain said in a voice that permitted no dissent. "All of them."

When Rascelon looked away, Par Keld slid past the defensive line, took hold of the heavy door, and started to push it shut.

Rascelon stepped forward and put a burly arm out to hold the door. "Stop it, you fool," he barked. "Stand down."

Par Keld, sweating and desperate, ignored the captain and redoubled his efforts, straining to move the door, all his strength and weight pressed against it. Hands encumbered by his weapons, the captain couldn't hold it back.

"Stop him," said the captain, looking about for aid, though all the men nearby were sithian mercenaries and lugron — not his men. They would not take his orders; more likely, they would take Keld's.

Keld never saw Rascelon's arm come up until the captain's sword butt slammed into his forehead. Par Keld staggered; his eyes unfocused, a confused expression etched his face before he crumbled down in a heap.

The battle reached the hold's door, the attackers now revealed as Dagon's horrid dwellers of the deep. They bounded down the corridor, moving on four limbs as often as two, chasing down the last of *The Rose*'s fighting men. The dwellers' scaly hides were mostly green or brown, their fronts lighter, white or gray and glistening. Each had a large, ridged protrusion – some vestigial fin that extended from the crest of their heads down the center of their backs; their hands and feet webbed and clawed. Their heads were far oversized and narrow, dominated by expansive, toothy maws, and large, glassy eyes that moved independently and were rooted more to the sides than the fronts of their narrow faces. Most of them held long spears of bone, while some wielded daggers of shell or stone. A few advanced with but teeth and claws. Most wore armor fashioned of seashell and stone strapped about their naked bodies with strange cordage of unknown make.

Their nauseating putrescence flooded into the hold, along with cries, crashes, clanging steel, the sound of crunching bone, and the dwellers' high-pitched screeching, croaking, and gibbering. Even amid the clamor of battle, the clangor of the dwellers' eerie, rhythmic breathing stood out, for they all breathed together, inhaling and exhaling at the same time and far louder than do men.

More than a dozen battered men backed into the room, weapons bloody, Stev Keevis Arkguardt, former apprentice to The Keeper of Tragoss Mor, amongst them. Keevis dragged old Par Oris, pale, limp, and gray, by the collar. A smear of blood marred their wake.

Mason, the man of stone – a golem, a sentient magical construct created by The Keeper, backed toward the door; his wide girth blocked much of the corridor. His stony fists flailed back and forth and pounded the cadre of dwellers that thrust bone spears at his face and torso. He knocked most of the spears aside, but some few hit home, shattering on impact, or scraping along his stone torso or arms. Their great height a hindrance there, most of the dwellers were stooped over double in the eight-foot high passage, but they came on en masse, and crowded the corridor in such numbers that for all Mason's inhuman strength and mass, even he could not hope to hold them back.

Mason's great fist pummeled one dweller about the side of the neck. The creature went limp and fell forward into his grasp. He lifted the dweller and tossed him back with all his power into his fellows. The front two ranks were bowled over, affording Mason a brief respite to slip into the hold. Rascelon and the soldiers slammed the door shut.

"Secure the door," yelled Stev Keevis from Par Oris's side, where he frantically worked to staunch the flow of blood from the old wizard's wounds, though the door was already closed and barred.

The dwellers rained hammer blows and massive fists on the great door, which shuddered, bowed, and threatened to burst. On Rascelon's order, everyone pulled back, and a winch dropped a pallet of timbers aligned for the task in front of the door. Two tons of solid wood would hold them for some time, or so they hoped.

No sooner was the pallet in place than Par Keld dived into Rascelon, murder in his eyes, fists flailing. The two rolled about the deck, Par Keld doing his best to pummel the captain about the head before Rascelon tossed him off. Keld slid several feet across the deck and came lurching up to one knee.

The dwellers battered at the doors, tearing at the wood, wailing and screeching as only they could.

"You hit me," shouted Keld. "How dare you? I'm an archwizard. You can't treat me like that. You will show me the proper respect or—"

Keld's words choked in his throat and his eyes widened in shock as Rascelon flung a dagger underhanded at his throat. The blade would surely have killed Keld, if he hadn't seen it coming, and had not the mastery of the arcane arts to counter it. But he did, for Keld was a wizard of the Tower of the Arcane, and for all his quirks and faults, magic's weave bent to his command.

The dagger abruptly stopped, suspended in midair just a few inches from Keld's throat. Whatever mumbled words or odd gestures Keld used to invoke the magic that accomplished that feat, went unnoticed.

Frustration, but not surprise marked Rascelon's face during the brief moment before he charged Keld, sword in hand.

Par Keld pointed at Rascelon, and muttered some esoteric phrases. Suddenly, the captain's momentum fled and his feet left the deck. Keld raised his arm higher, and Rascelon rose up in the air, helpless. Rascelon's sword dropped from his grasp and he clutched at his throat with both hands. His face turned red as the life was choked from him by a force unseen and unnatural.

"Put him down," boomed Thorn from several yards away, even as several seamen moved towards Keld, knives, daggers, and swords in hand. Keld seemed not to hear him. Thorn moved to Keld's side and put a hand to his shoulder. "Par Keld, put the captain down. Now."

By that time, the dwellers had pulled in the doors, or torn them asunder. They pounded on the pallet of wood, trying to break it apart or push it aside.

"Brace the pallet," yelled Stev Keevis as a group of men strained to hold it in place. "Put your backs into it, men."

"He doesn't respect me," said Keld, the captain still aloft. "Did you see how he hit me? He tried to kill me. Did you see the knife?"

Thorn's hand lashed out and slapped Keld across the face, even harder than he had back at that tower. Keld's concentration broken, his spell was disrupted, and Rascelon dropped to the deck.

Keld turned toward Thorn; the merest hint of defiance remained on his face.

Thorn slapped him again, then again, and then again — four times in all before he stopped; no emotion on his face all the while, though his eyes were wider than was his norm.

Keld's face was beet red, his mouth open, his eyes wet. He looked like a small child, beaten for misbehaving, fearful, terrified, and on the verge of tears.

"Stop blaming me," said Keld. "I did nothing wrong. Nothing."

"We're still under attack, you fool," said Thorn. "Pull yourself together and focus. They will be on us in a moment. And we'll need the captain's sword at our side."

Even as he said those words, the wood pallet collapsed, falling over in a heap; its defenders scrambled back to avoid being crushed. The dwellers surged through the breach, a wave of inhuman fury and death, their slavering lips chanting, "Dagon, Dagon," as they charged.

> *The battle raged, long and bloody.*
> *Arrows and bolts,*
> *Bolos and daggers,*
> *Steel, stone, and bone*
> *Flew and crashed,*
> *Bashed, and slashed,*
> *No mercy asked, no quarter given.*
> *Claws and swords,*
> *Spear and axe,*
> *The battle joined,*
> *Desperate and bloody,*
> *No retreat and no surrender.*
> *Dwellers, seamen, and warriors too,*
> *Screamed and cried,*
> *Howled and died,*
> *In a red and milky blood tide.*
> *And then Glus Thorn stepped up,*
> *Little Lasifer at his side,*
> *And spoke his secret words*
> *From which no dweller could hide,*
> *And the last of Dagon's beloved children*
> *were swept aside.*

--- Fifth Scroll of Cumbria
Stanzas 198 - 202

27

Forbidden words spoken, blue flame arced from Thorn's hands and struck the nearest dweller; others of its ilk were already dead or dying about the wizard's feet from other spells he'd thrown and from blows from his staff. The arc of blue energy did not dissipate, but held steady between Thorn's hand and his victim. The dweller writhed in agony, but could not escape from the spell's infernal grip. The blue fire seared through it; smoke rose from its flesh, which blackened and charred in but a single moment. Then the blue fire leapt to the next closest dweller, and the next, and the next, fanning out in all directions like some crazed spider's web, holding each dweller in its deadly embrace, but sparing every member of *The Rose*'s company. Those dwellers far enough away to escape the initial attack, turned and fled, but the flames pursued them relentlessly; time and distance were of no hindrance.

***

The ship's claxon continued to blare, sounding the general alarm. Sir Jude Eotrus's face was pale and drawn as he paced the barred cell in which he had passed the last many days as a prisoner aboard *The White Rose*. He listened intently to the shouts, cries, and furious clash of weapons from up on the main deck. It sounded no minor skirmish. The ship had been boarded and a major battle was joined. Jude's pulse quickened; he felt it pounding at his neck. More than likely, the attack meant his imminent rescue or imminent death.

Jude held out a vestige of hope that his brothers had come at last to rescue him, but he knew the thought was foolish. *The Rose* had traveled too far from Lomion. Much too far. The Eotrus would never find him, if they even still looked.

More likely, the attackers hailed from a much closer port. The Southron Isles held all manner of strange civilizations – from the advanced and worldly, to the primitive and barbaric, to the downright horrific – or so Jude had been taught. Many islanders had never even heard of Lomion, or for that matter, much of anything beyond their own little domain. Jude imagined a horde of them – backward tribesmen – their faces painted, their weapons crude but deadly, leaping over the gunwales and howling for blood. They might want to claim the ship for their own, or else kidnap and violate what few women sailed aboard her. Or perhaps their purpose was even darker. Perhaps they were cannibals that craved the flesh of living men. The existence of such flesh eaters amongst the myriad uncharted islands of the southern seas was long rumored, if not proven beyond doubt.

If not primitives, then they could only be roving pirates seeking treasure. Pirates might be willing to ransom Jude back to his family, but because Lomion was so far away, they would probably decide that he wasn't worth the trouble, and just kill him outright or else sell him as a slave.

More than likely, because *The Rose* flew a Lomerian standard, whoever the attackers were, they would be no more friendly to Jude than to his captors. But the attack could provide an opportunity for escape — and Jude would welcome that if it came.

Though Jude had been well treated, clothed, and fed, the old gnome came each day to bleed him; his work supervised by the wizardess, Par Brackta, and enforced by several guards. That daily ritual began in the days immediately following Jude's capture, as he lay on his bunk, dazed and feverish from the wounds he received when the Shadow League's men ambushed him and his patrol on the road between Dor Eotrus and Riker's Crossroads.

Northern Lomerians, such as the Eotrus, had long ago abandoned bleeding as a medical procedure, having concluded that its debilitating effects overbalanced any good that it might provide. Some in the south still swore by the technique, and Jude had heard that it was widely used in parts foreign. Though Jude did not approve of the procedure, at first he made little protest, thinking they merely sought to cleanse him of unbalanced humors or other ailments, and thereby speed his recovery.

Although he had never been bled before, as the days passed and his mind and body cast aside the fever, Jude concluded that the gnome collected far more blood than any physician should. Though he extracted it with gentleness and care, Jude knew the procedure must hold some dark purpose, though what that might be, he could not fathom. Despite his questions and protests, Lasifer would not reveal his purpose, save to offer reassurances that no harm was meant. Brackta insisted that even she did not know the purpose of the bleedings. All she would offer was that they had been ordered by a wizard called Master Thorn, a mysterious figure that Jude had never seen in person, and was only spoken of by the Leaguers in hushed tones. The Leaguers feared Thorn; even Brackta did, but why, she would not say.

Whenever Jude refused to submit to the bleedings, Lasifer pleaded with him to comply, fear in his eyes – fear of his master's wrath. At last resort, Lasifer ordered the guards to hold Jude down. It was obvious to Jude that the little man didn't want to do that, but he believed that he had to. The gnome seemed a decent fellow (better than the rest of the Leaguers, at least), and only did what he did out of fear for his own safety. Jude would use that to his advantage, should an appropriate opportunity present itself.

The guards were slow to obey the tiny man. It seemed that they held him in little regard, no doubt, due to long held prejudices against his kind. But the mere mention that Glus Thorn might hear of their disobedience put a fear in their eyes and set them quick to purpose. As strong a man as Jude was, he had no chance of resisting them; there were too many guards. Consequently, Jude spent his days tired and weak from blood loss, his legs unsteady.

How easy it would be, he thought, to snap the old gnome's neck and put an end to it. But he didn't have the heart to do it. Besides, he knew that the gnome didn't act of his own accord — he merely followed the orders of his masters. If Jude killed him, he would just be replaced by another, and Jude would have to live with the guilt of murdering a harmless old man. He could never do such a thing — his honor and conscience would not allow it. And so he endured, as best he could, biding his time waiting for an opportunity to escape, such as the battle might provide.

Through the floor-to-ceiling, wall-to-wall, iron bars that comprised the front wall of his cell, Jude watched his two jailors. They stood at the heavy door of the little guardroom that housed his cell. Every few moments they unbolted and opened the door and one or both would pop their heads into the corridor beyond, then, not seeing anything of note despite the alarm that had been blaring for some time, they'd close and bolt the door again, uncertain as to what to do.

"Teek, can't you just go and find out what's happening?" said Jude to the larger of his jailors, a middle-aged lugron who was clad in a black leather jerkin that was a bit too tight, a white long-sleeved shirt, gray breeches, and big black boots. "We can't just sit here waiting for the boarders to storm the room. We need to know what's going on."

"We stand our post," said Teek, his voice much deeper than most lugron's, smoke rising from the ever-present cigar in his mouth, "until new orders they come. That's what a guard does, so that's what we do."

"Teek, the ship is under attack. They don't have time to send you orders. You've got to assess the situation yourself."

"Got to what?" said Tribik, the second lugron guardsman, a confused expression on his face, which complimented his disheveled appearance. He looked like he rarely bathed. He stunk even worse. Jude relished the meager fresh air from the tiny porthole set high in the cell wall. He even came to appreciate cigar smoke, for it kept down the stench.

"Orders will come, if we need them," said Teek. "That's how it works. Pipe it down now, Judy, and let me think."

"What if the ship sinks? I'll drown in here and then you will get blamed. What do you think Ginalli and Korrgonn will do to you then? What do you think Master Thorn will do?"

Teek paled, fear in his eyes. "Teek let you out if water comes in. Judy not get drowned, no worry, and Teek not get blamed. No, no, Teek not get blamed. Not this time."

"You won't have time. *The Rose* is heavy — she'll sink fast. I've seen ships like this go down in under a minute. If you don't unlock the door now, by the time the water comes, it'll be too late. It's the only way to protect yourselves. I'll get drowned and you will get blamed. I would hate to see you guys get killed over me. You've treated me good, all things considered."

Teek hesitated, thinking.

"Maybe we ought to unlock the cell, Teek," said Tribik. "We don't want Judy to die, and if he does, the Korrgonn will kill us two dead, for sure."

"It's the smart thing to do," said Jude. "I'll keep my behind planted in this chair, and you'll not hear a peep out of me. If the all clear sounds, you can lock the cell door back up tight, and no one will even know."

Teek stared at Jude, considering his words. The sounds of battle grew louder. Shouting erupted down the hall, and men ran down the corridor. Teek rushed to the door, but by the time he unbolted it and heaved it open, the men were long gone and the corridor was empty.

"Smart thing to do?" said Teek, as he reclosed the door. "Yeah, Teek open cell door for Judy. Then, Judy say, it's a smart thing to give him a weapon, so he can help if we get jumped. Then maybe it'll be a smart thing if old Teek and Tribik get in the cell with him, then Judy can slip out and lock us two stupid lugron in." Teek sneered. "Judy, a smart one, oh yes he is, very smart, all schooled up and fancy. Teek not so fancy, but Teek smarter. You stay put right there, Judy, and keep trap shut for now, and we stay all friendly like, see?"

Jude looked stricken. He slumped onto his spartan bed, his face scrunched up and on the verge of tears. "I'm no trickster, Teek," he said, sniffling. "If that's what you think of me, we're quits. No more Spottle, no dice, no Mages and Monsters, nothing," he said, pointing to the caged Spottle frog, the dice bag, and other gaming paraphernalia piled on the sideboard outside the cell.

Tribik turned to Teek, panic on his face. "Judy's not tricksy, Teek. He's always played us square."

Teek looked concerned and swayed from one foot to the other. "Don't get cross, Judy. We can get ya some extra-good rations, and keep that ugly witch-woman away. Then we be all friends still, right?"

Tribik nudged Teek's arm. "Can't promise that, Teek. Brackta not answer to the likes of us."

"I'll keep her out, somehow," said Teek,

glaring at Tribik.

"Nope, if you don't trust me after all the times we've spent together, then I'm through with you both."

"Teek!" said Tribik. "Now he's mad. We can't play Spottle with just two. Open cell like he asked. You'll not give us no trouble, right Judy?"

"I'll behave," said Jude mildly, an innocent smile on his face as he tossed some dice from hand to hand.

A high-pitched screech came from down the corridor. Men ran past their door, some shouting to others that they should fall back to the main hold.

Jude bounced up from the bed and grabbed the bars. "Get me out of here or bar the darn door, you fools," said Jude. "Or we're all going to end up dead!"

"Set the bolt," said Teek, panicking, as he raced to the heavy trunk whose top served as their gaming table. "And set the crossbars, quick. I'll put this here trunk in front of the door."

Then they heard heavy steps coming down the corridor. With them came a strange, loud, rhythmic breathing; it was nothing like that of a man – perhaps more like some large animal.

Tribik bolted the door and grabbed the lower crossbar.

"Forget the trunk," said Jude. "Set the crossbars. Quick!"

Teek ignored or didn't hear him and slid the trunk toward the door.

A single, massive blow blasted the guardroom door open. It slammed into Tribik, sending him stumbling backward. The door's deadbolt fractured, flew across the room, and hit Teek squarely in the forehead, knocking him senseless.

Two of Dagon's dwellers of the deep rushed in, long bone spears in hand, their nauseating fishy smell charging in with them as they screeched something incomprehensible. The first spear thrust took Tribik through the abdomen just as he scrambled to his feet and tried to draw his sword. The second thrust entered his upper chest and lifted him into the air. The spear's shaft went clear through him and lodged in the guardroom's wall, leaving Tribik suspended in the air, his feet dangling, as his life slipped away.

Half-dazed and lying on the floor, his head bleeding, his cigar still locked between his lips, Teek tossed his key ring through the bars at Jude.

The first dweller pulled his spear from Tribik and went after Jude, though the intervening bars vexed him. It loomed before the cell, fully nine feet tall, its head brushing the guardroom's ceiling. Jude's eyes were wide and he gagged as the smell of the thing filled the room. He'd never seen anything like a dweller before; prior to that moment, he didn't believe such things existed, save as monsters that haunted the ancient tales of *The Age of Myth and Legend*.

The dweller thrust its spear between the bars, determined to skewer Jude. Jude dodged the thrust easily enough since the bars hindered the creature's aim. It thrust the spear again, then again, Jude sidestepping each time. By the third attack, Jude had gauged its speed. When next the dweller struck, Jude reached out, grabbed the spear's shaft in one meaty hand, and chopped down with the other, close-fisted, and roaring. Despite its thickness, the bone spear snapped in two under the fury of Jude's blow.

Jude spun toward the bars and lunged forward with the broken spear tip. Too quick was he for the dweller. It had no time to dodge or retreat. The blow landed precisely where he planned – the spear's tip sinking deep into the dweller's eye. The creature reared back and wailed in agony – a discordant sound, high-pitched and grating, unlike anything Jude had heard before from man or beast. The power of that strike sent the spear tip out the back of its head and instantly killed the dweller, its body flopping lifeless to the floor.

Jude reached through the bars and grabbed the stone axe that hung from the dweller's belt. It was a clumsy, heavy weapon, but sharp as a razor's edge.

The second dweller came on, this one ten-feet-tall or larger, stooped far over to fit within the room. It shoved the corpse of its fellow aside without regard, and as it did, Jude lunged in with the axe and struck the dweller's arm just above the elbow – the cut so powerful that its arm was nearly severed and dangled by only a bit of bone and sinew as its blood doused the floor. The dweller turned and retreated, squealing, though its narrow, fishlike face remained expressionless, its black eyes, dead and eerie. Jude swung his arm between the bars and slammed the axe into the dweller's back before it was able to stagger out of range. It dropped to its knees — even so, it was still taller than Jude.

Jude picked up the key ring and unlocked the

cell door. He stepped over to the dweller who was by then hunched over, wheezing and coughing, as its milky blood pooled about it. The thing tried to turn, tried to lift its hand up in defense, but it was far too slow. Jude slammed the axe against its head, splitting it in two down to its shoulders.

Teek peeked out from behind the big trunk and pulled himself unsteadily to his feet, his eyes focused on his dead comrade. Jude spun in his direction, bone axe still in hand.

"You gonna bash in old Teek's head now, Judy? Them stinky fish-things beat you to that," he said, pointing to the wound on his forehead that dripped blood, "but you can finish me off, if you've a mind to. I ain't got much fight left in me just now," he said, his arm braced against the wall to hold himself steady.

"What in Odin's name are these things?" said Jude as he stood over the body of one of the dwellers.

"Never seen their like," said Teek. "Never even heard of anything like them. They be some kind of fish men it looks like. Never liked fish much. So you're not going to kill me then?"

Jude looked over the bodies. "They're not men." Jude walked over to Tribik's body, pulled the longsword from the lugron's belt, keeping an eye on Teek all the while, and moved toward the guardroom's door.

"Are you making a run for it?" said Teek, the sounds of battle still reaching them from up on deck and elsewhere on the ship.

"I have to."

"I misjudged you, Judy," said Teek. "I thought you just a tin can what earned his armor by getting born to the right fancy folks. But you're a heap more than that. You be a killer, Judy, tried and true. You showed me something here you did. But now you've got to finish things. I'll get blamed but good for you hightailing it. Thorn will have me flayed or worse – if Ginalli or the Korrgonn don't kill me dead first. Best you kill me now, Judy. Kill me quick. It would be a mercy."

"I can't do that to you," said Jude. "I won't."

"Pity that," said Teek narrowing his eyes. "Thought you a friend, I did, considering. Foolish, that."

Jude didn't understand what Teek meant, and at the moment, he didn't much care. He peered into the corridor, and saw dwellers kick in doors down the hall while others of their kind came from the opposite direction, dragging the bodies of dead men. There was nowhere to run. If he'd had some short window in which to escape, it was already closed.

Jude closed the door, which now had no lock. He grabbed the crossbar that still leaned against the front wall of the guardroom and hefted it into place. "Find the other crossbar, quickly," he said to Teek. The crossbar was a four inch thick timber that fit into iron brackets securely mounted to the wall on either side of the door about five feet above the floor. The second crossbar fit into brackets two feet below. Within a few moments, they had both crossbars solidly in place, the heavy oak and iron-bound door now far more secure than it was with just the deadbolt that the dwellers had broken through.

"Let's move everything heavy against the door," said Jude.

They pushed up the trunk and the table that the guards used for dining; then they carried over the bodies of the dead dwellers.

"You think that will keep them out?" said Teek.

"It'll slow them down, and that will give us a chance," said Jude. "We need that spear," he said, indicating the one pinning Tribik to the wall. Teek nodded his acknowledgment. "I'll hold him up. You try to pull it out."

"No," said Teek. "I'll hold him." Teek stood under Tribik and gripped his legs, holding him steady, the dead lugron's blood dripping down Teek's shirt. "Me and Tribik served together near thirty years," said Teek, as Jude pulled the spear free. "That was long before the League came around. We came up through Grontor's Bonebreakers — best darn mercenary company there ever was — at least, amongst them what lugron can join up with."

The two gently lowered Tribik to the floor. "He was a simple fellow, not much of a talker, and not the best fighter, but he was a solid friend, and held his own in a scrape when it came to it. Them fish-things are just too big. He never had a chance."

"He died fighting, protecting the ship, and doing his duty," said Jude. "No one could ask more from a soldier than that."

Teek stared at Jude as he spoke those words and nodded his head in agreement.

"We've got to try to keep them out," said Jude, "but if they get in, we retreat to the cell, and lock the door behind us. The key is still in the lock, so we'll be able to relock it fast if we need to."

"What if—"

A huge impact on the door signaled the arrival of more dwellers.

"They don't leave a stone unturned, do they?" said Jude.

The dwellers kicked the door over and over. The wood cracked and splintered; only the crossbars prevented it from being smashed to pieces. Eventually, the lower brackets gave way, the upper brackets bent, and its screws pulled loose from the wall. Jude and Teek stood poised to fight for their lives, spear and sword in hand.

"Get ready," said Jude. "Don't fall back to the cell until I say."

Then a sudden and bright flash of blue light flooded through the cracks around the door; so bright was that flash that Jude and Teek shielded their eyes from it and turned away. Then all went quiet.

A few heartbeats passed and no sounds issued from beyond the door.

"You think those stinkers got gone?" said Teek.

"I think they're dead."

"How you figure?"

"That light was from no lantern or torch. It was a blast of flame that shot down the corridor, maybe filling the whole passage."

"Fire don't kill stuff all silent-like. There would be howling and screaming from them as they got burnt crispy."

"Wizard fire can kill quick."

"I don't go in for that business," said Teek. "It's not natural. When I was shrimpy, the village shaman tossed the bones about and foresaw stuff with them and with chicken guts. Never understood the chicken guts – messy and stinking and they didn't do the chickens no good, so how could they tell a man's future? A bunch of bunk and bother I always thought, until I hooked up with the League. Their wizards got the real juice, they do. Every one of them got a darkness in them. I feel it whenever they're near — a crampy, twisty feeling deep in me gut, so I steer clear of them, best I can."

"The door is about to come down anyway," said Jude. "So let's open it and have a look."

They pushed aside the makeshift barricade and Jude removed the upper crossbar with some trouble since it was well-wedged in place.

Jude stood before the door, sword in hand. "Open it."

Teek did.

And there stood Par Brackta with blood on her face and more smeared across her shirt. Her eyes were afire and a curved sword was in her hand. Before Jude could move, she uttered some mystic word, and unseen magic tore the sword from Jude's hand; it clattered the floor on the other side of the room. An invisible force pushed Jude, and his feet slid out from under him. He fell backward, flat on his back, the unseen force holding him down. Brackta was on him in an instant, kneeling on his chest, sword across his throat. Then she leaned down and kissed him, full on the lips, long and passionate. For a moment, Jude forgot.

"I feared you dead," she said, tenderness in her voice.

"I'm not so easy to kill," said Jude as he stroked her long hair. It was a mess. He'd never seen her look unkempt before. Luckily, she didn't seem injured. Even at her worst, her beauty surpassed any woman he'd known. "Do we really need the sword?"

"Yes," she whispered.

Several men entered the open doorway, Ezerhauten amongst them.

"You seem to have things well in hand," said Ezerhauten.

"Our guest almost made good his escape," said Brackta, her voice harsh. "This lugron helped me recapture him," she said, pointing to Teek.

Ezerhauten eyed Teek and then nodded. "We can take it from here."

"Good," said Brackta as she stood up, then quickly exited the room, gifting Jude not another glance.

"Get up and get back in the cell," said Ezerhauten with a grin that dared Jude to try something.

Jude weighed his chances of escape. Besides Ezerhauten, who he knew to be a better swordsman than he, at least four sithian knights stood in or around the guardroom's doorway; probably more in the corridor. He had no chance of escape; no chance at all. Reluctantly, he stepped into the cell. After Ezerhauten securely locked Jude inside, he turned to his men, directed them to wait outside, and to close the door behind them, which they did. He told Teek to remain.

Ezerhauten held up the key ring. "Do you have another key to this cell?"

"I don't," said Teek.

43

"Who does?"

"Don't know. A crewman gave me the keys after I got picked for this duty."

"Did he take the keys from you or did you let him out?"

Teek stood up straighter and puffed his chest out. "I sprung him. I had to, cause if I didn't, more of them fish-things would've gotten in and killed us both dead."

Ezerhauten looked about the room, studying the wreckage. "More than likely." He placed the key ring in his pocket. "I'll hold onto the keys. If you need to let him out again, you send for me. And just to be sure you don't get lonely, I'm leaving three of my men to stand the guard with you."

"The Eotrus is prisoner of the League, merc," said Teek. "You're pushing past your pay grade, methinks."

"Then mayhap you should tell Ginalli what went on here. I'd be happy to turn the keys over to him."

Teek looked defeated and turned away, busying himself with picking up the mess.

***

Frem Sorlons stood up in the longboat to get a better look at what was happening on the main deck of *The White Rose*. He wasn't accustomed to being in the rear, and he didn't like it. He needed to be in the middle of the action, not watching it. Given his throbbing arm, courtesy of the muck monster's flailing tendrils, and the sorry state of his squadron, standing the rear guard for once might be best, all things considered.

There had been a big commotion on *The Rose*'s deck while Frem and the rest of the shore party battled the muck monster. Sounds of battle – shouts, clashes of arms, flashes of light and loud explosions that could only have been sorcery reached them, but they were too far away to see what went on. Soon after the muck monster's corpse sank beneath the waves, but before the shore party had drawn close enough to see much, *The Rose*'s deck went silent and still. The only sign of life, intermittent flashes from a signal mirror up in the crow's nest. Not being seamen, if the flashes held some message, the shore party couldn't read it, save to know its sender still lived.

When they drew close, Frem saw a number of men high in the rigging, waving, but no one stood on deck. It looked like several bodies lay on the bridge deck, visible between the rails, but who they were, Frem couldn't tell. Any bodies on the main deck would not have been visible from Frem's vantage point; they'd have been hidden behind the gunwales.

Korrgonn's boat was the first to pull up against *The Rose*'s hull. Ezerhauten argued with Ginalli — no doubt advising him of the stupidity of putting the expedition's leadership out front, and being overruled as usual. At least Ginalli waited until a second longboat pulled alongside before he had both boats' crews scale the cargo nets and slip over the gunwale onto the main deck. Korrgonn led the way up.

Men motioned to them from the rigging, but if any words were exchanged, Frem was too far away to hear them. Suddenly, the main door to below deck burst open and a troop of dwellers rushed out, howling.

The boarding party readied their weapons for a charge that didn't come. Within but a moment it was clear that the dwellers were in full rout, fleeing for their lives. They raced for the gunwales, ignoring the men on deck, and dived over the side, one after another. A narrow, crackling stream of blue fire burst through the door from below deck and slammed into the dwellers, cascading from one to another, seizing each one in an immovable and deadly embrace, though leaving the boarding party and the crewmen untouched.

In the blink of an eye, the flames burned away their flesh, leaving their white skeletons suspended in the air for but a moment, before they too were incinerated. The dwellers' ashes dusted the surface of the deck or sailed away with the breeze. Nearly all the dwellers suffered this fate, even those who had dived over the side and were in midair over the water. Only those few that had already plunged into the depths escaped, for the fiery blast failed to follow them below the watery surface.

"Wizardry?" said Frem to Sevare. "It must be."

"I've heard that Master Thorn can throw such a spell, but I've never it afore. Darned impressive. He must've used the coach to come aboard."

"Good timing, anyway. We didn't need another fight." Frem looked back at the island. "The big lizard is still watching us. Just standing there, like it's waiting for something."

"Strange, that," said Sevare as he looked back at Dagon who stood far away on the beach. The creature's size was beyond belief. Thirty or forty feet tall it was, maybe more, for it was hard to tell, so out of scale was it to everything else living; its claws and teeth the length of swords. A dragon of legend come to life, though no wings did it have. There was no fighting such a creature. Not with weapons; not with sorcery. All one could do was flee and hope to escape its wrath. And they had done just that, though several men amongst their party were not so lucky and fell to its crushing feet or ravenous jaws.

A breeze flowing in from the ocean carried with it a fleeting odor of burnt fish. "Best cover your faces with cloth, men," said Sevare. "Unless you like inhaling hot ash."

Frem and his squadron remained in the longboat as the crew raised it up into its berth, and then climbed over the gunwale onto the main deck. Only then did they get their first clear view of the death and the destruction that the dwellers visited upon *The White Rose*. Bodies were strewn everywhere – mostly seamen and sithian mercenaries, with a few dead dwellers scattered here and there. Few of the bodies were intact. The dwellers' blows were so powerful, so vicious, their victims were often unrecognizable. Some of the corpses were without heads; others were missing limbs. Many of the bodies had been crushed beneath the dwellers' feet.

And the dwellers fared little better. It took so much punishment to bring them down, that their corpses were almost as badly mangled – hacked to shreds with swords and axes, riddled with crossbow bolts, and burned and charred from magics thrown. The slaughter was so thick that the deck was covered in a putrid, brownish yellow slop, derived from the red human blood and the dwellers' white mixed with the spilled contents of their innards and bowels.

These sights were horrific and nauseating, even to veteran fighting men like Frem's Pointmen. The smell though, was perhaps just as bad – an acrid, fishy stench of spilled innards and violent death that was indescribable, save to say that it caused nearly every man to cover his mouth and nose in vain attempt to block it out.

Seamen scrambled about the deck securing the last of the longboats, working the rigging and sails, and raising the anchor. Mort Zag, the red-hued giant, lay on the deck, a blanket wrapped around him; Ezerhauten and two of Frem's Pointmen (Torak and Clard) stood over him.

"How is Big Red?" said Frem as he cradled his wounded lugron friend, Little Storrl, in his arms.

"He should be dead," said Ezerhauten. "But he's not, if barely. I can't explain it. Have him and your wounded taken down to the main hold straight away. We're setting sail afore the lizard king decides to go for a swim and comes calling. Ginalli has called a council, so join me in the mess hall as soon as the wounded are squared away."

III
WAR, TRUTH, AND EXECUTION

Captain Dylan Slaayde sat in a rickety wood chair in the rear storage locker of his ship, *The Black Falcon*, a cane in his hand, his injured leg stretched out before him. Bertha Smallbutt, ship's Quartermaster, stood at his side, her face troubled. Three feet away, facing Slaayde, sat the battered and bloody form of Darg Tran, until lately, the ship's navigator. Darg's hands were tied behind his back and his feet were tied to the chair. One of his eyes was swollen shut; his cheeks were bruised and bloodied. His shirt and breeches were streaked with blood. Blood spatters marred the floor. The room was dark and cold. Slaayde's bullyboys, Little Tug and Guj, stood on either side of Darg, awaiting Slaayde's orders. The sorry remnants of a chalk-drawn mystical pattern lay smudged and trampled beneath their feet.

"Let's just review what you've told me," said Slaayde. "You stole some kind of magical dust from Theta's trunk. Then you used it, somehow, to conjure up a demon that killed my men. You did this because you think that Theta is evil and deserves to die. You think he's some legendary monster that you call the Harbinger of Doom – a creature straight out of ancient myths and fables concerning the god, Thoth."

"Azathoth," sputtered Darg through bloody lips. "Thoth is different; he's a false, pagan god.

49

Azathoth is the one true god."

"Whatever," said Slaayde, rolling his eyes. "You say that you acted alone in this. No one put you up to it, helped you in any way, or even knew about your plans. Have I got that right? Is that your story?"

"Yes," said Darg. "You have to believe me, Captain. Theta is the Harbinger of Doom. He has to die. If he doesn't, then all of Midgaard will be destroyed. If I don't kill him, you have to. There's no one else. Don't you see that? Can't you understand what I'm saying? Dead gods, please tell me you understand. Don't let this all be for naught. Please."

"Do you even know how many of your shipmates died because of you?"

Darg shook his head. "Because of the Harbinger, not me."

"So many are dead, or gone over the side, we haven't even been able to sort it out yet."

"The Harbinger will kill us all anyway."

"Not today, Darg Tran," said Slaayde. "Only one more man will die today on *The Black Falcon* and that's you." Slaayde looked up at Tug and Guj. "Bring him on deck."

"What are you going to do, Dylan?" said Bertha.

"Hang him from the yardarm," said Slaayde. "He betrayed his ship, his shipments, and me. For that, he swings, and even that's better than he deserves."

"The Eotrus will want to question him," said Bertha.

"They can question his corpse. Men, haul him topside."

✳✳✳

Ob and Tanch stood about Claradon's bedside. For the first time since he nearly died at the hands of Chancellor Barusa's mercenaries, Claradon was fully awake and coherent. Ob and Tanch recounted for him the outcome of the melee in which he was sorely wounded; the group's subsequent hard-fought battle to escape the city of Tragoss Mor; and the recent fight with the Brigandir, the creature conjured by Darg Tran.

"So the Alders killed two of Seran's soldiers – the ones that came with him to find us in Tragoss?"

"Aye," said Ob. "Fought well, they did. One fell to a Kalathen Knight, the other to Bartol of Alder. Them Kalathens are tough buggers, as solid as their reputations. Though I don't much stomach giving him credit, if it were not for Mr. Fancy Pants, we might not have got clear from that scrape."

"Those two were Ector's age, if even that," said Claradon. "I didn't even know their names."

"It's a hard thing to leave good men lying dead in the street," said Ob. "Especially in a stinking foreign city far from home. Troubled me too it has, I'm not ashamed to admit, but it's best not to dwell. There's nothing that we could have done different, and there's no going back."

"They were in my charge," said Claradon. "It's my duty to bring their bodies home to their families – to give them that little comfort at least, but now I can't even do that."

"No, you can't, boy – we can't. It's a sad

thing, but that's the way it is. We barely got out ourselves. The fight in the street and the one on the pier were close things, very close. The luck of the Vanyar was with us or we would all be toasting Odin, up Valhalla way, about now."

Claradon stared down at the bed, only half listening to Ob. "We may never get home at all." Claradon's eyes were watery. "We can't even give them a proper service; can't even bury them at sea. That would be something at least. I could tell their families that. What will the Thothian monks even do with their bodies? Leave them in the street to rot, to be eaten by rats or dogs? Burn them, bury them, or what?"

"I don't rightly know, boy, but I don't expect they will get a proper service – not by our standards, anyways."

Par Tanch cleared his throat and interrupted. "Maybe it's best in such times to put the truth aside and tell the families of the dead something more comforting, some tale that will ease their minds a bit."

"That's the wizard way, is it?" said Ob, a bit of sharpness to his voice.

"It's the human way," said Tanch. "A little compassion never hurt."

"Compassion gets a soldier killed," said Ob. "Best tell them the truth, which ain't so terrible bad anyways. They died in battle, doing their duty, carrying on heroically. We should all go as well as that. When you start spinning lies, even with good intentions, eventually you get all tripped up in your own stinking web. Steer clear of that business, I say. Stick to the truth."

"How many more did we lose today?" said

Claradon, his eyes tightly closed. "At the hands of – what did you call it?"

"Brigandir," said Ob. "We don't know yet. Seran is counting them up right and proper. We lost Trooper Anders for certain — as I saw him go down — but as best I know, no other Eotrus man got killed dead. Three or four at least from House Harringgold fell. All the Malvegillians made it, stinking archers and such, hanging back; they'll probably outlast us all. It's Slaayde's men what took the brunt. They scattered early on and the demon picked them off one by one like we done told you. Them seamen are darned good in a straight up fight, but against something like that Brigandir thing – well, they didn't know what to do, and that cost them dearly."

Claradon's face was filled of anguish and guilt. "Anders's little sister is my chambermaid; a wisp of a girl, too shy to even look me in the eye. How am I supposed to tell her I got her brother killed? I should have been with you, fighting that thing, not lying here in bed like some helpless fool."

"Men die in battle every day, my boy. Think too hard on it and you will paralyze yourself with fear and indecision. You've got a big heart, a good heart, and that's a strength for most any man, but it can be a weakness too, especially for a leader."

"It's just not what I expected," said Claradon. "I thought I knew what battle was. Even what war was. But I didn't. I didn't really understand. I didn't expect that anyone could die at any moment. I didn't expect father to die, not out in our own woods, not at the hands of some creatures out of a nightmare. I never thought Sir Gabriel would die. I thought he would always be with us. I mean, what could kill him? He was the toughest man I've ever met. And I always thought, stupid as it was, that I would live forever – that somehow, I was immortal, even though I knew in my heart that no one else was, so how could I be? I thought that nothing could hurt me. Surviving the Vermion and the duel with the Chancellor just made me feel all the stronger – all the more invincible." He looked down at the bloodstained bandages that wrapped his chest. "But now I know that's not true. I can die the same as anyone. And anyone can die at any time. It doesn't matter how important you are, or how famous you are, or how much you're loved or admired or feared. You can die just the same. I didn't understand that. Now I do."

"That's war, boy, and that's life," said Ob. "That's the way it is. Want a happy ending, want everyone you like and love to survive and to be a hero? Then you will have to read some fairy stories, some children's tales. That's not how it is out here in the world. Here there's blood, and pain, and death. Like you said, the best of us can be taken – no warning, no goodbyes. Gabriel's passing and Aradon's, not to mention all the rest, showed us that as clear as can be. Now that you understand the way things are, you will be the stronger and the wiser for it."

"Why would any man that has seen battle, real battle, start a war? That's what the Leaguers are doing after all, isn't it?"

"Men what understand the way of things don't start wars unless they have to, to defend their own, or unless they're not right in the head. Wars are started by them what don't know no better, or don't care, or are crazy. Hotheaded younkers or old farts what never seen a real battle and never will. They ship off other men's sons to war and don't much care as long as it profits them. But they're wrong. War profits a man nothing, same as fear. Best do without either."

"Sometimes you have to fight."

"Yep. Sometimes you do. That's why we're soldiers. That's why there are men like Gabriel and stinking Theta, and me. We do what needs doing no matter how ugly it gets. Somebody has to. This is a tough lesson to learn, boy. Best learn it quick. Harden yourself to it, make peace with it, and you will be one of us, a warrior, in truth, not just in title. Most men never learn as much, not afore old Death comes and takes them. Old Sickle Boy comes for everybody sooner or later. When he comes for you, spit in his eye, and tell him to get gone, that you will call him when you're done with the world and not before."

Claradon smiled. "You think that will work?"

"Worked for me plenty of times. I practically blinded the bugger more than once. Gnomes is hard to kill, though."

"Even so, we could be next."

"Maybe. But until then, we will fight. We will continue on and do what's right and proper, so long as any life remains in us. That's what makes a man a man. That's what your father would tell you if he was here, so I'm telling you in his stead."

Ob picked up a decanter of wine from the nightstand and poured them each a goblet.

There's something I've been meaning to ask you both," said Tanch. "It's a strange thing."

"Then get it off your chest, for you're strange enough already," said Ob.

"When we were in the temple in the Vermion, something was holding us back from moving toward the altar. Theta was out in front of all of us. Did you see what was holding him back?"

"Wasn't nothing to see," said Ob. "Some invisible force, same as what slowed us all. Some crazy magic thing it was. More than that, who can say? And who cares, anyways? It's over and done, and we won."

"But did you see him up front with your own eyes?" said Tanch. "Did he look any different to you?"

Ob scratched his head and paused, thinking. "I was behind him a ways, but I didn't see nothing different about him any more than I saw about any of us."

"I was too busy trying to keep my head from bursting," said Claradon. "I wasn't focused much on anybody else. Why do you ask? What did you see?"

"What about when we were on the river, and we were passing through the Dead Fens, and those creatures appeared out of nowhere and attacked us – those things that Theta called Einheriar?" said Tanch. "Did they look like monsters to you, or like men?"

"They weren't like no men I've ever seen," said Ob. "Had an evil cast to them, like something you would expect to come out of Nifleheim."

"That's what I saw as well," said Claradon. "They were blurry, hard to focus on, but what I saw was more monster than man."

"What about when we were in Hecate's temple in Southeast, during that cultist mass – did they sacrifice people? Did they really kill them or was it just all show?"

"I don't understand where you're going with this," said Ob. "They passed around cups, big chalices, filled with the blood of those poor folks. Them folks was dead for certain. We all saw them get stabbed right through the chest. No sleight of hand was that. I know the sound a blade makes when it sinks into a man's chest; Odin knows I've heard the damnable sound enough times over the years – and that's what I heard then. Them poor folks was killed dead and their blood collected and drank by them nutcases, and there ain't no debating it."

Claradon nodded his agreement. "What is this about, Tanch?"

"It's nothing really. I just had a strange dream a few times, that's all. In the dream, I relived each of those three events, but saw them happen differently. I know it sounds crazy, but the dream made me feel as if things didn't happen the way I remembered them, but a different way, a way that changed everything."

"You had the same dream more than once?" said Claradon.

"Three times that I remember since we left Tragoss."

"Odd that," said Claradon. "Wonder what it means."

"Dreams is strange stuff," said Ob. "Don't put much stock in them myself. Look here, Tanch old boy, trust your memories, not some fantasy what got conjured up in your sleep. Dreams don't mean nothing from nothing. You probably just had a bad blot of mustard, or some rancid crumb of cheese."

"You're right, of course," said Tanch. "Just a stupid dream."

***

Little Tug hefted Darg Tran by the collar, his hands still tied behind his back, and dragged him across the deck, careful to avoid stepping on the floorboards that had been damaged in the fight with the Brigandir. Guj snatched up a coil of rope and quickly tied its end into a noose. They brought Darg up to the bridge deck and stood him atop the railing overlooking the main deck. The crew took notice and began to gather to find out what was going on. Guj sent two men up the rigging to tie the rope to the yardarm. Visibility was limited, for fog had settled in when warm air from the water (due to Korrgonn's magic that had killed the muck monster) mixed with the cold wind coming in from the sea.

"Listen up, men," shouted Slaayde from the Bridge Deck's rail. "Darg Tran is the scum what betrayed us all and conjured up that beast. He betrayed his captain, his ship, and all his mates."

One of the Eotrus men standing watch outside the door of the Captain's Den entered to rouse Theta, as Guj fixed the noose about Darg's neck. Other men called out to those below deck to spread the word of what was happening.

"He's got a weighty debt to pay to us for his

58

treachery," said Slaayde. "He will pay it with his life."

"What's this, Captain?" said one man. "Darg's one of us, how could he do that? What evidence is against him?"

"Darg's no wizard," shouted another seaman. "He don't know no conjuring."

"I had it from his own lips," said Slaayde. "Tug, Guj, and Bertha heard it too."

The captain turned to Tug. "Aye," Tug said. "The captain spoke it straight. Darg called that thing up somehow or other and confessed to it. I heard it myself."

"He's a stinking no good traitor," said Guj. "And he's to swing for it."

"We lost a lot of good mates to that monster," said one sailor. "If Darg brought it over, then hanging is too good for him."

"We should skin the scum," shouted an old sailor that held up a long, rusty knife. "I'll peel him like an apple, Captain; just give me your leave."

"*The Falcon* is a civilized ship," said Slaayde. "There will be no skinning here. But he's to swing all the same."

"What say you, Darg?" shouted one sailor. "Why did you go traitor on us?"

"Let's have it from him direct," said another.

"Aye," said many men, heads nodding all around.

Darg's looked down at his crewmates. His eyes searched for his unwitting accomplice, Bire Cabinboy, but the lad was nowhere to be found.

"Stop," boomed Lord Angle Theta as he strode from the Captain's Den, his blue armor glistening in the light of the sun. "I need to question that man."

"He's been questioned," said Slaayde. "By me. He's guilty, and the penalty is death by hanging. There's no more to say about it."

"It's Theta that's the traitor," shouted Darg. "He's the one. You heard what the creature said of him, just as you heard much the same from the creatures what jumped us by the Fens. We've all been whispering of it for weeks. It's not just me."

"Did you set them ones from the Fens on us too, Darg Tran?" shouted Bertha.

Darg shook his head. "Kill me if you want, but Theta is your real enemy, not me. I'm loyal to the Captain, and this ship, and this crew; I always have been and always will be. I've done nothing wrong, and I'm sure not no traitor."

Theta mounted the ladder that led up to the bridge deck. Tug stood at the top of that ladder and stared down at Theta. "Best you stay down there," he said, his voice menacing.

"Stand aside or I will break you," said Theta, anger in his eyes.

Slaayde nodded to Guj. The burly lugron pushed Darg off the railing. He fell about three feet before the rope went taut. Just as it did, an arrow fired by Dolan Silk from halfway across the ship, severed the rope. Darg crashed to the main deck having hung barely a moment, but that was long enough. Men ran forward and checked him, but found him dead, his neck broken.

Theta slammed his hand against the ladder.

Some of the gathered crew and soldiers turned away immediately, others milled about for a while, staring at Darg's body, shaking their heads, or whispering amongst themselves. Murmurs of shock, surprise, and anger lingered about the deck.

Tug stepped back from the ladder as Theta ascended. Theta's jaw was set, and anger still simmered in his eyes as he approached Slaayde, Tug shadowing him.

"I needed to know what he knew," said Theta quietly but sharply. "Killing him was stupid – all to assert your power. You are a child and a fool."

"I've had about enough of your insults," said Slaayde turning fully to face Theta, defiance in his eyes, confidence on his face. "This is my ship, not yours. If you continue to forget that, I will put you people off at the next port, and you can find another way home."

Theta stared at him for a moment saying nothing, but his narrowed eyes said everything. He took a deep breath before speaking again. "We need to talk in private, Slaayde. I need to know whatever you learned from that man. Let's sit down in the Captain's Den and talk it through over a drink or two."

"When my duties permit, I will grant you an audience, but right now, I've other matters to attend to." Slaayde turned toward Guj. "Clean up that mess," he said, pointing to Darg's broken corpse, "and let's get the deck repaired right and proper. We've fresh deck boards in the hold — have them hauled up and let's put this ship back in order."

Theta stepped closer to Slaayde and Tug put his hand on Theta's shoulder – a warning, and a restraint.

"We will talk now," whispered Theta in Slaayde's ear, so quietly only Slaayde could hear. "Or else I will lose my temper, and you will lose your life." Theta reached over and grabbed Tug's restraining hand. He moved so fast one's eyes could barely follow. In an instant, the huge seaman was down on his back, his hand restrained, Theta's foot at his throat, surprise and bewilderment on the giant's face.

Slaayde's hand moved reflexively to his cutlass, but he stopped himself. He dropped his hand to his side, his eyes and Theta's boring into one another. "Fine," he said. "Let's talk."

Theta released Tug's wrist and extended his hand to help him up. Tug accepted the gesture, and Theta heaved him up.

"I didn't even see you move," said Tug. "You've got to teach me that one."

"No hard feelings," said Theta.

"None," said Tug. "But don't try it again," he said holding Theta's gaze and smiling with his cheeks, but not his eyes.

When Captain Slaayde walked into the Captain's Den, he found Theta sitting at the big table with piles of clothes, odd and unidentifiable gadgets, and innumerable warrior wares arrayed before him. A large trunk stood open beside the table. Dolan knelt beside it and carefully picked through its contents, a small ledger and quill in hand.

Slaayde limped to a chair opposite Theta, leaning heavily on his cane, his whited hair loose about his shoulders. Smartly dressed as always, the portly swashbuckler looked at least ten years older than he had when Theta first met him only several weeks before. Neither man said anything for some moments.

Theta broke the silence. "Brandy?" he said, pointing to an ornate bottle on the table. Slaayde nodded and Theta poured them each a glass.

"A gift from Lord Malvegil," said Theta. "Eighty years old – a good vintage, but I've always had more of a taste for wine."

"My tastes aren't so fancy," said Slaayde. "Mead is my drink, and cold beer when I can get it. Wine and spirits I leave for special occasions: fancy parties, fancy women, or fancy meetings with men of consequence."

Both men sipped their drinks in uneasy silence for some moments.

"This has been a difficult voyage for us all," said Theta. "Especially for you as the captain, and considering the grievous wounds you've suffered. I sympathize with your position, but it's important that you understand the import of our mission. We're not just out to rescue Jude Eotrus and take vengeance on his captors. I think you know this."

Slaayde nodded. "I've heard all about this gateway you say the League seeks to open. The Vermion Forest tale has plagued my ears at least ten times now. The men tell it like a ghost story and with each telling it gets a new twist. I took it as exaggeration at best, or else a total fabrication for reasons not obvious to me, but after the attacks on my ship, I feel differently. I know there's truth to it, at least at its core."

"If you haven't figured it out yet, Theta, I'm not just some simple river captain. Nor am I a low pirate or freebooter as some in Lomion City would have you believe. I've sailed all across the known world these last twenty-five years. I've visited islands and exotic ports and seen cities that the simpletons in Lomion haven't even dreamed of. How could they? They're too dizzy from thinking that the world revolves around them. It doesn't. It's a big world out there, and Lomion is just one small part; a very small part."

"Indeed," said Theta.

"In all my travels, and in all my adventures, I've rarely seen magic thrown; I'm talking about real magic, not charlatan stuff. And only a few times afore this journey have I seen a beast that I would call a monster. But on this trip, magic is as common as dirt and monsters drop by daily for dinner, and we're it! It's a bit grating on the nerves, Theta, not to mention what it has done for my hair and my leg. I'm quite attached to both, and am not at all happy with the changes."

"The things that attacked my ship were no normal beasts or men – no such things dwell anywhere in Midgaard, best as I know. So if they've been called up from Nifleheim or whatever other world does exist out there, and they get here by magic or whatever means, then this gateway story might be true too. It must be, or else why would these things be after you? It's clear to me that they're assassins sent to kill you, and that means somebody is afraid of you, or of what you can do."

"You've sized things up well enough," said Theta. "The League knows I mean to stop them from opening another gateway. They will stop at nothing to get me and the Eotrus out of the way. If we fail, and if they get it opened, more than likely the world will end – the whole world –

64

simple as that. Instead of one creature like the Brigandir that we fought today, imagine an army of them running rampant. That is what we have to prevent, and that is why I need your cooperation and your swords, not just passage on your ship."

"You've had my help more than once, though it has cost me dearly."

"Yes, but members of your crew have turned on us – over and again. That has to stop. What happened today must be the last of that. I need to know that I can count on you and your crew to aid in our mission. Your men have stepped up admirably when the ship has been threatened. They've proved their quality, but that won't be enough going forward, because things are only going to get harder. There will be more death and more suffering afore we take the homeward road. We must keep order on this ship no matter what trials we face. We need to be a team, all of us, working together. Your crew's lives depend on our success just as much as anyone's. Are you with me in this, Slaayde?"

"Aye."

"Good. I need to question the crew. I need to make certain that there are no more traitors or spies biding their time."

Slaayde didn't look happy at this request. He squirmed in his seat and answered sharper than he might have liked. "Tell me about the magic dust what Darg stole off you?"

Theta didn't seem surprised by the question and didn't pause a moment before answering. "What did he tell you?"

"Said he got it from your trunk, which I see

is not news to you," Slaayde said, gesturing toward the tabletop piles and the open trunk. "Says he needed it for the conjuring up whatever magic plucked the creature from Nifleheim and dropped him here. He called the thing, 'Brigandir,' just as you've named it a moment ago. He said it was a holy warrior, sent down by Azathoth to fight evil. Specifically, to fight you. For he said that you are the most evil bastard in all creation. He said that you're not a man at all, but some thing, some monster out of hell. By the time he was done jabbering, I got the feeling that he didn't like you so much."

Theta smiled. "I trust that you're smart enough to judge men by their actions rather than by some fool's words?"

"I can't have you question my crew. I can talk to them. I will talk to them, and I will sniff out any more Leaguers, if there are any."

"You don't have the means. With this," said Theta, pointing to the ankh that hung from a cord about his neck, "and other devices, I can root out any more traitors afore they strike. It has to be done – you know this."

Slaayde looked at the ankh. "I'm not impressed by crystal balls, rabbit feet, or whatever that thing about your neck is, and neither are my men. How can it, or whatever devices you're talking about, get the truth from a man? By torture, is that what you're saying?"

"No, not torture. Suffice to say that the ankh has a magic to it. A magic that can tell me when a man is lying."

Slaayde shook his head. "Even if I accept that, and I don't, then your men need to be questioned too. You can't treat my people any different."

"None of the soldiers has gone traitor. But some of your men have tried to sink the ship; they've transformed into Einheriar, and conjured up a Brigandir. It's yours that need questioning."

"That's offensive. One man is the same as another. If my men get grilled, so do yours. That's the only way I will agree to any questioning at all."

"So be it," said Theta.

"Now tell me," said Slaayde. "What was that magic dust? What was it really?"

"It was the remnants of the mystical orb that the League used to open the gateway to Nifleheim in the Vermion. The pulverized shards of it were enough to bring through the Brigandir from Nifleheim, and probably the Einheriar as well. I was keeping the shards until I had the opportunity to dispose of them properly."

"And are they all gone? Did Darg take them all? Use them all up in his rituals? Or do you have more squirreled away?"

"He took them all."

"Hard to believe such things are possible," said Slaayde. "Conjuring. Gateways to other worlds. But those things got on board somehow. Maybe it's true. It just doesn't make a lot of sense; not to me."

"There's more to the world than you know, despite all your travels. Midgaard is old, older than you can imagine. There are things buried in the depths . . ." Theta paused, considering, and then said no more.

IV
REBEL, REGENT, AND RULE

Mother Alder stood stern and stately at the lectern on the petitioners' dais in old Tammanian Hall's High Council Chamber. Her black locks were bound in a tight bun and her gossamer black dress gently fluttered about her, though the air was nearly still. In her right hand she held a black walking stick capped with a carved dragon's head (painted brick red with emeralds for eyes and gleaming silver teeth), though she didn't lean on it for support, and exhibited no noticeable infirmity when she sauntered across the chamber, a regal figure with a light step that made only the slightest of echoes. Her brother, Rom, stood close behind and to the side of her, arms folded across his chest, his expression, grim, as was usual. Gently leaning against Mother Alder's leg was her granddaughter, Edith, a tiny wisp of a girl.

Guildmaster Slyman grunted as he leaned forward in his seat high in the councilors' mezzanine. Though his chair was wider and deeper by some inches than those of the other councilors, his girth spilled over the sides, and he always seemed on the verge of tumbling to the floor. "Is it your testimony, dear lady," Slyman said, his voice echoing in the large, bare chamber, "that Brother Claradon Eotrus willfully refused to submit to the lawful writ of arrest presented to him by the duly appointed agents of this esteemed council?"

"I suppose, "refused to submit," is one way of saying it," said Mother Alder.

"Please explain, dear lady."

"Eotrus and those with him viciously attacked the council's agents without cause or provocation," she said, her voice gravelly but strong. "There were a series of pitched battles; many men were killed on both sides. Tragoss Morian soldiers got involved in a brave but vain attempt to help our lads, and were slaughtered for it. The Eotrus showed them no mercy; no shred of human compassion or decency. That day, they proved themselves the barbarians we've always suspected them to be. These monsters must be brought to justice. They must answer for their crimes."

"Let me make certain that I understand your testimony," said Slyman. "You're saying that Claradon Eotrus and the men under his command murdered agents of this council? Murdered agents of the crown?"

"Yes," said Mother Alder. "Lomerian blood flowed freely in the streets of Tragoss Mor that day. The Eotrus's actions bring shame on us all. I trust that this council will not let these crimes stand?"

"We will not," said Slyman. "I can assure you of that."

"A crime is only a crime once proven in court," said Lord Jhensezil, a tall, broad, muscular man with graying hair who was seated immediately to Slyman's left. "And until proven, it is merely an accusation. Tragoss Mor lies hundreds of leagues from here. How do you even know that this skirmish happened, little less that Claradon

69

Eotrus started it?"

"I know it to be true," said Mother Alder, "because I saw it with my own eyes. I saw it through my Seer Stone."

"Through your Seer Stone, you say," said Jhensezil shaking his head, his brows uplifted.

"Yes, through my Seer Stone, the Alder Stone," said Mother Alder, her voice sharp and stern. "Scoff at my powers all you like, Garet Jhensezil," she said, pointing the tip of her walking stick at him, "but they are real and need no validation from the likes of you. I am an Arch-Seer of the Orchallian Order and have been since before you were born. The powers of my order are well known and respected by those of note. You are free to disbelieve all you like, it matters not; it changes nothing. I have the sight. I can see the present from afar, and sometimes, I can foresee the future. Mayhap even your future, Jhensezil. Do you want to know it? Mayhap I could tell you the time and manner of your death. That is knowledge of great value, is it not? Do you have the courage to ask that of me? Shall I call on that power even now, in this chamber, for all to hear?"

Jhensezil looked flustered and found no words to respond.

"Enough," said Lord Harringgold, the Archduke of Lomion City. "This chamber is plagued with theatrics enough from the councilors; we need no performances from the dais."

"Go carefully," said Chancellor Barusa, his voice cold, and sharp as Valusian steel, his ire directed at Harringgold.

Mother Alder shot Barusa a vicious glance. "I

70

need no protection from you, firstborn. Especially not against such as these."

"Of course you don't," said Barusa, though his gaze was now affixed on Slyman.

"Your written statement," said Slyman as he quickly fumbled through a small pile of papers set before him, "bespoke of witnesses that could corroborate your account of these events, does it not?"

"Yes," said Mother Alder. "I spoke with three agents of the crown after the battle was over."

"Spoke with them how?" said Jhensezil.

"Through the Alder Stone, of course," she said, rolling her eyes.

Jhensezil smiled. "I do not wish to unfairly disparage the old religion that you practice, Lady Alder—"

"Mother Alder," she said sharply. "Then don't."

"I find it difficult to accept such testimony," said Jhensezil. "Sights that only you can see; sounds that only you can hear. Really, Mother Alder, this testimony is most vexing."

Field Marshal Balfor, the commander of the Lomerian army, sat to Jhensezil's left. "I believe that the good bishop has some information to share regarding the testimony of Seers before the high council," said Balfor, his broad black beard covering the array of medals affixed to his shirt and masking the wide arc of his ponderous belly. Balfor poked Bishop Tobin in the back, rousing him from sleep.

"Yes, yes," said Tobin. "Indeed, I do, and there's no need to batter my back, you ruffian. I wasn't asleep, you know, just resting my eyes. It has been quite a long day, but I'm quite alert; not like some old folks whose brains are addled and whose ears are merely ornamentation for their heads."

"Do you have some relevant information, Bishop?" said Jhensezil.

"It's right here," he said, opening a large leather-bound book to a bookmarked page somewhere near the middle. "Quoting from The Book of the Nobility: the word of an Arch-Seer, duly certified by the Arcane Tower, is considered infallible with respect to reporting of current events witnessed through her Seer Stone. It goes on and on from there," said Tobin, "but that's the meat of it."

"I would add that the High Council has routinely relied upon the testimony of Arch-Seers over the ages," said Councilor Slyman. "Is that not right, Bishop?"

"Quite true, quite true," said Tobin as he leaned back and closed his eyes. In moments, his chin slumped to his chest, as if he'd fallen sound asleep.

"What is the name of the officer that you spoke with?" said Jhensezil. "And was he the one who served the writ?"

"Bartol Alder," said Mother Alder.

"Your son."

"Aye, my son."

"And the other two?"

"Blain Alder. Also my son. And Edwin Alder, my grandson."

"And who appointed them to deliver the writ of arrest?"

"Barusa Alder, also my son — as you well know, Garet Jhensezil."

72

"And how would you describe the relationship between the Alders and the Eotrus? Cordial, is it?"

She paused for a few moments before responding. "We like them less than we like the Jhensezils," said Mother Alder. "Though not much less."

"Thank you, Mother Alder," said Jhensezil. "Thank you for your testimony today. If there are no further questions," he said looking around to his colleagues, "you are dismissed."

She snorted, turned, and stepped off the dais, Edith following on her heels. Rom stood rooted, staring at Jhensezil for several seconds with a look that would have killed him, if it could have.

The councilors remained in silence until after the petitioners had left the room and the chamber's door was secured. The High Council meeting was held in private that day, no witnesses permitted, so the audience hall now stood empty, save for a few Myrdonian Knights on guard.

Slyman stood. "Infallible testimony says our sacred law book. Infallible. That makes our course of action clear, my friends. I move that this council declare Claradon Eotrus an outlaw and an enemy of the State. His title to be stripped. All his holdings to be forfeit to the crown, effective immediately."

"That is an extreme measure," said Lord Harringgold, unwarranted by the facts as we know them."

"Unwarranted?" said Slyman. "Have you been paying attention? He attacked our emissaries. That testimony came from a certified Arch-Seer — therefore, by law, it's a fact. It's not in dispute."

"Emissaries carrying the name of Alder, who came at him with an armed force sent by another Alder," said Harringgold. "The whole thing witnessed only by the matriarch of House Alder — her clan being long-standing rivals to the Eotrus. And rivals is a mild term for their relations. We all know that they are bitter enemies. Surely, no one here has forgotten the duel that took place in these very chambers not long ago. Here, at the very least, is the appearance of bias, wouldn't you say?" he said as he looked around at the other councilors. "Can even you, Chancellor," he said, turning toward Barusa, "deny the appearance of bias in this matter?"

"The writ was served and prepared properly, voted on, and approved by the Council," said Barusa. "Who carried it out is of little or no consequence, so long as they faithfully fulfilled their duties."

"And the witness's truthfulness cannot be questioned," said Slyman.

"Let no one dare try," said Barusa.

"We cannot strip a Dor Lord of his title without trial and with only one witness against him," said Jhensezil, "regardless of that witness's reliability."

"With respect to Dor Eotrus, we will proceed as I originally advised some weeks ago," said Barusa.

Harringgold rose. "Do not bring up the idea of a Regent again. I will not abide that."

"Eotrus stands accused of murder and evading the law," said Slyman. "Thus, he's an outlaw. That gives the crown and this council all the authority we need to confiscate his lands, his title, and his holdings — until the matter is sorted out. If somehow, he's proven innocent, all will be given back to him."

"Proven innocent?" shouted Harringgold. "Proven innocent! Have you no understanding of the law? That is not our way. We must prove a person guilty, in court, before a magister, in order to convict them of a crime. They need not prove themselves innocent. This council is not a court and none of us are magisters. Thus, Eotrus is not legally a criminal. His holdings cannot be stripped."

"That is your opinion," said Barusa. "And it holds no more weight than does the opinion of any other high councilor."

"The Alders have long desired Dor Eotrus," said the Duke.

"And you have long opposed any measure brought forth by the Chancellor," said Slyman. "You speak of bias, though you yourself reek of it."

"Let us put it to a vote," said Balfor, "and be done with this matter. Is he an outlaw, yea, or nay?"

The roll was called, the votes were tallied, and Claradon Eotrus was formally declared an outlaw and an enemy of the State. His title to be stripped. His ancestral lands to be confiscated. His only recourse, to be tried, but acquitted, in Lomerian court.

"We must now choose a Regent," said Slyman.

"How do you propose to confiscate Eotrus lands?" said Jhensezil.

"We will send troops," said Marshal Balfor.

"Troops?" said Jhensezil. "How many?"

"A full brigade," said Balfor.

"One brigade?" said Slyman. "Even after their recent losses, the Eotrus garrison can field far more men than that without even calling in their bannermen. Not to mention, their walls are strong."

"We don't want an all-out war," said Balfor. "The idea is to take control of Eotrus holdings, not to wipe them out. For that, we'd need to deploy a full corps at least, equipped with supplies for a lengthy siege. There's no call for such tactics here. It's Claradon that is the outlaw, not all his people."

"His brothers are as responsible as he," said Barusa. "They must all be taken into custody."

"Responsible for what?" said the Duke. "No court has convicted Claradon of any crime as of yet, yet you've already condemned him and want to hold his kin accountable too? For what, I say?"

"The Eotrus are a stubborn breed," said Bishop Tobin with just one eye open. "If you deploy troops to their doorstep, they will fight. One brigade of guardsmen will accomplish nothing."

"Then what do you propose?" said Balfor. "Will you deploy the Church Knights?"

"Oh dear, no," said Tobin. "Such is not their purpose as you well know. It is the Lomerian guard that must do this thing, if it need be done at all. I merely mention that one brigade will not suffice; not even for the limited purpose that you propose."

"Hopefully the Eotrus will be smart enough to lay down their arms," said Balfor. "They are devoid of leadership now, and high winter is coming in the North. I think they will have little stomach for a drawn out confrontation."

"Then you've little understanding of Northmen," said Tobin. "They will fight you. They will take your one brigade, or two, or three, if you muster that many, and slaughter them to the last man. Northmen are a bit less civilized than folk from the big cities of the South. Know your enemy, Field Marshal, or know defeat."

"That's the point," said Balfor. "They are not the enemy. It's Claradon who's the outlaw, not all his people. If we go there in force, you're right, it could get bloody ugly. A smaller force will send a message that we're not there to conquer them. It's a police action — one of law enforcement, not a military campaign."

"They'll take it as an insult," said Tobin. "As if you think they're so weak that a single brigade could overrun them. Like as not, you'll have a bloodbath on your hands."

"Well then, what's the alternative?" said Balfor. "To deploy an army to siege them? I'll not deploy a full corps against one of our own Dors. Not unless they're in outright and open rebellion, which they're not. These are our own people, not invaders from parts foreign."

"And if they attack your brigade?" said Slyman. "If they wipe out your men?"

"If they dare such a thing, unprovoked," said Balfor, "then they'll mark themselves as our enemies, as traitors to the realm. If that be what they are, then I will unleash the full might of the Lomerian guard on them. We'll bring them down and their strong walls with them. We will crush the Northmen and send them wailing back to the mountains whence they first came. But only if traitors they truly be."

"This is madness," said Jhensezil.

"Then we must choose our Regent carefully," said Tobin, "for it will be his or her diplomatic skills that will win the day, or thrust us into civil war. We must choose very carefully."

"The rule of law must be maintained," said Barusa. "That above all else."

"Seizing all the holdings of a Dor Lord makes a mockery of the law," said Jhensezil.

"It must be done," said Balfor.

"An example must be made," said Slyman. "We'll rout out all the Eotrus, and whichever of their bannermen are foolish enough to stand with them."

"The Eotrus have many allies," said Tobin. "Both in the Northlands and farther afield. These Northmen are hard men – hardened by the harsh weather and by battles in the mountains too numerous to count. It's they that have kept the lugron in check all these years. It's they who've held back darker things — things far worse than lugron — that have crept from the mountain peaks and the deepest caverns and the icy realms beyond. This action will rouse a sleeping dragon. A dragon we'll all regret rousing before we're done. Think carefully, councilors, before we deploy these troops."

"My men can handle the Northmen, if it comes to a fight," said Balfor.

"You're a fool to think that," said Tobin. "A darned fool."

***

House Alder's parlor was one of the smallest rooms in the manor, though it was huge by common standards, outfitted as it was with three generous leather couches and several wide, high-backed cushioned chairs. A fire crackled in the fireplace and supplemented the light provided by the oil-fired sconces positioned about the walls. The parlor's doors were closed and closely monitored, as was usual when a prominent guest visited the House. The room smelled vaguely of mothballs.

"Your new position suits you," said Mother Alder from her chair, which was taller and more ornate than its fellows. "I've rarely seen you look as sharp or as fit."

"What man wouldn't try to look his best when visiting you," said Garon Kroth with a smile that showed off his white teeth and chiseled jaw. "But had I known better the daily length of a High Magister's toils, I might well have refused the position."

"No, no," said Mother Alder. "Lomion needed you, and you answered her call, as was your duty. You would not have done differently."

He nodded. "Today's council meetings went well, I'm told."

"Well in outcome, if not in form," said Mother Alder.

"That jackal, Jhensezil, insulted Mother Alder," said Rom through gritted teeth. He sat in a chair to the right that matched his sister's, but was set a foot or so back toward the wall. "He insulted all the Alders."

"We expected no less," said Mother Alder, her voice conciliatory. "I was surprised that

Harringgold didn't say more against us. He surely had his chance, but didn't take it. The fool must be frightened."

"As he should be," said Rom.

"We must use that to our advantage," said Mother Alder.

"He didn't have the votes, and he knew it — so anything he said was a waste of breath," said Barusa from across the room. He stood by the mantle, wine glass in hand. "Why antagonize us? There was no point to it. Yet even knowing that, he couldn't hold back — not completely. A weak, sniveling fool, just like the rest of his clan."

"We accomplished many of our goals today," said Mother Alder.

"Aye. In the private session," said Barusa, "more measures passed than I thought would. More mayhap than I hoped, though there were some painful losses."

"The measure regarding healers?" said Magister Kroth.

"Passed," said Barusa, a broad smile on his face. "The services of Lomion City's healers will now be free to any and all that need them. Now the common folk will get the care that's always been denied them for lack of coin. Getting that law passed is mayhap my greatest accomplishment since becoming Chancellor. That alone makes today a good day."

"I congratulate you, sir," said Kroth, "but I must ask how the measure will be funded?"

"From the treasury, of course," said Barusa. "We planned to fully fund it via the half tax on the Dor Lords' holdings, but that measure, unfortunately, was struck down. Tobin, the old fool, and Lady Aramere voted against us, and so Harringgold's old guard carried the day on that vote. We'll have to find another source of revenue — until then, we will issue letters of credit."

"Why not hold the measure in abeyance until the funds are available?" said Kroth.

"In part, because we've no idea when they'll be available," said Barusa. "But more importantly, I'll not let the poor suffer a single day more than they have to. Not when healing is available. If the kingdom must go into in debt to help the common folk, so be it."

"A view that may yet come back to haunt us," said Kroth. "Especially considering the weighty debt Lomion already carries. The merchants and landholders already joke that foreigners own more holdings in the city than do the nobles. More letters of credit will only exacerbate that."

"An exaggeration," said Barusa. "And of less import than the welfare of the people."

Kroth nodded. "And the moneylenders? What of the measure concerning them?"

"We now own them," said Barusa. "They all now fall under the council's domain. Even more importantly, the progressive tax measure passed despite all Jhensezil's railing against it. The old malcontent lost his voice trying to shout us down."

"So finally the wealthy will pay their fair share?" said Kroth.

"Not their fair share, not by a longshot," said Barusa. "But a lot more than they pay now. Eventually we'll get there — fairness — but we must take one step at a time. We must proceed in a measured fashion."

"These may be the most important measures to come into law in decades," said Kroth. "They could transform our society."

"They will," said Barusa.

"In ways few have the wisdom to foresee," said Mother Alder. "And that, my dear High Magister," she said holding her wine goblet in the air, "is precisely my plan."

V
DISCONTENT

As the crew of *The White Rose* cleared the decks of the dead dwellers and their own casualties, the expedition's surviving leadership gathered in the ship's mess hall – the room filled of smoke, sweat, and rattled nerves. Lord Gallis Korrgonn, son of Azathoth, sat silent and still at the head of the long but narrow rectangular table. Father Ginalli was at his right hand, all ego, and nervous energy. Par Glus Thorn was at his left, wooden and unreadable; Thorn's elderly assistant beside him. Lord Ezerhauten sat at the middle of the table, the knight-captains and officers of his Sithian Mercenary Company positioned on each side and opposite him, Frem Sorlons and Par Sevare amongst them. Scattered about the table sat Par Keld, Par Brackta, Par Weldin, Par Rhund, and Stev Keevis. Captain Rascelon scowled at the far end of the table, his officers, and several bodyguards around him, tense and wary.

"Tremont of Wyndum fell on the bridge deck," said Ezerhauten. "He took at least five dwellers with him, judging by the bodies piled around him. Miles de Gant fell there too, along with his entire squad. Twelve men dead on the bridge deck alone, twelve dwellers beside them and more on the main deck that must've fallen to their swords and dropped down. You should hear the seamen that took refuge in the rigging describe that battle. A last stand worthy of song and story."

"Hear, hear," said the knight-captains.

"de Gant's family would rather have their son than a song," said Par Brackta. "Count de Gant will demand a full accounting of the day's events."

"As will Par Landru's brothers," said Sevare.

"I will inform the families of my fallen, as is my custom," said Ezerhauten. "No one else need concern themselves with this," he said sharply.

"Your men fought and died valiantly for our noble cause, Lord Ezerhauten," said Ginalli, his voice unusually calm and soft. "As did many members of Azathoth's faithful, and Captain Rascelon's crew. They will be remembered one and all. The honor their sacrifices bring to their Houses will temper the grief, though it be great."

"You speak of honor when nigh two thirds of my crew is dead," said Captain Rascelon through clenched teeth. "Song and story won't bring them back, nor will it sail my ship."

"The costs of war," said Par Keld.

"We're not at war," said Rascelon.

"Make no mistake, Captain," said Ginalli. "We most certainly are at war – with those who've corrupted our society and turned away from the lord, and with those misguided souls that seek to stop us from setting things to rights."

"The loses are not yours alone, Captain," said Ezerhauten. "We all knew this expedition would be difficult. More than a third of my company has fallen since we left Lomion. In twenty years, I've never suffered such casualties."

"The League of Light has paid a steep toll too," said Par Brackta. "Half our lugron have fallen, and more wizards and archmages than I dare count. More even than fell at the Tower of the Arcane during the troubles."

"You failed to protect my ship," said Rascelon, looking first at Ginalli and then at Ezerhauten. "You put too many good men ashore and left incompetent fools behind. Because of that, my crew was decimated."

"Mayhap fewer would have fallen if they had stood and fought instead of running away," said Ezerhauten, bristling.

The captain smashed his fist to the table. "My men aren't soldiers. An army of sea-devils boarded my ship – giants, eight, ten, some twelve feet tall. What were they supposed to do? There was no way to fight those things. Even your armored knights couldn't best them."

"Everyone did what they could," said Ginalli, his voice quicker and sharper than before. "We need to get past this and agree on how to proceed. We can't lose sight of the larger goal here. We have a mission of vital importance to complete."

"Vital importance to you, not to me," said Rascelon. "How is it that you had the means to stop those things and waited until you did? Why didn't you let loose your blue fire sooner?"

Ginalli glanced at Glus Thorn and sat back, ignoring the captain's glare.

"I acted as soon as I became aware of the situation," said Thorn.

Par Keld fidgeted in his seat, his eyes downcast.

The captain's face looked incredulous. "As soon as you became aware? Were you dead drunk or in a coma, wizard? There was enough noise on deck to wake the dead. Was the screaming as my men got cut to pieces not enough to slip you from your sordid dreams?"

"Excuse me, gentlemen," said Stev Keevis, leaning forward in his seat. "Master Thorn wasn't—"

Par Keld bounded to his feet, fully extended his arm, and pointed at Stev Keevis. "At last, the traitor speaks!"

"What's this?" said Ginalli.

"He was asleep on watch," spat Keld.

"Him and Par Oris – drunk, the both of them. When we roused them, they refused to inform Master Thorn of what was happening. They even tried to stop me from doing so. All to protect themselves, the cowards."

Stev Keevis rose slowly to his feet, his eyes boring through Par Keld. He spoke slowly and calmly. "It was you that refused to call Master Thorn, not me. You said that you were in charge; that you would handle things."

"Lies," shouted Keld. "He lies! You can see it on his face. See how he fidgets?"

"It's one thing for you to try to save your reputation by blaming me, a man you barely know, for your own negligence," continued Stev Keevis. "Many men of low character would do the same. But to blame Par Oris too – a kindly old man that lies now on the brink of death. Par Oris told me you had been his apprentice years ago. He taught you, guided you, helped you to grow in magic, and you abandoned him, and now accuse him. You left him to fight and die while you fled to save your own hide. You're a special kind of scum, Keld. Truly special."

"How dare you disrespect me." Keld looked

around the room at the gathered officers. "Do you see how he speaks to me? He isn't even really one of us – just a stinking hanger-on. You've no voice in this council, elf. Your lies won't save you. Oris was never my master. He was just old. Everyone is sad for Par Oris' injuries, I'm certain, but I know far more magic than he ever did. If it weren't for me, the whole ship would have been lost. It was you that fell asleep on watch. If you had any honor, you would admit it. You are responsible. You practically killed Oris and all the others with your own hands. For that, you should pay and pay dearly." He turned to Ginalli and Thorn. "You know that I'm not one to speak out against anyone, and it's up to you, of course, but I say we should string this traitor up from the yardarm and drop his golem into the sea afore they do us any more harm."

"Enough," said Ginalli. "As I said before, we all did our best given difficult circumstances. I don't want to hear any more accusations or recriminations. I want to hear how we can best move forward and complete our mission."

Stev Keevis looked shocked and stood there staring at Ginalli.

Ginalli scanned the faces of those gathered, searching for a response.

"We stopped at that island to find a mystical talisman," said Par Sevare. "We found it. Why would we not just go on to Jutenheim as planned? I'm not sure what there is to discuss?"

"Not on my ship," said Rascelon.

The room went utterly silent and all eyes turned to the captain.

"My mind is made up," said Rascelon. "We're

heading back. We've lost far too many men. My ship is trashed and barely seaworthy. This isn't what me and mine signed on for. If we go on, we will all end up dead. I'm done with your mission and with you and your stinking League of Light. We're going home."

"You forget your place, captain," said Ginalli.

"You forget yours, priest. This is my ship, not yours."

"You committed to this voyage – to our holy mission. You're a believer, a disciple of Azathoth; this is your cause as much as ours. You cannot turn aside now."

"I committed to ferry you to Jutenheim and back – not to take part in a war. After all the loses we've suffered, it's obvious this quest is cursed, and I'm through with it. If you want to continue, I will put you off at Tragoss Mor. You and your charlatan," gesturing at Korrgonn, "can hire another ship there. I will have no more of this madness."

"Azathoth is a jealous god," said Thorn, his voice slow and low. "He demands unswerving loyalty from his servants."

The captain stood. "Azathoth can kiss my—"

Thorn gestured with his hand, a small gesture – a mere flick of the wrist – and the ship's officers and bullyboys that stood around Rascelon slid backward against the cabin's wall, and were held helpless there as if by unseen hands of great strength.

"You will utter no blasphemies in the presence of Lord Korrgonn," said Thorn. He made a slapping motion with his hand and Rascelon reacted as if struck in the face – the sound of the slap filling the room. The captain's face reddened with fingermarks, though Thorn was no less than twenty feet from him.

Shock filled Rascelon's face.

Thorn waved his hand again, and Rascelon was slapped on the cheek, this time even harder. Rascelon struggled to move, but his hands were pinned to the table by the same unseen force that held back his men. Thorn waved his hand again, and again, eight times in total; the beating far more severe than what Par Keld had experienced. It left Rascelon dazed and bleeding from his mouth, nose, and one ear. He slumped forward, finally free of the magic's grip. His eyes locked on Thorn; his hands drew into fists.

"Will you make good on your commitment, Captain?" said Ginalli. "Or will you turn your back on your god?"

Rascelon's sword was out in an instant. He vaulted onto the table, cursing, murder in his eyes. He had gone three steps before Thorn waved his hand upward. Unseen hands gripped Rascelon and rocketed him to the ceiling, head first. The impact shattered his head, sending blood and brains spurting in all directions, dousing or splattering nearly every person in the room. His corpse dropped to the tabletop.

Frem rose to his feet and jumped back from the table, as did most of the others, shocked expressions all around.

"Varak du Mace," said Ginalli to *The Rose*'s First Mate, his voice soft and calm again. "Step forward."

Thorn waved his hand, releasing du Mace from his magical grip, though the other seamen were still held fast. Du Mace stepped up to the table, sweat pouring down his face.

"Congratulations, du Mace, you're the new captain of *The White Rose*," said Ginalli. "Are you prepared to set course for Jutenheim and see our holy quest through to the end, no matter the danger?"

"Aye," said du Mace, his voice quaking, his eyes wide with terror.

***

The officers' lounge was empty save for Frem, Sevare, and Ezerhauten. They huddled at the corner table in the back of the room and spoke in whispers, mugs of mead in hand. Sevare had two mugs before him – one of mead, the other served as his spittoon.

"An evil thing that was," said Frem. "Killing the captain like that. I've seen a lot in my time, but that was some of the worst, especially since it didn't need to happen at all."

"Ginalli said it plainly enough," said Sevare. "Azathoth is a jealous god; you can't put anything ahead of serving him. Rascelon put his ship and his own skin first, and then took a sword to Thorn – not only disloyal, but downright stupid. He had it coming. Don't trouble yourself thinking on it any further."

"Azathoth didn't kill the captain," said Frem. "Thorn did. They're not one in the same, are they?"

"I know you've got religion, Sevare," said Ezerhauten. "That's your business, but remember, we're not with Ginalli and his bunch out of some religious obligation. They needed a coherent unit of professional soldiers for this expedition, couldn't get them from the noble houses in league with them, so they hired us. Your loyalty is first and foremost to the Sithian Mercenary Company – or at least it better be." Ezerhauten stared at Sevare, waiting for a reply.

"I haven't forgotten," said Sevare. "This quest of theirs has got my head turned around. It's not like any job I've ever done. This one has a deeper purpose."

"Our company is not just hired swords, don't forget," said Ezerhauten. "We don't work for whoever pays the most. We're not that type; never have been. I've always taken jobs that served some good purpose besides lining my purse. I took this one for the same reasons."

"That's why I signed on with you," said Frem. "Without a good cause, I couldn't lead this life. I couldn't look my little girl in the eye if I wasn't proud of what I was doing. Today, I'm not so proud."

"I've had second thoughts about this venture as well," said Ezerhauten. "I've had them for some time now, as I think you know."

"If Rascelon didn't pull his sword on Thorn, he would still be alive," said Sevare.

"Do you geniuses understand that the whole thing was a setup?" said Ezerhauten.

"Don't start, Ezer," said Sevare. "There was no setup."

"A setup is all there was. The council meeting was a sham. You said it yourself; it's obvious what we need to do – stick to the plan. We found the talisman. Now we go on to Jutenheim. Nothing has changed. There was nothing to discuss. We were called together because Ginalli and Thorn suspected Rascelon wanted to end the mission. They wanted to test that theory, convince Rascelon to change his mind, or kill him if he didn't. It played out like a stage performance.

They knew that they didn't need Rascelon – they just need his ship and a competent crew to sail her. So they made an example of him. And it worked. They will get no more trouble from the ship's officers after what they witnessed today. Now they're more scared of those wizards than they are of death itself. Crafty was their scheme, but brutal. We've signed on with a cadre of fanatics, boys, make no mistake of it. Very dangerous fanatics."

"You're seeing conspiracies that only exist in your head," said Sevare.

"Ezer's right," said Frem. "I think Ginalli and Thorn planned most every word that they said in there."

"Then you're both daft," said Sevare. "To complete the mission, we have to get to Jutenheim, and Rascelon was going to stand in the way. They had to eliminate him. He forced their hand."

"Oh yes," said Ezerhauten. "The ends justify the means. An old and often used philosophy – often used to justify all manner of mischief and evil."

"Afore we rowed our butts over to that island," said Frem, "we guessed that Korrgonn held our Pointmen in reserve on purpose – not knowing what dangers lurked there, we figured he didn't want to chance losing his best scouts, so he sent another squadron instead of us. We thought that was right smart. But the truth is, Korrgonn knew that that big lizard, Dagon, was there all along. He knew that thing had the talisman that he needed, so he set that other squadron up to get killed dead. Somehow, he knew that the dwellers would kill them and use their blood to do their summoning – to call up Dagon from that well or whatever it was. Only then could Korrgonn snatch the talisman from the lizard. The timing of it all was much too good to be chance."

Ezerhauten smiled. "You've sized it up straight, Frem old boy. I'm impressed. I see it the same."

Sevare's eyes narrowed. "You really think that Korrgonn is so manipulative? That he would have men killed to achieve his goals? He's not just some petty lord or merchant, you know. He's the son of Azathoth. Why couldn't it be chance? The hand of Azathoth intervening to suit his own purposes. Is it so hard to have a little faith? Or is it just too easy to be a cynic?"

"I have faith in myself, my sword, and on a good day, my men," said Ezerhauten. "That's about it."

"Then I pity you," said Sevare. He rose, downed what remained in his mug, and took his leave.

"He's got a bit too much religion, I think," said Ezerhauten.

"Aye, it seems so," said Frem.

"I know that he's your friend, but when a man gets too much religion, sometimes he goes wacky and you can't trust him anymore. I'm not saying Sevare's gone that way, but for now, we have to watch him, and we have to be careful about what we say around him. He might be a lost cause. We might not be able to save him. He could turn on us. I've no interest in getting my skull splattered on the ceiling."

"Me neither," said Frem. "It could be that he's just upset that more fancy wizards have dropped in battle on this quest than in the last fifty years combined – not counting those lost during the coup at the Tower, that is."

"Maybe," said Ezerhauten. "But I think it's more than that."

"I was worried that Korrgonn had the come hither on you," said Frem. "That you were under his sway."

"Because of that time that he grabbed my shoulder and told me to promise loyalty, and I did?"

Frem nodded. "We haven't spoken at length in private since then. I wasn't certain of what to do if you were under his thrall."

"You were right to be worried. He did put the come hither on me – it just didn't take. When he grabbed my arm, his voice sounded in my head and tried to bend my thoughts to his will; tried to make me his lackey. There are certain wizards what have such skills, but Korrgonn's power is stronger. A lot stronger. The worst is that I think he only used a fraction of that power on me, thinking that's all he needed. So I played along and made it easy for him – made him think that my mind was easily swayed, hoping he would back off before he did me any real damage, and he did. My mind and my will is still my own, and always will be."

"How were you able to fool him?"

"I have my ways," he said with a smile.

"Where have I heard that before?" said Frem smiling and shaking his head. "I heard one of the men saying they saw Mort Zag on his feet."

"It's true. Not an hour ago, I saw Korrgonn press his palms to Big Red's chest. His breathing immediately grew stronger. Then he touched his head, his arms, and his legs. No sooner was he done than Big Red opened his eyes and started talking. Not a lick of medicine, no setting of bones, nothing but a touch. Now that's a feat. That's a kind of magic that I've never seen or heard of afore."

"I've heard of old priests and healers what can fix a man up good. We've seen some of that."

"Not from wounds like Big Red's. Half his bones were broken. Korrgonn has got the touch; there is no doubt about that. Then again, who knows what healing powers Big Red has – he might've survived anyway. The lord only knows what he is after all."

Frem looked confused. "Sevare told me he's just a giant from the mountains. He says he's red because he eats bushels of tomatoes and red apples."

"Does he think you believed him?"

"Sevare thinks I'm stupid because I don't have schooling and don't talk all smooth and sweet as him. Let him think that. No skin off me."

"You're more than what you appear to be, Frem Sorlons."

"Aren't we all?"

95

"I trust that you know now that it's Thorn that's the real power in the League?" said Ezerhauten.

"That came across clear enough," said Frem. "Ginalli is but a snake oil salesman. He's got power, but he's for show. Thorn's got the real juice."

Ezerhauten nodded. "I see it the same. I'm glad to have you serving with me. Especially in this, our most important mission. I mean that."

"Same here." Frem finished off his mead. "So what do we do? About the mission, I mean?"

"We do the job that the League hired us for, just as we have been doing. Keep your eyes and ears open, and watch what you say to Sevare.

"Aye, Commander; that I will.

VI
WHEN THE BLACK ELF KING COMES CALLING

"**I** want to go with you," said Lady Landolyn Malvegil as she sat in bed beside her husband. "I can help you — in many ways."

"No one knows that better than I, my love," said Lord Torbin Malvegil as he wiped the sleep from his eyes. "But if you go to Lomion City with me, I'll be worried about you every minute."

"I can take care of myself."

"I'll be worried that my enemies will try to kidnap you or to harm you to get at me. That worry will be a distraction that I cannot afford. I need to be at my best to accomplish my goals and to keep the Hand's assassins at bay. My mind needs to be clear. I need you here, where you're safe, behind our walls, and closely guarded by our own people."

"I'm not afraid of the Chancellor, or the League, or anyone. I can defend myself better than you know. After all these years, haven't I earned to right to be at your side?"

Torbin's jaw was set. "So do you want to put me at risk? I just told you that if you're along, I'll be distracted. I can't have that."

"Do you think that if you take me to the city, that I'll run off or something?" said Landolyn. "Is that it? You don't even trust me?"

"That's just ridiculous. You're staying here and that's it. I'll waste no more time on this."

"My feelings are not a waste of time," she

said sharply. Her face had gone red. She kicked the covers off her legs and scrambled out of bed, muttering curses under her breath. She grabbed a throw pillow and flung it at the nightstand, spilling a jar of mearn, and knocking over various powders and brushes. She turned to Torbin, furious, but before she spoke, there was an anxious knock on their chamber's door.

"My lord," said Gravemare through the door, "an emissary approaches the Dor."

"It's not that stinking Alder again, is it? The tax collector?"

"No, my lord."

Torbin turned to Landolyn. "Put on your robe," he said quietly. He plucked his own robe from the hanger beside the bed, donned it, and cinched it about his waist. "Enter."

Hubert Gravemare, Dor Malvegil's grayed Castellan, opened the door slowly, but not nearly as slowly as was his custom, and stood waiting for his lord to give him leave to speak.

"Are you unwell?" said Malvegil to Gravemare, concern on his face. "You look pale."

"I'm fine, my lord, considering."

"Considering what?"

"Considering that myths and legends have come calling to Dor Malvegil."

"Myths and legends? What are you saying? I'm in no mood for games this morning. Who is here and what do they want?"

"Svarts," said Gravemare. "They request an audience."

There was a long pause as Lord Malvegil studied Gravemare's face, perhaps searching for some sign that he was jesting or else just waiting for him to continue. "Svarts, you say? Are you serious?"

"Aye, my lord."

"Black elves? Here? At my keep?"

"Aye," said Gravemare, nodding.

"I thought they died out ages ago. No one has seen them in . . . how long? Three hundred years?"

"Four hundred, my lord, mayhap longer. But today, they are at our doorstep. And not just any svarts. The king of Thoonbarrow himself."

"The king of Thoonbarrow!" said Malvegil. "Now that is a legend come to life. How does that old poem go? Do you remember?"

Gravemare cleared his throat and spoke the ancient rhyme.

When the black elf king comes calling,
Hide your children and your gold,
For the old elf's stony heart is icy cold,
He'll steal your wealth and leave iron rust behind,
He'll steal your babes, in the morning, an imp to find
In a cradle as cold as the depths of his mines,
A creature of darkness, on your soul to dine,
So beware the black king and all his evil kind,
Shun the deep darks where the black elves bide their time
Hold on dear to your immortal soul,
Or down to darkest Thoonbarrow it will slide,
Down to where the black elves hide,
Never again to see the light of day,
To Odin, to Thor, you must pray,
For courage and strength to keep the Svarts at

bay.

"**W**ell done," said Malvegil.

"It goes and on," said Gravemare, waving his hand, "but I don't recall the rest. I have a book that—"

"The svarts are not elves," spat Landolyn. "They are creatures of the black, of the deep rock. They dwell in Midgaard's darkest depths where no elf or volsung would venture."

"Dark gnomes then," said Malvegil. "I've heard them called that many a time. Or is it deep gnomes?"

"They prefer to be called svarts, my lord," said Gravemare. "Though they take no offense in being called deep gnomes. We've been warned not to call them black elves, for that term causes them great offense."

"Pfft," went Landolyn. "Believe nothing they say, Torbin. They are lying, wicked twisted little things, devoid of feelings, compassion, and common decency. They are worse than lugron."

"The king of the svarts, here, at my keep," said Malvegil as he walked to his wardrobe. "How odd a thing. Curious timing, too, isn't it? Wait — you said you were warned not to call them black elves. Warned by whom?"

"By the dwarven ambassador that travels with them," said Gravemare. "McDuff the Mighty."

"McDuff!" said Malvegil. "Gravemare, if this is a jest, I am not amused."

"No jest, my lord. Though, I fear we'd be far better off if it were."

At lord Malvegil's command, guards accoutered in full battle regalia pulled open the doors of Dor Malvegil's audience hall. Four squadrons of the finest Malvegillian soldiers stood at attention about the great hall. Two squadrons were positioned near the entryway, one to each side of the massive double doors, facing toward those who were about to enter. The other squadrons stood in the rear, arrayed protectively about the lord's dais on which Torbin Malvegil and his advisors assembled.

Malvegil sat in his chair, which was in truth, more akin to a throne — high-backed, massive of limb, and bejeweled of garnet, emerald, and opal. His lady sat beside him in a smaller seat that matched his. Gravemare stood beside Malvegil, lean and stoic, his black and red robe and tall staff, similarly colored, the formal trappings of his office. Opposite him, standing beside Landolyn, was Brother Torgrist, the Dor's high cleric. To either side, various other House officials. On the main level, just in front of the dais, stood Master Karktan of Rivenwood, the Malvegils' Weapons Master, and his brother, Stoub, Lord Malvegil's chief bodyguard — both men, massive and black bearded, looking much like larger versions of their lord, who was no small man himself. Their armor was black and red, and they wore tall helmets adorned with black and red feathers.

Though near mid-morning, the hall was unusually dim, for the sky was so overcast that little light filtered through the great skylights high overhead at the hall's apex. So, as in the evenings, much of the hall's light came from the oil lamps that hung by steel chains in orderly rows from the rafters. The pleasant scent of birchwood wafted from the fire pits and counterbalanced the acrid scent of the burning oil. Except for the crackling from the fire pits, the audience hall stood silent.

Then began the drums. The svart drums emitted a soft but eerie, echoey sound unlike any instrument the Malvegils had heard before. That rhythmic sounding ushered forth a grand procession into the hall. At its van marched McDuff, an usually tall dwarf, massively broad at the shoulder and upper arm, with flaming red hair and beard, dressed in burnished plate armor of intricate design and a flowing black cape that kissed the floor behind him. Six dwarven soldiers followed him.

McDuff stopped but a few steps into the hall and the drums went silent save for some odd reverberations that continued for several moments. Other figures stood behind the dwarves, but could not yet be clearly seen. "I am McDuff the Mighty, emissary of his grand majesty, Bornyth Trollsbane, High King of Clan Darendon."

"Welcome, emissary," said Gravemare in a loud and measured voice. "The Malvegils are happy to receive you and word from the great King Bornyth, our friend and ally, loyal and true, these many years."

"Thank you, Castellan," said McDuff. "You honor my clan and country with your words."

"Tell us, emissary, who is it that travels with you this day?" said Gravemare. "And for what purpose?"

"Those with me request to announce themselves," said McDuff as he and his fellows stepped forward and to the side. The drums began anew and the procession continued into the hall.

Those who followed the dwarves were unlike any persons that had entered Dor Malvegil in the four hundred years of its existence. Shorter even than dwarves, the svarts had sleight frames, spindly limbs that were a bit overlong, large hands with unnaturally long fingers, dark gray skin nearing to black, bald pates, hairless bodies, and disturbingly large eyes with black pupils and sclera of greenish yellow streaked with more black. Their faces were expressionless; their large teeth and long nails as black and yellow as their eyes. Their ears, sharply pointed. Their aspects were so odd, so alien, that the Malvegils could not be certain whether all those who entered were the male of the species, or the female, or whether there were some of each. Those at the fore carried staffs of bleached bone half again taller than they were, and wore long beige robes that trailed well behind them. From what manner of creature the bone staves were salvaged, no Malvegil could guess. "Their wizard-priests, the Diresvarts," whispered Landolyn to her husband. "Each deadly and treacherous."

The svarts hummed an eerie tune as they marched into the hall, their melody in harmony with the beat of the svart drummers that followed close behind them. They marched with a heavy step that belied their diminutive size – so heavy in fact were their steps, that the great hall shook as in they came, row after row, after row.

When the procession came within twenty feet of the dais, Master Karktan and his brother stepped before the svarts and put up their hands, palms forward, directing them to halt. They would allow their guests no closer to their lord and lady.

McDuff rushed over. He too gestured for the svarts to stop, and spoke some words in what must have been their language. The svarts halted, though they seemed confused, and looked around to their fellows, though no words escaped their lips, and no expressions formed on their faces. Their tune continued for some moments, then abruptly stopped. Their ranks parted in orderly fashion and up from the rear marched two of their number. The svarts began to hum another tune, this one deep and somber, as the two made their way to the front.

The first was accoutered as all the rest, save that he wore robes of yellow and black and his staff was a full seven feet long, also of bone. That one they called the Orator, as that was his function.

The second was the svart king, adorned all in yellow. He was the shortest of them all – less than three feet tall, smaller even than most gnomes, yet he exuded a presence, a charisma, that outshone all his fellows. No doubt, it was some combination of his regal bearing, or the strength and confidence in his voice, or the wisdom that shone on his lined face. The king's skin was darker than that of the others, his face heavily wrinkled, whereas his brethren's faces were smooth in the main. Despite his obvious age and limited height, the king's frame was broader and thicker limbed than his fellows, giving him a more robust appearance.

The Orator spoke first. He chanted all his

words rather than merely speaking them. His voice had an alien quality – bold, melodic, and haunting with a strange echoing effect not unlike the drums. His words were in High Lomerian (an archaic dialect of the common Lomerian spoken about the kingdom), with a strong accent, but by and large, the Malvegils understood him. He raised his hands, palms facing each other as he announced his lord.

"Oh great lord of the Malvegils," he said, "afore you stands Guyphoon Garumptuss tet Montu, high king of Thoonbarrow, Master of the Seven Stratems, Patriarch of Brood tet Montu, and Lord of all Svartleheim, offspring of Guyphoon Pintalia of the Windy Ways, Traymoor Garumptuss the Bold, and Trantmain lin Backus tet Montu, great king of the undermountains – may his memory outlast the ages."

Malvegil nodded respectfully but made no other response. Gravemare seemed uncertain of what to say or do, fidgeted where he stood, and ultimately only nodded as well.

"Three parents?" whispered Malvegil to Landolyn. "I can't pronounce his name, for Odin's sake."

"Some say their king has bedding rights," she whispered, "but others say their biology requires three."

The Orator continued unperturbed. "We come of heavy heart and dire tiding. Ancient, terrible evil from the time afore time has arisen from the bowels of Midgaard. It gathers and it grows. It festers, it plagues, and it hungers. Most of all, it hungers. Its thirsts cannot be quenched; its appetites cannot be sated. Soon it will spill

105

Lomerian blood, for toward you it moves."

"What is this evil of which you speak?" said Malvegil. "Name it."

The Orator did not answer. He did not react at all – as if he didn't hear or didn't understand Malvegil's words.

"Name it," repeated Malvegil after a few moments. The Orator turned toward his king.

The king said but a single word. "Duergar."

As one, the svarts winced and groaned as if physically struck. Some murmured in their own language – their words unintelligible. Nearly all of them made a sign across their faces and chests – a protective ward designed to stave off bad omens and dark magic.

"What or who is this duergar?" said Gravemare.

"They who devour life and make it duergar," said the Orator.

Gravemare and Malvegil looked to each other, confused. "Of what do they speak?" Malvegil whispered to Landolyn.

She shook her head. "I know not. That word means nothing to me."

"We do not follow your meaning," said Gravemare. "Please explain."

"The gates of Helheim are sealed," said the Orator.

Gravemare shook his head, indicating he didn't understand.

"What has stood open since time immemorial is closed," said the Orator. "None may enter. All are turned back."

"What does this mean?" said Gravemare.

"None may enter," said the Orator, louder.

"All are turned back."

"Turned back from what?" said Gravemare.

"Death," said the Orator.

Malvegil's hands gripped the arms of his chair; his face went pale, his jaw set. He feared he knew now of what the svarts spoke but he prayed to Odin that he was wrong.

"We still do not follow your meaning," said Gravemare.

The Orator paused for some moments, searching for the right words in a language alien to him. "All life touched by duergar are turned back from death," he said.

The king stepped past the Orator and waived Malvegil's guards aside. They parted, but Stoub closely shadowed him. The svart king made his way up to the dais, and stopped before Malvegil's feet. He waved McDuff over. The svart king spoke in svartish and McDuff repeated his words in Lomerian, as best as his translation skills allowed.

"Duergar," said the svart king, "are the dead that walk. They are the dead that hunger. The dead that kill. The dead that feast on the living and make them duergar. They will not stop until all are duergar. Where they go, no life remains."

The king repeated his last sentence, this time in Lomerian without McDuff's help. "Where they go, no life remains!"

"They will not stop until all are duergar," added the Orator.

Malvegil looked to McDuff who nodded repeatedly. "Dead gods," murmured Malvegil, for now he knew the truth, and from it, there was no escape. A truth he had feared for twenty-five years. A truth that he hoped to forget, but that he knew he never could. "Can it be?" he said so quietly that no one but Landolyn heard him. "Did we not get them all?"

Landolyn reached out her hand, placed it over her husband's, and squeezed. He looked up. The svart king stared up at him, his face expressionless. The hairs on the back of Malvegil's neck stood up when he met the svart's eerie gaze.

"Do they come in force?" said Malvegil as he leaned forward in his seat. "As an army? How soon? How much time do we have to prepare?"

The king turned toward the Orator and made some gesture, after which the Orator resumed his role as spokesman.

"We understand not the ways of the duergar," said the Orator. "They sometimes appear mindless. A force of nature. Chaos personified. At other times, they attack in force. How soon they might venture on your lands, we know not. A day? A week? A year? Or mayhap, they are already here. Gird yourselves against them. Raise your gates. Bar your doors. They are coming. The dead are coming."

"Where did these things come from?" said Gravemare.

"They came at us without warning, from the dark places – up from the great depths, through the olden rock, from down deeper than we have ever traveled. And we have delved deep. Their origin, somewhere beneath the place you call the Dead Fens, though they do not return there. They only spread, like a plague, outward, in all directions. They must be stopped or nowhere will be safe for the living."

"How do your people fare?" said Malvegil.

"We recognized too late what they were. We ignored the signs and portents to our folly. We disbelieved. And as a result, ancient Thoonbarrow fell the first day of their attack. The king's palace held for but one day more. We are refugees now. Everything that was ours is gone. Our people decimated. A hundred millennia of art, culture, writings, all gone. All destroyed. Those of our people that escaped fled far afield in all directions. The dwarves have taken many of us in, and given us sanctuary, despite hard feelings amongst our peoples going back through the ages. The dwarven king, Bornyth Trollsbane is wise. He knows that the duergar are the real threat. He allies with us to combat them, such as our skills and numbers allow."

"Hard feelings?" whispered Landolyn in Malvegil's ear. "The dwarves kill the svart on sight and burn their bodies to ash. Do not trust them, husband, for these are no tribe of men. They are an ancient breed of creatures from an old line otherwise dead. They are no more akin to a man than is a snake, and far more dangerous."

"Enough," whispered Malvegil.

"Do the dwarves vouch for this account?" said Gravemare.

"The svarts speak the truth on this matter, they do," said McDuff. "The duergar threat is real," he said, and spat on the floor in disgust. "They attack, they kill, and they eat anything alive that they find, the scum. Any that escape them, but suffer a wound at their hands, from a bite or a scratch, soon develop a fever and die – sometimes within minutes, if the wound is

109

severe, other times, within hours, but at most a day or two. Then they rise again as duergar. They rise up from the dead! And when they do, they hunger for the living. And so the cycle continues and their plague spreads."

"There is an ancient legend from the South about creatures that are neither dead nor alive, and that drink the blood of the living," said Gravemare.

McDuff put up a hand. "I know those tales. You speak of blood lords. The duergar are something different. Something unknown, save in the oldest svart legends. Whatever written lore the svart knew of them is lost along with their histories and most of their scholars."

"How can they be stopped?" said Gravemare. "How can they be killed if they are already dead?"

"Blades and bludgeons are of limited effect," said McDuff. "The svarts cut some to pieces, though even the pieces moved of their own accord. Fire does them in eventually. Torches and oil work. What else may stop them, we know not."

"Will you ally with us against the duergar?" said the Orator.

Gravemare looked to his lord.

"If your words be true," said Malvegil. "We will stand against them with you."

"But our walls are high," said Gravemare. "Let the duergar break against them, as all our enemies have in the past."

"We will develop our tactics in due time," said Malvegil.

"Thank you, oh great lord of the Malvegils, for you are wise," said the Orator. "We offer a gift to cement and strengthen this alliance."

110

"Here comes the hook," whispered Landolyn to Malvegil.

The svarts hummed a new tune – this one strong and rhythmic. Other svarts moved up from the rear carrying an ornate crate of lacquered wood painted with multicolored geometric designs. Behind the crate walked a svart female – obvious by her curves, however slight, though her head was as bald as the rest. Her eyes were even larger than the males, and her face was pleasing in its way, unlined, ageless. She wore a sheer purple dress that fluttered as she walked and trailed behind her.

The svarts set the crate down by their king and removed the top. The female reached in and removed a large spherical object draped in a thick cloth. She carefully removed the covering and held the object out for the Malvegils' inspection.

"The Sventeran Stone," said the Orator; a hint of pride on his face.

Landolyn gasped and rose to her feet, in part in excitement, and partly to get a better look. "A Seer Stone," she said. The stone was maroon and black, with streaks of gold that moved of their own accord about its surface, which was smooth and well preserved.

"The duergar are coming," said the Orator. "They are a darkness that we will not survive unless we stand together, and for that communication is key. The stones offer that. We are pleased that you recognize what they are. We feared that such things were beyond you. With them, we'll be able to communicate with each other from afar, to exchange news, and coordinate our activities against the enemy."

"We know of Seer Stones," said Gravemare, "though one has never afore graced this hall."

"Then you know that it takes a true Seer of great power to use one. To any who hold not the power of a true Seer, the stones are useless. Cardakeen rack Mortha," he said gesturing toward the female svart, "is a true Seer of rare gifts. She will remain amongst you to operate the Sventeran Stone . With it, you will be able to communicate with us at Darendor, where we have a second stone."

"Even now," said McDuff, "Galibar the Great, the prince of Darendor, first son to Bornyth and heir to Clan Darendon, journeys to meet with the Lindonaire elves. He carries the same warnings, the same offer of alliance, and a third Seer Stone with which we'll all be able to communicate with the elves."

"The Lindonaire will not ally with the svart," said Landolyn.

"Perhaps not," said McDuff, "which is why Galibar goes there and the high king of the svart has come here. In the end, the elves must ally with us all, or they will not survive this. The Lindenwood and the elves' arrows offer little deterrent to the duergar."

"You say you can communicate with Darendor with your stone?" said Malvegil.

"Yes," said the Orator.

"Contact them," said Malvegil.

"Use of the stones is difficult," said the Orator. "There is a price that must be paid for its magics by the Seer. As such, the stones must only be used when needed. Both we and Bornyth Trollsbane anticipated your need for confirmation of our words–"

"Which is why Bornyth sent me," said McDuff.

"Smart thinking to send an old friend that I trust like a brother," said Malvegil. He stood and jumped down from the dais with surprising agility, landing heavily on his feet. Stoub was at his side in an instant. "Nevertheless, you will contact them now," said Malvegil, his voice stern, his expression serious as he walked directly up to the svart king who did not flinch at his approach. Malvegil loomed over the king, standing nearly twice his height. Their eyes locked on each other's, tension in the air. It seemed as if anything could happen; violence only a word or nod away. Strangely, the svart king smelled like lemons, but why, Malvegil had no idea. The soldiers arrayed about the room stirred and fidgeted.

"Torbin," said McDuff, "the svarts have spoken true. They come here as friends."

"I hear you, old friend," said Malvegil. "Nevertheless, I will not consider an alliance unless they use the Stone to contact Bornyth. Now."

The Orator and the svart king chattered back and forth in their language. The king was obviously very agitated – his voice was raised and his fingers danced and pointed as he spoke. More than once, McDuff winced at some remark of the king's, though what he said remained unknown to the Malvegils.

"Very well," said the Orator after a time. He spoke some words to Seer Cardakeen and she placed the Seer Stone on the floor and sat down next to it. The hall went silent; all were watching the svart Seer. She chanted in the svartish, her voice soft and delicate, rising and falling with the words as her fingers caressed the stone. Streaks of what looked like lightning appeared within the stone's depths. They grew more frequent, brighter, and stronger, as the moments went by. After a time, an image solidified within the sphere. Malvegil drew close to see, Stoub at his side gripped his arm, so as to be able to pull him away quickly if need be. As the svart Seer gazed into her crystal ball, Malvegil's stomach went queasy. Stoub's face went gray; his brother's the same. As one, the men stepped back, well away from both the Seer and her stone. Somehow, they knew it was the source of their nausea.

"What trickery is this?" spat Malvegil.

"It's the way of Seer Stones," said McDuff. "The svarts are not causing it. It is some byproduct of the Stone's magic. Stay well clear of the stone and the nausea will soon pass."

The svart Seer spoke some svartish words and somehow her words were answered. The voice of another female svart projected through the Stone.

Malvegil looked to McDuff. "Well?"

"They are calling for a spokesman. Jarn Yarspitter, Bornyth's councilor has been the liaison with the svart. They're trying to find him. You know him, right?"

"These many years."

But then something unexpected happened. Bornyth Trollsbane himself could be heard on the other side of the Stone, and Jarn Yarspitter as well. "I told you that Malvegil would want to hear it from me? You fools never listen. He's probably got the imps trussed up from the rafters by now. If only I could see through this darned thing. Stand aside and let me near the thing, but not too close for it makes my stomach tumble."

A clanking was heard through the stone, as if a mailed fist were knocking against it. "Is this thing working?" said Bornyth. "Malvegil!" Bornyth yelled. "Malvegil, are you there?"

"Aye, I'm here," said Malvegil.

"Was that him?" said Bornyth. "Was that him?"

"Aye, sire," said Jarn. "I know his voice."

"So do I," barked Bornyth. "I just can't hear straight through this damnable thing. Malvegil – you listen close because I can't talk into this thing long or I'll puke my guts up again. You still there?"

"Still here," said Malvegil.

"Good," said Bornyth. "The threat is real. The duergar are out there. We don't know how many, but it's spreading. Get your people ready and for Odin's sake, warn Lomion City straight away. If we don't find a way to stop them, all Midgaard will be threatened." Bornyth began coughing and retching, interspersed with colorful curses and threats against whoever was around him. The svart seers spoke a few more words to each other and then contact was broken.

"Gravemare," said Malvegil, "send word to our bannermen of this threat. Direct them to secure their borders and their keeps. Every town must be fortified, every village prepared to evacuate. No time must be lost."

"At once, my lord."

"It's settled then," said Malvegil as he

approached the svart king. "You have your alliance," he said extending his hand.

The svart king looked at Malvegil's large hand for several moments as if confused, and then he extended his own and they shook.

"But do not cross me," said Malvegil with a toothy smile. "For my rafters are high."

The svart king looked up at the rafters. He had no idea what Malvegil meant.

VII
THE DWARF, THE TROLL, AND THE ALCHEMIST

Old Cern, the town elder hunched forward in his seat, his sinews cracking as he moved, his voice cracking as he spoke. He smelled of garlic. His hair, what little of it remained, was limp, greasy, and gray. "How many?" he asked, his face scrunched up as if he dreaded the answer.

"Fifteen," said the alchemist, burly, bushy browed, and black cloaked. "Including the three from last night."

Old Cern winced and shook his head. "Fifteen of our own gone missing in not three weeks, and no trace found. I've never seen the like of this in all my years. Not once." The old man looked forlorn, his cheeks sunken more than usual, and that's saying a lot. His face was sallow and shadowed in the dim, flickering light cast by the oil lamp that hung above the alchemist's dining table. He looked as if he'd aged ten years in the last fortnight, and was even thinner than usual, which seemed impossible, since he was never much more than skin and bones.

"At least fifty livestock have gone missing as well," said the butcher, his belly jiggling beneath his coveralls with each word, his girth spilling over the arms of the chair. How he squeezed into that seat was anyone's guess. That he could squeeze out again seemed less than likely.

"Who cares about the stinking sheep and goats?" said Pellan, a beardless female dwarf with a bald pate, and a lit tobacco pipe in her right hand. "Something is killing our people."

"You'll care deep in the winter if the meat starts to run low," said the butcher.

"If we don't get whatever is out there, we might not make it through the winter," said Pellan.

The butcher rolled his eyes and shook his head.

"Let's not get carried away," said Old Cern. "I refuse to believe that we're in that much danger."

A distant howl interrupted the conversation. The councilors went quiet, listening, but the howl didn't return.

"Back again tonight," said the butcher. "Whatever that darn thing is."

"We don't know that our missing folk are dead," said Old Cern. "It could be that they were kidnapped. There may yet be ransom demands. Let's not jump to conclusions and think the worst."

"Dead gods, how daft are you?" said Pellan. "Fifteen people didn't get snatched one and two at a time. And by who? Nobody has seen no strangers about. Besides, we found bloodstains, for Odin's sake, or have you forgotten? And what about that howling? Every night after dark for weeks. You think it's a coincidence?"

As if on cue, another howl, this time louder, closer.

"Have you ever heard anything like that afore?" said Pellan, "because I haven't, and I'll wager no one around these parts has. Not in any of our lifetimes."

"Don't start that talk again," said Old Cern

with a palm upraised toward her. "This is a serious matter; I don't want to hear any more faerie stories."

"Whatever is doing the howling is what took our folk," said Pellan. "That's obvious to anyone what got half a brain. Our people are dead and they got dragged off. It probably eats them, which is why we've found no bodies. It's a predator. A deadly one. And there may be more than one of them."

"We need to act now," she said. "We need to stop this thing, whatever it is, to protect our folk. We've got to decide on what we're going to do. How to find it. How to kill it. Then we need to go out and do it. We can't waste any more time. People are dying; we gotta take action."

More howls, several in quick succession, all coming from the northeast of town.

"Where are the Eotrus?" said Old Cern as he held his head in his hands. "Why don't they come? They have a duty to protect us."

"They have their own troubles as you well know," said the alchemist. "With Lord Aradon dead and the best of his knights with him, we can't expect Mindletown to be a priority."

"If we had sent for them when I said, that first week," said Pellan, "they'd be here by now – in force, and the town would be well protected. But no, "it will pass," you said. Then it was, "Constable Granger and his watchmen can handle it; they're professionals — let them do their jobs." One old man, an even older deputy, and two watchmen not old enough to pick their own noses? What can they do? Nothing. With something like this, they are useless. Worse than

119

useless, because they're giving you a false sense of security."

"This isn't my fault," said Old Cern.

"I'm not saying it is, but we need to do something," said Pellan. "These killings have to stop."

"Granger and his men are out there patrolling the fence," said the butcher. "Trying to keep us safe. What more do you want? We've sent for the Eotrus. We told them what was going on. What more can we do?"

"Fence?" said Pellan. "That pile of rotten kindling couldn't keep out a drunken goat. How can it stop trolls?"

Old Cern and the butcher groaned and squirmed in their seats.

"Yes, I said it," said Pellan. "We've all been thinking it; somebody had to say it. Trolls. They are real — they're no faerie stories; they never were. They are flesh and blood creatures, not make believe. Do you really think we've got a rogue bear out there or a mountain lion? Do you think an animal like that could take fifteen people in secret?"

"Yes, I do," said the Old Cern. "I've hunted all my life and, on occasion, I've seen animals do things most folks wouldn't believe. A cave bear down from the high mountains could be our killer. Or worse, it could be a saber-cat. Those things are vicious man-eaters with teeth as long as swords. And they've been known to hunt in packs of two, three, sometimes even more."

"Neither bear nor saber-cat howl; not like what we've heard," said the alchemist.

"Dire wolves," said Old Cern. "They howl."

"They're extinct, aren't they?" said the butcher, looking to the alchemist."

"No dire wolf has been seen in these parts for fifty years or more," said the alchemist, "but that doesn't mean they are extinct."

"I say it's one creature," said Pellan, "maybe two or three at the most, with smarts enough to stay out of sight and only go after folk what are on their own or in a small group."

"A single dire wolf," said Old Cern. "That I could believe. Unusual, certainly. Unlikely, yes, but not a crazy thing. Not a crazy thing at all. They're as big as ponies, and with teeth nigh as long as those of saber cats. One or two of them, hungry and desperate, could explain what's been happening. That has to be the answer. It makes perfect sense."

Another series of howls, closer still, again from the northeast. This time, however, they were answered by similar howls from the southeast.

"Wonderful," said the alchemist. "Now we know for certain that there are at least two."

"You've got to agree that wolves make a lot more sense than trolls," said Old Cern. "So there are two, maybe three, whatever. Wolves are known to travel and hunt in packs. There's nothing unnatural about that. It's just wolves; it doesn't need to be anything more than that. We can deal with wolves, can't we? Even dire wolves? They're just animals after all. The whole notion of trolls is ridiculous. Once you start imagining mythical beasts, why not say it's a ghoul, a dragon, or a frost giant while you're at it? Or maybe you think it's Loki himself come down from

Asgard to freeze our hearts and pluck out our souls?" He laughed and then took a long draught from his ale mug. "It's some kind of wolf is all — just as I've said from the first."

"It's not wolves, though I wish it were," said the butcher. "It's men what done these things. Animals ain't smart enough – they couldn't take so many folk without being seen by no one else. Bandits from out east, I say it is, maybe lugron amongst them. They're the ones out there, howling it up. Those are scare tactics, meant to frighten us, and keep us locked inside at night, so they can skulk about unseen. But there aren't many of them, or else they would've come at us direct like."

"The skulking about at night, in the shadows – it proves there ain't much to them. We stick together and keep our wits and we'll be fine and dandy until the Eotrus get their behinds out here and clean them bandits out."

"You didn't see the bites on old Thom Prichard's back," said the alchemist. "And farmer Smythe had his head torn clean off."

"Some scavenger must have got a hold of old Thom after he was dead, or else the bandits keep dogs," said the butcher. "As for Smythe — a bandit's sword could have taken off his head."

"You're fools," said Pellan. "The trolls will be coming for us all one of these nights — you mark my words. Unless enough Eotrus show up to track them all down and send them packing back to the mountains."

"They're not real," said Old Cern as he pounded his fist to the table, sweat beading on his brow, and running down his cheeks.

"They are real," said the alchemist in a somber voice that immediately captured the attention of the others. "Or at least, they were. My grandfather told me of them when I was a boy. He saw one himself when he was young. Luckily, it didn't see him. But that was a long time ago. I expect — I hope, that they're all long dead. I don't know what's out there, but I don't think it's bears, lions, or even dire wolves. Nor do I think it's bandits. It's something that we haven't seen afore, and as Pellan said, it's deadly. We should think about gathering all our folk in The Odinhall each night. It's the strongest building in the village, and there's safety in numbers."

"That's smart," said Pellan. "We could barricade the windows, reinforce the doors . . ."

"That will cause a panic," said Old Cern. "I can't abide that. A curfew – no one out after dark. That should do it. We need do no more than that."

"You're in denial," said Pellan. "You're going to get more people killed. We need to make sure that every able-bodied person is armed, so they can defend them and theirs."

"Stop blaming me," said Old Cern as he rose to his feet, bristling.

Someone ran up the porch stairs, pounded on the door, and then flung it open. It was Mileson Tanner from the north end of the village. He was breathing heavily; his face was flushed and dripped with sweat.

"Wheelwright is dead!" he said pointing out the doorway where three men stood, a wooden and canvas stretcher at their feet. On the stretcher lay a body covered with a sheet – a sheet red with blood. "Something came out of the

123

wood, busted clean through Wheelwright's door, and tore him up bad – really bad. We brought him so that youse folks could see. It's terrible. You wouldn't have believed it otherwise. And it took his wife too – dragged her into the woods while their kids were watching, scared out of their minds. You've got to take a look at him, and then we've got to get back over there. The thing may still be nearby. We've got to get it afore it done kills more folk."

"Dead gods," said the butcher as he rose to his feet. The others followed.

"This can't be happening," said Old Cern. "Is the constable at Wheelwright's? Does he have things under control?"

"Miller and his boys are out looking for him," said the tanner.

"He'll clear this up," said Old Cern. "That's his job. He'll stop it, whatever it is. It was wolves, right? Dire wolves?"

"No one saw it, except for his kids, but they're hysterical. Said it was a monster what came from the wood. That's what got their parents – whatever it was what come out of the woods. That's all they can say. I don't know what got him, but when you see him," he said pointing out the door again, "you'll know it weren't no wolves."

They all went outside and gathered around the stretcher. "We could barely recognize him," said the tanner. "I never seen nothing like what was done to him."

Pellan pulled back the sheet.

There were gasps all around.

"Dead gods," said Old Cern as he stepped

back and turned away. He walked a couple of steps, then bent over and retched.

"What am I looking at?" said the alchemist of the bloody corpse that lay before them.

"It's like he's been shrunk or squashed down," said the tanner.

"I saw a body like this once, many years ago," said Pellan. "In the high mountains west of the Crags. The mountain folk hired Halsbad to rout out something that was killing their kin."

"What was it?" said the alchemist.

"We never found it," said Pellan. "The killing stopped on its own. We never knew whether the thing just went to ground, moved on to another territory, or got itself dead somehow. Wasted four weeks on it, and didn't collect a copper since we came up empty."

The butcher put his hand down on the body and prodded it. They all turned their attention to him.

"What are you doing?" said the tanner.

"It deboned him," said the butcher.

"Deboned him?" said the tanner. "You sure? How can you tell?"

"Because he ain't got any bones left," said the butcher.

"That's part of the troll legend," said the alchemist. "The old stories say that one touch of a troll turns a man's bones to jelly."

"That's ridiculous," said Old Cern between coughs and spits. "Ridiculous. The butcher was right – it's bandits out there. This is all part of their evil plan – trying to intimidate us. It's not going to work. I won't be intimidated. This town won't be intimidated. We're too strong for that."

Several people sped by them from the north. Then they heard the sound of a brass horn also coming from the north.

"The constable's horn," said Pellan. They all went quiet and listened. It sounded again and again over the next minute. The last sounding was cut short.

"Was it three blasts or four?" said the butcher.

"Three," said Old Cern.

"I think it was four," said the alchemist.

"It was four," said Pellan.

"Dead gods, what is that man doing?" said Old Cern. "Four blasts mean a general attack. He's supposed to be a professional. He's not supposed to panic over a few bandits."

"I'm going back to Wheelwright's," said the tanner. "Who's with me?"

"I'll go," said the butcher. He looked to the others. "We can't just sit here and do nothing. Are you coming?"

"I'm going to council the folk," said Old Cern as more people ran by in a panic. "We've got to get them off the streets and back inside their homes or else this panic might get out of hand. If we just stick together and keep our wits about us, this trouble will soon pass. You'll see, it will soon pass. Our town is strong. Mindletown strong. We'll make it through this, together."

People screamed in the distance, toward the north end of town. They heard strange howls, now seemingly coming from all directions.

"No need to head to Wheelwright's looking for monsters," said Pellan. "From the sound of it, they're out looking for us. I'm going home for my axe and my armor."

"I'm not waiting for you," said the butcher. "Alchemist, are you with us?"

He shook his head. He wasn't going.

"Fine," said the butcher. "Don't help. Stay here and hide under your bed, for all the good that it will do you. You wouldn't be of any help out there anyways." He stormed off, the tanner and his companions on his heels.

Moments later, a man ran past the house. "Get inside! They're coming!" said the man as he ran, panic on his face.

"Nonsense," said Old Cern as he stepped down to the street. "We have to face these bandits head on, and show them we're not afraid. That will set them to rights." The man never slowed.

The alchemist looked furtively around and stepped back inside.

Pellan felt naked without her axe while so close to danger, but it seemed too risky to try to make it back home. Three blocks in the dark, with howls coming from all sides – it might as well be ten leagues. Maybe the alchemist had weapons inside. "Cern, get your wrinkled old butt inside afore you get yourself killed dead," said Pellan.

"I'm not afraid of dire wolves or bandits," he said shaking his walking stick before him as if it were an adequate weapon against bandits, wolves, or anything else. "Everyone, get back inside your homes," he shouted to whomever was in earshot. "Lock your doors and shutter your windows. The constable will take care of this commotion. He'll set things to rights."

Just then, several people raced out of the shadows and barreled into him as they fled down the street. It looked like the baker's sons, but Pellan couldn't be certain because it was dark, they kept running, and didn't look back. Old Cern was knocked to the ground and landed on his rump, dazed, but seemingly unhurt. Before Pellan could move to assist him, a terrible growl came from the shadows nearby. It was loud. It was close. It didn't sound like a wolf – dire, common, or otherwise. The monster vaulted out of nowhere and was on Old Cern in an instant. It had bounded from the shadows, behind the old oaks that lined the lane – a leap of fifteen feet or more.

The thing had the general shape of a man, but it was no man; even a quick look in the dark was enough to tell that. The beast was hairless, with mottled skin of green and brown, and it was big. As tall or taller than a tall man, and broader as well. It had claws and a maw filled of large teeth. She had been right. It was a troll; it had to be. There's nothing else it could be; there was no other explanation.

Pellan reached for her sword, but her hand found nothing. Her sword and sword belt hung from a peg by her front door. She didn't know what to do. She couldn't fight the thing unarmed, but she had to try. Before she could do anything, the troll's first slash tore out Old Cern's throat; an obviously mortal wound.

Pellan could not save him. No one could; not with a wound like that. She could go out there barehanded and die with him, or else try to hide. A seemingly easy decision, but a hard one for Pellan. She was not one to run from a fight. But she knew that she had to. She carefully stepped back into the doorway as more howls and growls came from nearby. There was a whole pack of trolls out there and they meant business. She prayed that the troll wouldn't turn and spot her; that it wouldn't notice her closing the door.

"Don't close it all the way," whispered the alchemist from behind her. "Leave it ajar; they'll think we fled and won't linger."

Once back inside, Pellan looked around. The house was dark – the lamp that hung above the table was out, but she saw well that the alchemist had pushed the dining table aside and lifted the rug beneath it. A trap door lay open directly beneath where the table had been. He had a root cellar. Thank the gods. Pellan left the outside door ajar as the alchemist had advised, ducked down low, and moved toward the cellar. The alchemist knelt on the dining room floor and was busy crushing handfuls of leaves and scattering them about the place. He had a whole bag of the stuff. Pellan had no idea what that was about.

"Weapons?" whispered Pellan.

"Downstairs, and food and water too. Get down there, quick and quiet."

They both did. The alchemist had a way rigged up to move the rug and the table back from below, even with the hatch closed. He was able to position the table atop the hatch, completely concealing it. He was prepared. Pellan had always liked him.

The alchemist had a single candle lit. He held out a handful of leaves toward her. "Crush them and smear them on yourself. It'll mask our scents. With any luck, it will even repel the things." They both did so. The alchemist grabbed two short swords that hung from a peg on the wall, two small jugs of water, and some dried fruit. He laid them beside them and blew out the candle. It was pitch black. They could see nothing and all that they heard were distant howls and screams and their own breathing.

"I didn't know you had a cellar, but I thank Odin that you do," whispered Pellan.

"Nobody knows. I dug it myself years ago – at night, in secret. I hauled out one bucket of dirt at a time so no one would get suspicious. Took two years. No other building in town has a cellar, so no one will go looking for one here. Sometimes, you just need somewhere safe to hide – a refuge from storms, angry mobs, or trolls."

"Alchemist, I'm glad that you're a paranoid, crazy old fart."

"I love you too dwarf."

A crash of glass and wood upstairs. Something had come through one of the windows. Then they heard the outside door fling open, and low growling came with it; heavy footsteps on the floor planks above their heads. At least two trolls prowled the house.

Pellan gripped the hilt of the short sword so tightly that her hand hurt. She was frightened. Truly frightened. Who wouldn't be in such a situation? Not Pellan. Not usually. When it came to fighting, she didn't fear much. She'd seen more than her share: seven years of mercenary work down South with Halsbad's Freeswords; five years of dour dwarves and constant battles under Bornyth Trollsbane during the lugron campaigns;

and ten years in Dor Eotrus's guard. The Dor was to be a retirement job – not that she was old even when she left there, but she'd had her fill of the roaming warrior's life. She wanted a quiet life in a civilized place, but one not so cosmopolitan that she felt out of place or crowded. She was surprised to learn that but for her resume, the Eotrus wouldn't have accepted her. Most Dors took anyone who was willing to sign up. Not the Eotrus. Even after a recommendation from one of Bornyth's top lieutenants, she still had to prove herself on the practice field before they accepted her into their service. She thought she knew all there was to fighting by then, and didn't expect to learn anything from a bunch of spit and polish northern knights. In fact, she expected to school them good and proper.

Sir Gabriel and the Dor's lead knights taught her different. There were dozens of them that were first rate. Artol, Stern, Sarbek, and Lord Aradon fought like no one she had ever seen before, and even they didn't match Sir Gabriel. Sparring with him was like taking on Odin himself. A humbling experience since there was no chance of winning, not ever – not even with two or three against him at once.

Training with the Eotrus took her from brawling, street-fighting mercenary to poised sword master. But she'd never fought a troll, and with only a borrowed short sword, no armor, and a grizzled old alchemist at her side, she had no desire to try one on. So she hunkered down, as quiet as a shadow, and bided her time.

The trolls spent a long time searching the house. They opened every door, closets and all –

yes, opened them, using the knobs and handles. They were no mere animals. They had smarts and that made them all the more dangerous. And more surprisingly, they spoke. Their voices were deep, harsh, and guttural – exactly what you'd expect from a troll, if you ever expected them to speak at all. Pellan had heard many languages spoken during her travels, but trollspeak held little resemblance to any of them.

At one point, the trolls knocked over the dining table. For some moments, she was certain that they were going to find the hatch. And then find them. By Freya's grace, they never lifted the rug, so the alchemist's hidey-hole remained hidden. How long the trolls remained in the house, Pellan couldn't say with certainty. The problem was, when the trolls finished searching for any people in the house, they rummaged about, slowly and quietly, nosing through things, for what reason and to what end, Pellan couldn't fathom. After a goodly while, maybe an hour or so, she heard them no more.

Not only did that provide no relief to her stress, it was maddening. Were they up there still, lying in wait for someone to return or to creep out of some hidey-hole? Did they settle down to sleep in the house? Or did they just walk out quiet-like? She didn't know. Neither did the alchemist. That served only to increase their tension. Now they were afraid to even breath, for fear that if the trolls were sitting above in silence, they might hear them.

So Pellan and the alchemist sat in silence for what seemed like hours, waiting, listening, afraid to whisper, eat, or even breathe. All the while, they heard distant growls, crashes, screams, and shouts. The trolls were systematically invading every building in the town, and from the sound of it, wiping out the populace – Pellan's neighbors, her friends. And she could do nothing, save to go out and die in the street with them. No sense in that. No sense at all.

As she sat there listening to the horrors outside, and straining to hear any sound from within the house, she wondered – no, feared –- whether there was some other entry into the root cellar. Presumably, the trolls could see in the dark since legend said they lived in the deepest mountain caves. What if they'd gone quiet because they had found another way in and were lurking there in the dark, even now, watching her. Waiting. That kept her alert for a long while. She prayed to Odin that the Eotrus would come – but she knew they wouldn't – not soon enough anyway. Even at their best speed, they wouldn't arrive at the village that night or the next day, and probably not for a few days hence.

After what must have been an hour or two, the alchemist lay down. She did the same. You can only sit still in silence for so long. Her muscles ached; she could only imagine how the old alchemist felt.

Pellan opened her eyes and she saw a bit of light streaming through the little joints between the floorboards. It was daytime outside. She had fallen asleep. How she did that while her friends and neighbors were being hunted, murdered, and perhaps even eaten, she didn't understand, but it made her angry. It felt like she had insulted them – every victim of the troll attack. She was supposed to be a great warrior, yet while everyone else died, she hid, all warm and cozy and rested; food and drink close at hand. The guilt and shame of it was almost more than she could bear. She forced those thoughts out of head, the way she had learned to do over a lifetime as a warrior. She had to - for she knew, she may not be out of danger yet.

She forced herself to lay still and only listened for a time. From the sounds of the alchemist's breathing, he was awake and sitting up, so she sat up as quietly as she could.

The alchemist leaned toward her and whispered into her ear. "Something is up there still," he said. "One of them at least in the back room."

She winced. "Anything outside?" she whispered.

"Not for hours."

"We've got to kill it and get out of here."

"Maybe we can get out afore it knows we're here. Legend says they can't go out in the light – it burns them."

"If you're wrong, it'll run us down," said Pellan. "Best to face it head on."

"What if there are others hold up in the other buildings? They'll hear. We won't have a chance."

"If they can't go out in the sunlight, we'll only have to face the one. If they can go out, we're probably dead regardless. Got your sword?"

"Aye," he said.

"Know how to use it?"

"Stick them with the pointy end."

"Good enough."

"Maybe we should stay hold up here."

"If it doesn't go away on its own, it'll smell us soon enough. Don't know about you, but I can't hold it in forever."

"There's that. Fine. You're the warrior; you kill it. I'll help if I can."

She rolled her eyes. They crept to the stair as quietly as they could. The dirt floor made that easy enough: no creaking. The stair was a different story. It was solid and stout, but like most all stairs, it creaked. The alchemist went first because he knew how to move the rug aside without lifting the hatch.

He crept up the steps as quietly as he could and listened. He listened for a long while and then listened some more. Not a sound. He got the rug moved and the hatch opened, still without anything stirring. The moment that they stuck their heads through the hatch, the smell hit them. The place stank of troll – an animal stench that for whatever reason they hadn't noticed much in the cellar, but on the main floor, it was strong.

Still nothing stirred. They couldn't see much because the dining table lay on its side, blocking view of most of the room. That meant they could climb up unseen. They did so and closed the hatch behind them.

The front door was shut. Light streamed in from the window that the trolls had broken through. It was quiet outside. The slaughter was long over.

Just as Pellan stood up, sword in hand, she heard a deep gravelly chuckle that could have been a man's voice, but it wasn't. It was a troll. Perched on the sideboard like a bird, it leered directly at the alchemist, the larger prey, its

135

overlarge teeth exposed in a wide grin. It had dark eyes, no eyebrows but a heavy brow ridge, and long pointy ears. It said something in trollspeak, then leaped up high and whooped as it came down, legs extended. Its feet crashed into the table in a sort of flying dropkick. The force of that blow was incredible. The table smashed into Pellan and the alchemist, slid them across the floor, and slammed them hard into the kitchen cabinets. The troll got up laughing. It was toying with them. Playing with its food. That delay gave the alchemist the seconds he needed to find his sword and bring it up to guard. Pellan noted that he didn't hold it correctly – he was an amateur. At least he had guts enough and sense enough to defend himself. That was more than Pellan could say about more than a few supposed warriors she had served with over the years. The troll effortlessly swiped the alchemist's sword aside, sending it clattering to the floor. Pellan came at it. Its larger prey disarmed, it turned its attention to her. Black claws, wicked sharp parried her thrust, grabbed the blade, and tried to wrench it from her grasp. She twisted it and pulled it free. The troll growled, opened its maw wide, and gnashed its teeth.

The alchemist flung a handful of reddish powder at the creature. The powder hit it full in the face; a good portion falling into its open mouth, and some in its eyes. The troll reared back coughing and spitting.

The old fart was proving more useful than Pellan would have guessed. With the troll distracted, she moved in, and slashed the troll's chest once, twice, and then again with her blade, opening deep wounds.

It looked shocked. It hadn't expected that sort of resistance, especially not after the easy bloodbath the previous night.

Next, the alchemist grabbed the oil lamp that hung from a ceiling hook over the table and threw it at the troll. It smashed on impact, dousing much of the troll's body with oil.

Pellan wished that she had a torch, or anything afire, but there was nothing. She had to cut it down with her sword. There was no other option.

She couldn't believe her eyes when she saw the wounds on the troll's chest begin to close, to heal of their own accord. That's when she understood the old legends – about how hard trolls were to kill. That's when she knew that the old tales were true. They said to burn them, or to cut off their heads. Anything short of that, and they'd get up again; ready to fight, ready to kill.

She had no fire. And no easy way to take off its head, so she did what she knew how to do – what came naturally and instinctively to her. She attacked with her blade, using every skill and trick that she had amassed in her decades of experience, and bided her time for an opening to get at its neck.

She slashed again, but the troll parried the sword with its claws even though it still spat and coughed from the alchemist's powder. Pellan unleashed a furious series of strikes – cuts and thrusts, slashes and overhand blows – a sequence taught by Sir Gabriel to all the best swordsmen at Dor Eotrus. The troll dodged or parried most of the blows, but several struck home, opening several vicious wounds, any one of which would have killed most men.

But those wounds barely slowed the troll.

They served only to make it angry.

Maybe the thing didn't feel pain. Maybe it healed so fast it didn't care about pain or injury. Pellan didn't know and she didn't have time to think about it. She just kept fighting.

The alchemist made some motions with his fingers, and suddenly a tiny flame, as but from a single candle, appeared in his hands. Then he made a throwing motion; the flame flew across the room; it hit the troll in the chest. The oil that covered the troll burst into flame.

They ran from the house. Pellan in the lead.

Pellan half expected to run into a pack of trolls feasting on corpses in the street. She was almost surprised when there was no sign of them. Old Cern's body was gone – only a reddish-brown stain marred the pavement where he fell.

The street was empty. No trolls. No townsfolk. No bodies. And it was dead quiet. The smell of smoke was heavy in the air – buildings had burned overnight, though none nearby. She kept telling herself to trust that the trolls couldn't go out in the day, and that as long as they got well away or to a secure location before nightfall, they'd be okay. Thank the gods it was a bright, sunny morning. What if it were overcast? Would the trolls be out?

Across the street, the cobbler's door hung off its hinges, his first floor windows busted in. The merchant's house across the way was much the same. The front porch was covered in blood spatters. Most of it reddish brown – human, but some of it was troll's blood, on the porch, at the door, and on at least one of the windows. Pellan poked her head through the doorway. More bloodstains. The place was a shambles. No sign of life. Old Marvik and his family had put up a strong fight. They were a tough bunch.

"Where should we go?" said the alchemist. "The Odinhall? The constable's?"

"I'm going for my armor and weapons," said Pellan. "Then I'm heading to Dor Eotrus." She had to get her mother's amulet – it was the only thing she had of her and meant more to her than anything. Her shield – with her clan's coat-of-arms; the sword she'd used for the last twenty years; the coins she had saved up over a lifetime. She wasn't going to leave any of that behind, unless she had no choice. She didn't work her whole life to have the first looter who came along get all her stuff.

"There might be survivors," said the alchemist.

"If we find them, they can come with us, or not, as they will. Regardless, I'm heading for the Dor." The alchemist followed her and made no further comment except to ask her to slow her pace a couple of times.

He would slow her down if she had to make a real run for it. A liability. But she wouldn't abandon him. He was a friend and Pellan didn't have too many of those. Besides, he had guts.

None of the houses between the alchemist's and Pellan's showed any sign of life.

Her front door was broken in.

"They might be in there," said the alchemist. "Like at my place. Maybe we should just head for the west road. The edge of town is close."

"I need my equipment."

"I won't be of much help if it comes to it. My bag of tricks is running low."

"You did great back there. Just watch my back. I'm going in."

Luckily, no trolls had taken up residence. There wasn't even much damage: a few things overturned and broken; all the doors open or torn off their hinges. Pellan donned her armor, strapped on her sword belt and axe. Hers was no common armor – dwarven steel plate and chain, sculpted to her frame, reinforced where needed, and riddled with old dents and gouges. At the bottom of the trunk, she found her Eotrus tabard and cape and put those on as well. She wasn't certain she'd wear them again after she retired from the Dor six months previous. Ob insisted that she keep them. Said that she was to look out for Eotrus interests in the town, and even sent her a modest stipend each month for so doing. It was Ob that arranged her position on the town council though she wasn't grateful for that. She retired because she wanted peace and quiet, not petty squabbles and politics.

She found her mother's amulet, in its little chest, just where she'd always kept it. She clutched it close. Her mother gave it to her when she was but ten years old. It was inscribed with the likeness of Odin, the all-father – one eyed and regal. It had been passed down in the family for more generations than anyone could remember. Her grandfather said that it was enchanted – made by the dwarves of Dwarkendeep ages back. What its magic was, if truly it had any, she never knew, but she wore it under her armor each time that she headed into battle. Maybe it gave her luck. Maybe its magic offered some protection. She couldn't say, but it was precious to her.

She put it on and tucked it under her armor. She and the alchemist filled packs with supplies and grabbed a couple of water jugs.

They were outside and on their way within ten minutes. Still no sign of life on the streets.

"Where are they?" said the alchemist. "The trolls?"

"In the buildings," said Pellan. "Sleeping because it's daytime. They have to be. There's nowhere else they could have gotten to in time to keep out of the sun. We've got to get well clear of town afore dusk or they will be on us."

"What about survivors?"

Pellan looked up and down the deserted street. "I don't think there are any. And we can't take the time to look for them or we won't get far enough away afore dark. Let's head straight for the west road and on to Dor Eotrus."

"I want to get out of here as much as you do," said the alchemist, "but we have a responsibility to the town, to the people. We can't just run off. I've been on the council for twenty years – these are my people. There may be folks that need our help. Families, children, folks we know."

"You weren't so worried about that last night?" snapped Pellan.

The alchemist looked like he had been slapped.

"Sorry, but we can't help them, just as we couldn't help them last night. If we had run out into the street all heroic and such, we've have died right there, beside Old Cern. Or maybe we'd have made it into the merchant's house and fought beside him and his. The outcome would have been the same. We and they would all be dead. We did what we had to do to survive. If anybody don't like it, I don't much care. Now our responsibility, besides keeping our own butts alive, is to warn the Dor. They need to know these trolls are active and out for blood. Who knows, they might even be planning on venturing farther south. The knights of the Dor need time to prepare, to be ready to ride out and meet them. The best chance of that is if we warn them and quick. So let's get going."

"We'd move a lot faster with horses."

"And if we find any on the way out of town, we'll take them. If not, we walk. The stables are too far away. I'll not chance it."

They passed a dozen buildings as they made their way to the west road. Every one had its doors broken in. Many had windows broken and debris strewn about; some even had gaping holes broken through their outer walls or through their roofs. The trolls got in wherever they could. A few homes were burned to the ground. It looked as if many folks had barricaded themselves inside and put up a fight. Unfortunately, it appeared that they all lost. Not one building looked untouched. As best they could tell, there was no human life left in Mindletown. That proved, if there was any doubt by that time, that the trolls were intelligent and acting with some purpose. No animal pack would go to every house, nor would any animal kill all the available prey at once. What the trolls' purpose was, beyond wanton destruction, wasn't clear. But they surely had a purpose and it wasn't just to feast on human flesh.

"Some folks may have run off into the woods," said the alchemist. "They may have got clear."

"There was no moon last night," said Pellan. "The woods are thick and that's where the trolls came from. Would've been tough to get away."

"So we might be the last," said the alchemist.

"Aye."

They reached the west road without incident and picked up their pace as they grew less concerned that their passage might rouse any trolls from their slumbers and encourage them to step out for a morning snack.

"If we make it to Berrill's Bridge, we should be okay," said the alchemist. "To cross elsewhere this time of year, you have to go way down river, nigh as far as Markett."

"How deep is the water?"

"Over a man's head and running fast, white water. I doubt the trolls would try it, and they'd probably not make it if they did."

"Unless they're on the road ahead of us," said Pellan.

"You think ours is the first town they hit?" said the alchemist as he breathed heavily from the pace that Pellan set. Her legs were a lot shorter than his, but the alchemist struggled to keep up.

"If they came only through the wood from the north, then maybe. If they use the roads, then probably not."

"Come to think of it, Mikar Trapper is a

couple days overdue for his usual visit."

"Innman was complaining yesterday that his ice delivery was late," said Pellan.

"Iceman comes down from Stebin Pass – northwest," said the alchemist. "Good old Iceman. I hope they didn't get him. We play Spottle every Thursday eve for years. Trapper comes from the east-northeast, from a ways beyond Trikan Point Village."

"We know at least one or two of the trolls have been around for a ten-day at least, since that's when the first person went missing. They might have taken out Trapper and the Iceman as they got close. Or they might have overrun their towns afore they last left. If that's the case, then the trolls are invading in force."

"There's no way to know," said the alchemist. "Not now, anyway. At this pace, we should make the bridge at least a few hours afore dark. Problem is, I don't know if I can keep up. You might have to leave me."

"I'm not leaving you."

They saw no one on the road all day, but that wasn't unusual. Merchants hauled supplies along the road a couple of times a week, but no one was due up from the south for two more days. Travelers on the road were uncommon. They'd hoped to run into someone – someone with horses, but no luck. After several hours of travel, they came within sight of the bridge. It was still daylight, though dusk rapidly approached. The alchemist hadn't dropped dead from exhaustion, and there were no trolls in sight. That was better than Pellan had expected.

The road descended rather steeply as they

approached the river; the Ottowhile had carved out a small valley over the years. Berrill's bridge was wide and sturdy – maintained in good fashion by the Eotrus for it carried their mounted patrols and loaded wagons for commerce.

The bridge was clear. The area was deserted. The guard post stood empty. Pellan wasn't certain whether it was normally continuously manned. She stopped and turned around as they stepped onto the span. From there, she had a clear view up the road, all the way to the top of the valley, a good half mile.

"See something?" said the alchemist.

Pellan smiled. "Not a thing. Looks like we're in the clear, but it's still a long ways to the Dor. Let's keep moving. You set the pace, but make it as fast as you can manage."

"I've been moving faster than that since we set out from the village. I'd feel a lot better if there were guards on duty; then we'd know that no trolls were on the other side. Just look at the river; no one is going to swim that."

Halfway across the bridge, Pellan heard it: a growl. The growl of a troll. She couldn't tell from what direction it had come. She pulled her sword, dropped to a crouch, and spun around. Nothing.

"Oh, dead gods," said the alchemist. "They found us. Odin help us," he said as he fumbled with some pouches attached to his belt.

There were no trolls on the bridge and no sign of them at either end of the span. They were thirty feet at least above the Ottowhile, which was running as fast and deep as they hoped. Then Pellan realized where the sound came from and the little hairs stood up on the back of her neck.

"Let's move!" said Pellan as she turned and started to run toward the west end of the bridge, the alchemist following. Before she got five yards, a troll climbed over the bridge's railing up ahead, toward the end of the span. Pellan thought to keep running, to charge past it, hopefully crippling it with her sword as she went, but then a second troll hopped over the opposite railing. There was no getting by two of them. The path ahead was blocked.

"Back," she shouted as she pulled up and turned. But two more trolls now stood at the other end of the bridge. They were trapped.

"Dagnabbit," said the alchemist. "They were waiting for us."

"For anyone who came along," said Pellan. "So much for them not being able to go out in daylight. Seems it doesn't bother them at all."

"What do we do? Should we jump? Take our chances in the river?"

"I'll sink like a rock," said Pellan, her armor far too heavy to swim in. "You go; it's your best chance. Get to the Dor. Warn them."

"I'm not leaving you."

"Go. You can't help. Not against so many. Save yourself."

"I've got a few more tricks up my sleeve."

"Just go," she said as the trolls began to move closer, leering, and slavering."

"No. I shouldn't have hid last night. I should have been out there fighting for my town. I'm not going to make that mistake again."

"Then a warrior's death it will be for the both of us," said Pellan. It would be a short battle with two trolls in front and two behind. The only chance Pellan had to do some damage was to engage one pair of trolls, perhaps get past them and turn, so that all the trolls were in front of her. She couldn't win this, but she needed to make a good account of herself to die at peace and to win her spot in Valhalla. She had to take at least one of them with her.

"Let's go," she said as she charged toward the trolls on the west side of the span. This was a different Pellan than the one who fought the troll in the dark of the alchemist's house the previous night. Now she had her armor and helmet, her shield and her battle blade, and her lucky amulet. Now she knew what she was facing, had some idea of its capabilities. Now she faced it out in the open, in the light of day, not the dark confines of a small house. That changed everything. She yelled a dwarven battle cry, something she picked up in her years with Bornyth Trollsbane. She wished she had her old dwarven squadron with her, charging shoulder to shoulder as she ran down that span. With that wrecking crew, she'd make short work of the trolls. But that was not to be. This time she faced death alone, excepting an old alchemist.

She barreled in, shield and sword working together in expert fashion. She punched with the shield, and then stabbed with the short sword. The trolls dodged back as she arced the shield across them – a strike akin to a roundhouse punch. She grazed one and missed the other, but the shield strike confused them and they lost sight of her sword. That was all the opening that she needed. She lunged forward and thrust as hard she could, stabbing one of the trolls in the groin. It screamed and fell back on its rump, whimpering. She slid past it and turned. The second troll was on her, the alchemist behind it. She saw him slash it across the back, but it barely reacted. The other two trolls charged forward, bent over very low, running on their knuckles as much as their feet – a strange gait, not at all like a man, but also unlike a four-legged animal.

The troll hammered down on her shield and pain shot through her arm. Lugron twice her size had battered that shield with swords and battle hammers, but those blows, as hard as they were, were nothing compared to the bare fisted punch of that troll. She backpedaled, then slashed her sword in a spinning arc, looking for an opening. The troll lunged forward, right into the sword's path, but the blade bounced off its scabrous hide. It slashed its claws across Pellan's shoulder. That strike tore off her armor's shoulder plate and gouged deep furrows into her breastplate.

She saw the alchemist fling another handful of his burning powder at the other two trolls, hitting them squarely in the faces. That stopped them in their tracks.

Pellan stabbed and slashed and whirled, but most of her blows deflected off her opponent's hide, and what ones struck home, healed before her eyes. The troll she'd stabbed was now back on its feet, but it went after the alchemist.

"Look out!" she yelled, but it was too late. It clubbed him on the back of the neck and he dropped to his knees. How he didn't get knocked unconscious or die outright from that blow, Pellan couldn't understand. Tough bugger, that alchemist. But they weren't done with the old man yet. A second troll slashed the alchemist once and then again across the chest, sending blood, bits of flesh, and shreds of his clothes flying. One of the trolls lifted him overhead, blood pouring from the alchemist's chest, and held him there, high over its head, opened its maw, and drank the stream of blood that freely flowed from the wound. Few sights had Pellan seen that matched the horror of that. And the strength of the trolls was unmatched. The alchemist was a big man by any measure yet the troll flung him about as if he was but a rag doll.

Despite his wounds, the alchemist was still alive and struggled in the troll's grasp. The alchemist put a hand to his lips and a moment later, a crackling stream of red and yellow flame erupted from his mouth and sprayed directly into the troll's face. It shrieked and dropped the alchemist to the deck, but still held onto his arm. The troll's entire head was afire. The flesh of its face blackened and melted as it howled in agony. It spun, lifted the alchemist up, and flung him over the rail – to break on the rocks below and drown.

Pellan saw the alchemist fall, but she didn't react to it, save to let anger fuel her energies and keep her going. A warrior never grieved during battle, not if she wanted to live. And Pellan wanted to live; she was determined to survive the trolls.

Pellan willed the amulet about her neck to do something – anything – to save her. She called out for Odin, Thor, and Tyr. She called on her ancestors to help her, to give her strength. But nothing happened. Maybe the amulet was just a hunk of metal after all, with no power save to provide false comfort. She had no tricks, no powders, or flame, no magic, only sharpened steel and steady resolve. Both seemed next to useless against the trolls. She backpedaled as three of them advanced on her. The burned one was out of the fight, at least for the moment. She didn't know whether it could heal those burns and get up again. In the end, it didn't matter; the three remaining trolls were at least two too many. She had no chance of winning. She couldn't outrun them. And if she died, Dor Eotrus would not be warned of the trolls' advance. So she did the only thing she could do and have any chance of survival. She ran to the railing and jumped.

She spun in the air as best she could and managed to hit the water feet first, far more from luck than skill – for she was certainly no experienced diver. She hated the water; most all dwarves did. The water felt icy cold as she plunged in and struck the bottom. It was just deep enough that she wasn't injured from the dive, but how she'd avoid drowning was another thing. She wasn't a good swimmer to begin with, and she was weighed down with more than fifty pounds of armor and weapons. Her sword and shield were already gone. She struggled to swim to the surface, but the water was so turbulent and the current so strong, she couldn't see anything and didn't even know which way was up. She concentrated on holding her breath, pulled a knife from her belt, and cut the straps of her breastplate, ignoring all else. She just let the water take her where it willed and concentrated only on the cutting. When she severed the last strap, she pulled the breastplate from her body and the water carried it off. She still had too much weight on her to swim, so she sliced through the straps of her leg armor. When she was done, it took all the willpower she had to take the time to sheathe the blade instead of dropping it. Then she powered to the surface, her air gone, bubbles escaping her mouth. Somehow, through all of that, the current didn't crash her into a single rock, not one. She finally got her head out of the water, still being dragged along by the current, but she was able to take a breath, and then another. Then she started swimming for the bank. She had to get out of the water before she got dashed into a rock and torn up or knocked out, but it was hopeless – the current easily overcame her efforts. The water was freezing; she was already beginning to go numb.

Then something bumped her on the back of the head. A floating log of deadwood. She reached out and grabbed it, and held on for her life. She pulled herself up onto the log as best she could and positioned her feet downstream, so that they'd strike any rocks first. The current was just too strong for her to do anything, save to let it whisk her and the log downstream. Every yard it carried her put her that much farther from the trolls and that was a good thing. She knew her luck would run out eventually and she'd come to a waterfall or get banged up on the rocks, so she kept her eyes peeled for any calm water that she could reach or fallen trees that she could grab on to.

For a long time there was nothing. The river carried her far before it gave her any chance of escaping its current, her arms and legs growing number and number from the frigid water. Then up ahead, she saw a bunch of driftwood piled up on the side of the main channel – an area of calm water at last. Something dark and large clung to one log. Dead gods, the alchemist!

Pellan pushed free of the driftwood log as the calm water neared and swam as fast as should could toward the alchemist. As she got close, the water grew shallow and she was able to stand, coughing up water. She couldn't have made it much farther. She waded the last fifteen or so. "Alchemist!" she called. "Alchemist," but he made no response and did not stir. She placed a hand on his back and his head moved.

"Where have you been?" he said, his voice weaker than normal.

"I thought you were dead."

"No, I just went for a swim," he said.

"How bad are you hurt?"

"Bad enough that I was planning on staying just here for a while." The still water was tinged red around him.

"Let's get out of the water." She took hold of his arm and carefully placed it around her shoulder. She led him to the bank, but by the time the water got as shallow as her waist, she realized that his legs were dragging behind. She leaned forward and hefted him onto her back, both of them groaning, the alchemist's legs still dragging behind due to his much greater height. She trudged to the bank, slow but steady.

She gently lowered him to the ground in a dry spot under a tree. She was exhausted and wanted to lie down to rest. She could have slept for hours. But that would have been the death of her and the alchemist both. She had to see to the alchemist's wounds and she had to keep moving. The day wasn't cold, but coming from the freezing water, she was shivering. She had to get herself and the alchemist out of their drenched clothes. She needed a fire, and blankets, but had neither. She couldn't chance a fire even if she could build one, for fear of attracting the trolls.

The alchemist's chest wound was deep – the troll's claws had shredded his flesh down to his breastbone. Its claws must have been razor sharp for the cuts were clean, not ragged like you'd expect from a bear or mountain lion. It looked ugly, but if she could stop the bleeding, and if it didn't get infected, he might yet live. The back of his head had a huge lump. His shoulders were badly bruised. He started dropping in and out of consciousness. She felt around the back of his skull to check if it were broken, but it seemed okay, but for the swelling.

"You've got to try and stay awake, you old fart. You've probably got a concussion."

He nodded, but his eyes were nearly closed. Pellan took off her Eotrus tabard, cut it into strips, and made ready to bind it about his chest. The alchemist stirred and stopped her. He directed her to some herbs in one of his pouches and told her how to apply them to the wounds. She did, and then bound the tabard as tightly as she could about his chest. She pulled off her clothes, down to her underwear, and his as well. She hung the clothes from a branch in a spot where they'd catch as much wind as possible while she set to building a litter. The alchemist wouldn't be walking under his own power anytime soon and she couldn't carry him over her shoulder, for the pressure and abrasion on his wounds would make him worse, the wound would keep bleeding, and ultimately, that would kill him. Leaving him or making a litter that he could lie on were the only options. Luckily, she was somewhat of an expert at such construction, having made many during her years with Halsbad and Bornyth. She used the alchemist's thick rope belt as cordage. In an hour they were ready to move. The alchemist was shivering; she was sweating – both conditions were dangerous going into a cold night. The afternoon sun had dried out most of their clothes. She had to keep the alchemist from going into shock, so she piled all the dry clothes atop his torso, to keep him as warm as possible. She dried off her sweat on one garment that was still damp and braved the elements with only her undergarments on, any sense of dignity put aside.

"Ready, alchemist?"

"Yup, let's go."

"Try and keep awake. What was that powder you used on the trolls?"

"Ground dried peppers, the hottest kind grown in the north," he said. "Little things, but potent. Simple, but effective.

"And the flames? How did you do it?"

"Oil and matches, my dear, and brains - that's all it takes. Don't tell anyone though. Some folk think I've got the magic, and I don't mind them thinking that."

She hefted up the litter and marched forward – exhausted before they even set out, and the litter was heavy. They needed to get clear of the river in case the trolls followed them down the bank. Pellan had to cover their trail – that forced her to heft the whole litter, alchemist and all, over her head. Pellan was strong, stronger even than most of her kind, who were long known for their powerful frames. She carried the litter aloft for some hundred yards before putting it down and running back to obscure her footprints. She prayed that the trolls didn't hunt by smell, or else they'd have no chance of getting away, not at the slow speed at which they'd be moving. She took one last long drink at the river and filled a little jar that the alchemist had stowed in his bag of tricks with some more. It wasn't much, but it would have to last them.

She decided that their only chance was to make for the west road and hope that the trolls had not yet headed down it. It would take a week of slogging thought the woods with the litter to reach civilization. Neither she nor the alchemist would last through that. She had to get to the road and she had to find help. It was their only chance.

After two hours, with no sign of the road, and no sign of trolls, she decided that they should set a camp for the night. She'd have to build a fire – for she feared without one, the alchemist wouldn't survive the night. She gathered some kindling and searched through the alchemist's pouches for anything that looked incendiary, but what supplies remained intact were hopelessly damp. She'd make fire the hard way, sticks and sweat. She knew how and she'd done it before. Just as she set to work, she heard them. The trolls. They were howling the way they do. The howls came from behind them, from the direction of the river. The trolls had followed them down and were hot on their trail.

"Dagnabbit," said the alchemist as he perked up. "We've got to get moving. Find somewhere to hide. I'll try to walk – it'll be faster. Just help me up."

"Stinking, no good stinking trolls," spat Pellan. "Wiping out the whole town wasn't enough. They can't even let one stinking dwarf get away. What the heck am I supposed to do now? No armor. No sword. Not even any stinking pants. All I've got is a hunting knife. What can I do with that – file their stinking claws?"

"You're right," said the alchemist. "You've got to leave me. You've got to run. You've got to warn the Dor."

"I'm not leaving you."

"You've got to."

"No." She bent over and hefted the alchemist up. "Sorry, but I expect this is going to hurt." She lifted him onto her shoulders – a comical site, for he was well over two feet taller than she. But she had the strength.

She started trudging through the woods, the howling growing louder behind her, the light growing dimmer. Faster and faster she went, the weight of the alchemist weighing her down. Sweat poured from her body, despite the chill in the air. She ignored the pain in her muscles and joints and pressed on. The howls grew steadily closer. The trolls had to be moving at more than twice her pace. She went faster and faster still, almost running now, stumbling once or twice, but catching herself before she fell. All her will was bent on moving forward as fast as her legs would carry her, hoping against hope that some way to save them would present itself.

She could not outrun the trolls. And she was so exhausted, she'd doubted she could put up much of a defense. On she went until the trolls were close. Just as she was about to drop the alchemist, so that she could turn and fight, she saw the road through the trees. Not thirty yards ahead. She made for it with all possible speed, her breathing heavy, and her head spinning from the strain. And then she was there. They had made it to the road. She turned down it heading west and ran.

"Put me down," pleaded the alchemist. "Save yourself. It's not too late. Save yourself."

She ignored him and kept running.

"They're on the road," said the alchemist. "A hundred yards back. They see us. They're coming."

"How many?" said Pellan.

"Two at least. No, three."

That was it then. Even if she left the alchemist, one or two of the trolls would follow her. There was no escape. No way to warn the Eotrus. But she wouldn't have left him anyway – duty be damned. She would make her final stand. She would earn her spot in Odin's hall.

She put down the alchemist at the side of the road, behind a small tree for whatever cover it could provide. She saw a fallen branch that was several feet long, and picked it up – a makeshift spear. She braced it before her and drew her knife. On came the trolls, barreling toward them on legs and knuckles.

"Fight well, alchemist, and together we will drink tonight in Valhalla, amongst the honored dead."

"Stinking trolls," said the alchemist.

All three trolls leaped at them at once.

VIII
A MATCH MADE IN MADNESS

Lord Harper Harringgold was never comfortable walking down the long hallway that led to the King's audience chamber. He didn't like being surrounded by guards that were not there to protect him, but rather to accost him if he made any move that they deemed a threat the king.

A king needed guards, of course – especially Selrach Rothtonn Tenzivel III, what with the League having come to power. But he was the Archduke of the realm's capital city, and an old friend of the king, yet the Dramadeens eyed him as if he were a murderer caught red-handed. Who were they to look at him like that? After all, they were little more than foreign mercenaries. It was insulting; infuriating actually, but he could do nothing about it. He had to bite his tongue and tolerate it. And that was something the Duke was no accustomed to doing.

Despite that annoyance, that wasn't why he disliked visiting the king. He was embarrassed by him and for him; by his behavior. To see an old friend who was once a great man, so far fallen; now reduced to a loud and angry drunk, paranoid, befuddled, and reclusive. Tenzivel had completely withdrawn from the government several years prior, leaving all affairs of State to him, and to Chancellor Barusa, and to the High Council. The king had not appeared in public in years, and he was rarely seen in private by anyone other than his immediate family, his bodyguards, and handpicked servants of long years.

For those reasons, he had rarely seen the King in recent years and didn't expect to see him again so soon after he and the wizard Pipkorn had sought his advice. This time he was being summoned. This time, the king wanted him. But for what, he wasn't certain. Upon their last meeting, Tenzivel had charged him with assuring that Barusa failed in his attempt to radically modify or overturn the Articles of the Republic. So far, the only success the Duke had in that was to overturn a writ that Barusa had blustered through the Council – an insane measure that placed a permanent levy of fifty percent on all revenues collected by every Dor, keep, and manor hold within the realm. That writ was designed to break the back of the aristocracy, destroy the wealth of the rich, and put their funds in the hands of the Lomerian government – for redistribution to other endeavors, including to those individuals deemed by the Council more worthy or needier.

A bitter fight it was in the council chambers. It raged for hours and nearly came to physical blows more than once. There was no way to make those on the other side see reason. Everything they said was in support of their own positions regardless of where lay the truth. In other words, they lied freely to achieve their ends. Some notion akin to the ends justifying the means colored their every move. Such thinking was so ingrained in them, that they assumed that everyone behaved in that way – that everyone lied to achieve their ends. So when presented with truth or logic that disproved their opinions, they were blind and deaf to it. Only a few were open to alternative views, and it was over their votes that the battle raged. In the end, the Duke and his supporters won, but barely, and only due to the greed of the councilors – because some of them, would themselves be negatively impacted by the tax writ. That battle cost the Duke much of his political capital. But it was a battle that he needed to win, so it was a price that he had to pay. In so doing, though, it would make future battles all the harder.

Many other measures that sought to modify the Articles of the Republic remained in play within both the High Council and the Council of Lords. A definitive vote would come in three months' time, when both councils met in open session. The outcome of those proceedings would decide the fate of the realm. Would it remain a troubled Republic or would it transform into a country devoid of personal freedoms, all in the name of supposed equality and fairness. That path led only to one end: revolution, followed by martial law, followed by despotism. Any student of history knew that, but so few people, even the smart ones, learned the lessons of the past. What the Duke didn't know, was whether Barusa was deluded into thinking that he was doing the right thing for the realm or whether he knew that he was steering them toward ruin. There was just no way to tell.

There were plenty of people that meant well and that agreed with Barusa's proposals; they only wanted the best for the people, and the realm. But others had darker desires – to overthrow the government, to end the Republic, and to install them and theirs to power – unlimited power over everyone and everything. The Vizier was one of those – of that, Harringgold had no doubt. Barusa was a different story, but an enemy all the same.

Before the guards pulled open the doors, Harringgold prayed that Cartegian would not be in attendance. His maniacal antics were too much to bear in close company. Besides, there was no way to tell how much he could be trusted. He might very well report everything he overheard to the chancellor.

The brightly lit, high ceilinged hall felt eerie and echoed with any loud sound. Despite its good size, the place always made Harringgold feel claustrophobic. The sergeant-at-arms announced him as usual and stepped out of the hall, closing the doors behind him. Tenzivel sat on the granite throne, hands on the armrests, a beer stein in hand. Save for he and Harringgold, the audience hall was empty.

"You are late," said the King, though Harringgold had arrived precisely on time.

"My apologies, my Lord," said the Duke. "What may I do for you?"

Tenzivel shook his head – a look of disapproval on his face. "You may serve me far better by telling me what you think, not what you think I want to hear. You were not late; you should have told me so. Why didn't you?"

Harringgold was surprised by the King's apparent lucidity – all too rare an event in recent years. "Such a small thing was not worth causing offense to you."

"So you fear offending me? Why?"

"You are the king."

"I am the king. I'm also an old fool who has hidden too long in these chambers. Hidden behind these walls, and locks, and guards. Tell me true, is it me you fear, or my words, or my Dramadeens?"

Harringgold's jaw was set. He didn't look happy and was not quick to answer.

"You don't like me saying that you're afraid of something, do you?" said the king.

"I would not call it fear."

"Then what? Avoidance of conflict? Maintenance of propriety? Appeasement of an old fool that you once called friend?"

Harringgold didn't answer.

"A great man must go boldly forward in word and deed," said the king. "He must be unafraid to be controversial or even sometimes to be confrontational. Greatness lies there, when coupled with the reason and a keen mind. Go boldly, Harper – the kingdom needs that from you. I need that from you."

"Is that what you wanted to speak to me about?"

"No, though it is relevant." The king took a long swill from his stein. "Last we spoke, you advised me to get Cartegian out of Lomion, to preserve the royal bloodline, should the League's assassins accomplish their goals, or age finally catch me. I told you that we would never leave here. And we will not. But Cartegian needs an heir."

Tenzivel stared at Harringgold for several seconds before continuing. "Your daughter is of suitable age. And she is a suitable match."

Harringgold's eyes went wide; he shook his head. "No," he said. "Never."

"Found your boldness, have you, old friend? No matter. I have given this much thought. The Harringgolds are amongst the few that I can trust. Amongst the few that the Republic can rely on. It must be her. There is no other appropriate choice. Your daughter has strength, intelligence, beauty, and station. It must be Marissa."

"The Harringgolds are honored by your offer. But we decline."

"You must not decline," said the king.

"I will not see my daughter wed to a madman," he said sharply.

"Despite my son's eccentricities, he is not a violent man. He will not harm her; he has never harmed anyone. He speaks fondly of Marissa – always has, since long before his affliction. He was quite jealous when she focused her attentions on Claradon Eotrus. But that is in the past now."

Harringgold seemed conflicted.

"I hoped that this conversation would not be necessary. I planned to arrange for Cartegian and Marissa to be in each other's company on regular occasions, and let nature take its course. If friendship developed between them, this might be an easy matter. If love bloomed, all the better. I thought that there would be time for this – plenty of time. I hoped to sit the granite throne for ten, maybe twenty more years. But I fear now that matters have tipped too far to be righted, and that my days are numbered. Perhaps, I can hold off the nooses and knives long enough for Cartegian and your daughter to procure an heir.

If so, I will name you steward of the throne until my grandchild comes of age or until Cartegian can assume his rightful place."

"It seems that this plan has been long in the making," said Harringgold.

"It has. I know that this is a weighty thing to ask, given the circumstances, but as your King, I must ask it of you, and of her, for the good of the realm. The line of succession must endure and must be solidified. We cannot let the League take over. I will not preside over the fall of the Republic."

"Is this your command? This marriage?"

"No. No, I will not command this marriage, or any marriage. Such bonds must be freely made. But I ask it of you and of Marissa. No, I beg you, in the name of the realm."

Harringgold nodded his head respectfully. "I will consider this matter very carefully, and I will speak with my daughter. That is all that I can agree to for now."

"Waste no time in this," said the king. "For the hour grows late."

IX
TO KILL A KILLER

Mallick Fern had killed many men and more than a few women. Some killings were personal – he didn't abide insults; others were business – as an enforcer for various moneylenders or merchants; and still others were for duty, or so he told himself – as a soldier for this mercenary company or that. He got quite good at it, the killing. He built a reputation for it. As a result, one day, a representative from The Black Hand showed up to talk to him – an old man that he had never seen before or since. A few days later, Weater the Mouse came by and made him an offer to join up with The Hand. A generous offer – almost too good to refuse. He thought about it for a few hours, but then he accepted – he joined The Black Hand, and killing became his full-time profession. A lucrative one.

Through it all, he had never killed a child and he never would. He had his standards.

While he killed for coin, he always made certain that his targets had it coming – in other words, that they were bad. Midgaard had too many bad folks and not near enough good ones. So getting rid of a few of the bad was doing the world a service – or so he told himself.

The Black Hand always afforded him discretion, information, and most important, respect. They didn't just give him a name, a face, a target, and told him that he had to kill that person whether he liked it or not.

The Hand treated its agents as professionals. It was a brotherhood. They'd kill for each other – moreover, they'd die for each other. They weren't a bunch of cutthroat murderers, despite popular misconceptions. (Not to say that the cutting of throats wasn't one of their methods). They had honor. And few amongst them had more honor than Mallick Fern. And unlike many of the brethren, as they called themselves, he always worked alone.

When they first told him that his target was Torbin Malvegil, he planned to turn down the assignment. Anyone who knew anything about Lomerian politics knew that Malvegil was a pompous blowhard, far more interested in his own purse than the good of the realm, but even so, the man didn't have an altogether bad reputation – save where his wife was concerned.

The old fool had married a crazed elven witch that flew into hysterical rages and ensorcelled most any man that came into her sight. The very thought that a volsung nobleman would wed an elf – and one who practiced the dark arts to boot, was unfathomable by Lomerian aristocracy. It made the Malvegils social pariahs. Even worse, at least for Malvegil, they say that his elf is a stooped hag – a crone old enough to be Malvegil's grandmother, but that she wove spells about her that gave her the illusion of youth and beauty. The very thought of her made Mallick want to puke. Maybe killing Malvegil would be a mercy – to put the deluded fool out of his misery. At least in death, he'd be free of the crone.

Despite his wife, Malvegil was popular in the Council of Lords. Not socially, of course, but rather, as far as the business of State was concerned. He was sometimes even spoken of as a candidate for The High Council (perhaps a sign of how far the council had fallen from its heights), though he'd never take the position if offered, for he'd have to leave his Dor and his witch wife behind. She could never move to Lomion City with him – the nobles would simply never accept her in their midst.

Mallick decided that if Malvegil's witch wife was the target, he'd take the assignment, but he'd not kill the old lord, despite his faults. From what he knew of the man, he just didn't need killing. He had turned down other assignments before; this would just add another to the list.

Everything changed when Mallick sat down with Weater the Mouse, the Hand's second ranking agent behind the Grandmistress herself. (How and why the "brotherhood" was led by a Grandmistress is a tale for another time).

"What has Malvegil done?" said Mallick. "And who holds the contract?"

"The client remains anonymous," said Weater, "though we suspect it's either a member of the Council of Lords, or more likely, one or more members of The High Council. As for what he's done – better to ask, what hasn't he done?"

"Tell me."

"We have evidence showing he's into piracy and smuggling – transporting illegal goods up and down the Hudsar. And he's been doing it for years, maybe decades. As for the piracy – his reavers take ships traveling alone on the river at night. It's how he's built his fortune. Worse, he leaves no survivors to tell the tale, which is part of the reason he's gotten away with it for so long."

"It seems someone important was on a ship recently gone missing. No ransom; presumably, no survivors. Now that person's family is out for revenge. Hence, the current contract."

"How solid is the evidence?" said Mallick.

"Solid as steel."

"So, we know that the ship was pirated?"

"A shepherd saw the attack, but luckily, the pirates didn't see him. The freebooters flew a Malvegil flag, which they took down just afore the attack, and re-flew erelong after. Only a pirate behaves as such."

"How do we know Malvegil sent them?" said Mallick. "It could have been a rogue ship or a pirate that stole a Malvegil standard? What if the shepherd misidentified the standard, or is lying for his own reasons?"

"Good questions all," said Weater. "And I'm glad that you asked them. Some of the brethren don't ask enough. They don't think things through, or maybe they don't care as much as you and I do. It's questions like yours that keep us honest; that make certain we've left no stone unturned. The last thing we want to do is to take a contract without due cause. If we started doing that, we'd be no better than most of our targets. I'm happy to say, we were especially thorough in our review of this one – given, of course, that the target is a Dor Lord."

"We traced the pirate ship back to the Malvegillian docks," said Weater. "It was captained by one of Malvegil's top officers – a trusted henchman of long years. They hauled the booty up onto those big hoists they have there

169

and pulled it up into the Dor, no doubt, to display afore the old lord himself. There's more evidence, a lot more; I could go on for hours, and there's likely even more evidence that we haven't uncovered yet, but trust me, there's no doubt that Malvegil is behind this and many other crimes. Dozens of ships have gone missing on the Hudsar these past few years. He's behind virtually all of it. There were women on many of those ships and children on some. Granted, most of the vessels were only cargo barges, but some carried passengers. Malvegil's reavers put them all to the sword, except for the fairest, who were violated, abused, and sold into slavery down in Tragoss Mor. That's the business that old Torbin Malvegil is really in; his facade of a kindly, boisterous old blowhard, notwithstanding."

"You're sure on all this?" said Mallick.

"I'm certain about the main issues, and sure enough on the details; not that details matter that much."

"Why hasn't the council done anything about this piracy?" said Mallick.

Weater smiled. "They have. They appointed a Dor lord with a strong fleet and direct access to the Hudsar to investigate and track down the pirates."

"Malvegil?" said Mallick.

"Assigned to investigate himself," said Weater, nodding.

"So he'd never be caught."

"Not ever, but for a sharp-eyed shepherd and a determined family out for justice. He's a snake, that Malvegil. If I had the opportunity, I'd cut his throat myself. He has it coming. So I ask you, will you take the assignment? It pays three times your normal fee – being as he is a Dor lord after all, and far better guarded than most men."

"I'll take it," said Mallick. "Gladly."

"Good man," said Weater. "We're making the world a better place, one contract at a time."

Mallick tracked Lord Malvegil and his troops for three days. He expected to have to sneak a ride on the hoists, or failing that, attempt to scale the crag – a feat that no man had ever accomplished, or so it was said. Mallick was a good climber, even for one of the brethren, and they were nearly all experts by normal standards, but he had no desire to try the crag – though he would have if he needed too. The brethren never gave up, no matter the difficulty. They always got their target, eventually.

Mallick was surprised when he arrived at Dor Malvegil only to find the old Lord on horseback leading a brigade of troops out to the field. Where he was going with that many troops, in peacetime, in the heart of Lomion, was beyond him. Most strangely, he was headed north, whence Mallick had come, toward Lomion City. In most ways, this made Mallick's task all the easier, for now he'd only have to sneak past the troops and into Malvegil's tent. A quick slice and slash would end things and he'd be off home.

It was easy enough for Mallick to grab a straggler on the second night – a soldier out alone without a torch, headed into the woods for a pee. Mallick knifed him good and proper, but was unable to make a move on Malvegil that night, for there was too much activity around the lord's tent.

He needed to catch him asleep to have a reasonable chance to get away clean – or more importantly, to get away at all. He knew postponing the deed had its own risks – if they noticed the man missing, as they probably would, they would likely increase their vigilance. But going in when a dozen armed men were in the lord's tent was suicide. All things considered, he decided to hold off until the next night.

The next morning, Mallick washed the dead soldier's tabard in the Hudsar, to get out as much of the blood as he could. It came out looking good. That was important. He couldn't afford to have anyone spot something amiss when he wore it to infiltrate the camp.

It didn't take long for the Malvegils to realize their man was missing. They sent a search party to scour the wood and the riverbank in the morning, to check if the man had fallen injured somewhere. The search didn't last long, and they didn't check the exact spot where Mallick had done his knifing. The Malvegils also sent a squad back down the road to look for the missing man. Mallick was surprised they bothered – and thought that they must want to punish him for desertion. With a lord like old Malvegil, no doubt they had a lot of desertions.

Mallick followed the main column for most of the day, being certain to stay well back and out of sight of their lookouts. After dark, when they had set camp and the men were preparing to bed down for the night, he infiltrated the camp adorned in his Malvegillian uniform.

He made his way toward the lord's tent,

acting casual and moving with purpose – as if he belonged there. Near the center of the camp, more than a few men were already curled up and snoring away, so no one paid him any heed. It had been a long few days on the road and the men were exhausted. No matter, if anyone did notice him and asked questions, he'd bluff his way through – he was good at that.

Mallick found a choice spot within a hundred feet of the lord's tent and lay down in a bedroll he'd swiped off a supply wagon. Other men were nearby, but he positioned himself out of the line of sight of those nearest. It was a better spot than he could have hoped for. He lay down and waited. Waiting was part of the trade, but this time, he didn't have to wait for long. It was lights out early in the lord's tent that night, just as Mallick had hoped.

Now he could sneak in, do the deed, and creep out with none the wiser, hopefully for many hours. He waited for the tent guard to walk over to the fire to get another mug of coffee, and then walked casually in the direction of the tent. The guard glanced at him for only a moment, apparently satisfied that he was one of them. He passed near to the tent, turned about, and when he was sure that guard was focused on his coffee – slipped through the tent flap as silent and quick as a mouse. The room was dim – one oil lamp was set on the small travel table, its flame burning low. Mallick heard low snoring coming from the lord's massive bedding at the middle of the room. He took two quick steps in – getting him just close enough to clearly see the blankets moving up and down in time with the old blowhard's snoring.

Mallick carefully pulled out a tiny hand crossbow from beneath his jerkin – aimed it at the lord's chest, and fired. He heard a dull grunt just after it struck home. He charged. He landed atop Malvegil, dagger in hand, ready to slit his throat and be done with it, but he immediately realized that he had been fooled. He straddled nothing but blankets and pillows. He rolled off, spun, and crouched, not understanding how he'd seen the bedding moving up and down as with breathing, yet no one was beneath it.

Movement startled him. A soldier, in the tent, near the side. A trap for certain! A twang. They were shooting at him. Somehow, the bolt missed. Motion on all sides. Men had been hiding within the tent's perimeter, behind fabric screens that looked like the outer sides of the tent in the dim light. Another crossbow bolt flew. He dodged. Then another. This one from directly in front. Mallick saw the bolt. He reached out his hand, faster than most could follow and plucked the shaft from the air, just as he'd been trained to do. Another bolt flew at him from the side; no time to try to catch it, he moved his arm, and the bolt clanged off the steel bracer he wore beneath his jerkin.

He ran for the tent flap. The men there had fired the bolts and were drawing swords. A bolt struck him in the back. It pierced his leather jerkin just below the right shoulder blade. The impact pushed him forward, but didn't break his stride. He barreled through the guards at the tent flap – a slash and a slice with his dagger as he went. One of them surely went down – his throat sliced open. Mallick ran for it.

Try as he might to ignore it, the pain in the right side of his back grew worse with each step that he ran. The bolt might have pierced his lung. He dodged and evaded as he ran, swerving this way and that to avoid any more bolts that flew his way. Yells of alarm came from all around. Men rose from their tents and bedrolls; others ran this way or that. In the confusion, no one tried to stop him. His injury notwithstanding, he leaped over men asleep and others arising. At one point, he vaulted over a tent at least five feet high and half again as wide.

As he neared the edge of the camp, escape in sight; a crossbow bolt whizzed over his shoulder, then another nicked his ear. He felt the warm blood stream down his neck. One Malvegillian soldier came at him, arms outstretched to grab and grapple with him. Mallick Fern was too fast for that. His tiny dagger was in his hand – a two-inch blade held in his palm in such a way that the blade extended between his index and middle fingers when he closed his fist. He ducked under the man's clumsy lunge, and punched him as hard as he could, blade first, under the armpit. Mallick spun and kept running, not even looking back to see the man fall.

Then a shaft hit Mallick in the back of the leg, mid-thigh. He wanted to fall down, but he didn't. He knew that if he fell, that would be the end of him. He wasn't ready to die. He wanted to live. He had to escape. He was past the edge of their camp now, into the trees. He had to lose them in the wood, but he heard men running behind him.

Close behind him. He tried to speed up, but he was hampered by his wounds; the shafts had sapped all his energy, his blood streaming to the ground. Then they hit him again from behind. He went down; a great weight upon his back. A man had tackled him.

Mallick's killing blade was still in hand, but the man saw it coming. The soldier enveloped Mallick's hand within a powerful grip, and pinned his arm to the ground. It was Malvegil's bodyguard, Stoub of Rivenwood; a great brute of a man – a professional soldier with arms like steel. There was no getting away. Not from him. In moments, other men showed up and grabbed Mallick's arms and legs. There was no getting away; no chance at all. It was the end for Mallick Fern and he knew it. They would torture him for information – to find out who held the contract on the old lord. But Mallick didn't know who the client was, so the torture might continue on and on, without mercy or end. He'd heard of the Malvegils' reputation for ruthlessness. They might make sport of him for days, even weeks, probing for information before they'd finally kill him. They'd make him beg to die. That's what men like them did. The thought of it all sickened Mallick – and not just because it was happening to him. When he killed a man, he killed him quickly. He didn't make anyone needlessly suffer – even though his targets were the worst of the worst, the most vile, degenerate examples of mankind that Midgaard had to offer. And yet even they deserved mercy, compassion, and dignity in their deaths. Mallick knew that he'd get none of that from the Malvegils. Despair took him. He had only one choice left; only one path still lay open to him, but he had to move quickly before the Malvegils took even that away from him.

Mallick used his tongue to move the tiny wooden capsule from where he had it lodged between his teeth and cheek, and bit down hard on it. It didn't fully break, so he bit down again, and the capsule splintered and crumbled. He had to do that. As a brother of The Black Hand, he vowed to die rather than permit capture, rather than betray his brothers. It was his duty. The round pellet released its contents into his mouth. It was a powder – essence of nightshade. It spilled onto his tongue; it felt dry and gritty. He swallowed. He couldn't believe it had come to this.

The Malvegils knew what he was about; they were yelling and tried to pry his mouth open, but he'd swallowed most of the powder already.

Stoub pummeled him in the face and someone got his hand into his mouth. That man pulled out the major remnants of the pellet's shell, but the damage was done. Mallick felt the burning in his throat and stomach and he began to cough; his face and throat felt like they were swelling, and it was growing more and more difficult to breathe. It happened so fast. The world grew dim and he couldn't breathe. Dead gods, he couldn't breathe. He looked up into the sky, past the angry faces of those gathered close around him, and searched for the Valkyries that would carry him home to Valhalla, to feast at Odin's table amongst the gods, the Einheriar, and the honored dead.

He saw only darkness.

***

"**A**re you alright, my lord?" said Stoub.

"What are our losses?" said Malvegil.

"Three men dead; three others injured," said Stoub. "Who?"

"Troopers Bern and Brant were killed. Trooper Conger, who went missing yesterday, is presumed dead. The assassin was wearing his uniform. Three others were injured, but they'll recover."

"Brant's sister works in the kitchens – an apprentice chef – a good one," said Malvegil. "And Conger's father has been my friend since I was a boy." Malvegil shook his head. "Was it The Hand?"

"Yes, my lord."

"For certain?"

"Aye."

"I'll need to write the families."

"Karktan can do that on your behalf, my lord. You've more than enough to worry about."

"No. It's my responsibility." He met Stoub's gaze. "This isn't over, is it?"

"Once The Hand has a contract, they never stop, my lord. Never. Another assassin will come; maybe a group of them. If we kill them, there will be another wave, and then another."

"I've heard those stories about The Hand. Everyone has. But I always thought it propaganda. To put the fear in people."

"The stories are true, my lord. The Hand never gives up. I know of people they've tracked halfway across Midgaard."

"Can they be bought? Can we call them off

somehow?"

"We can't. No one can. Not even the person who contracted them to target you. Once The Hand accepts the fee, the assignment is irrevocable – unless the client pays them their entire fee again. Then they'll remove the contract. Only then."

"Is he dead?"

"He took nightshade to avoid capture. Had it lodged in his mouth, just in case. He was dead afore we were able to question him."

"Stinking zealots," said Malvegil. "They don't even value their own lives. So we don't know who hired him? That was the point of the nightshade, I suppose?"

"Even he probably didn't know," said Stoub. "He took the poison to avoid torture."

"What? We don't torture people. What are you talking about?"

"I imagine he was told that we do. Our enemies have quite the propaganda machine going against us."

Malvegil nodded. "That's nothing new, I suppose. The Alders and their cronies can't win over folk to their cause with facts, so they do it with lies; the tired tactics of the morally bankrupt."

"You'd be safer at home, my lord. Out here, security is a lot harder to maintain. In Lomion City, it will be impossible. I won't be able to protect you; not even if we march the whole brigade in with us."

"I need to go to the city. That hasn't changed."

"We could fake your death; put the word out

that the assassin got you, but that we killed him when he tried to escape."

"And then what? Hide under my bed for the next twenty years? Flee Lomion for parts foreign and hope that they don't find me? Never."

"Then what do you propose?"

"Let's take the fight to them."

"My lord?"

"You heard me. I just declared war on the Black Hand.

"I like the concept, my lord, but these men fight in secret; they attack from the shadows. There's no way I know to rout them out. And Lomion City is their home territory, not ours."

"We don't have to find and kill them all. We just have to kill their leader and his lieutenants."

"A decapitation strike?"

"Exactly."

***

"**A** large patrol has spotted us," said Captain Gedrun, Knight Commander of the brigade, to Lord Malvegil. "They be on us straightaway. Too many men this close to the city. I'm surprised they didn't mark us sooner."

"Are you sure they didn't?"

"Our outriders have seen nothing."

"Lomion City security is growing lax — a bad sign," said Malvegil.

"How far do we take the troops?"

"To the forest border south of the city. Set up camp there under cover and wait. Any closer to the city than that, and we'll gather too much attention."

"Riders approach," shouted one of Malvegil's soldiers at the van. "Heavy horse; Myrdonian Knights – a full squadron, including men-at-arms."

"That's the patrol that we saw," said Gedrun.

The Myrdonian patrol pulled up when they saw the large number of armed men approaching them.

"Their captain is nervous," said Gedrun. "Because he sees no standard. He doesn't know who we are."

Gedrun, Malvegil, Karktan, and Stoub moved up to the head of the column and waved the Myrdonians forward.

Malvegil studied them as they rode nearer, and drew close his cloak and hood to obscure his appearance. "There are enough veterans in that bunch that we'll get recognized one way or another."

"If you want no welcome when you arrive at the city," said Gedrun, "we can't let them leave ahead of us."

"Then let's encourage them to visit with us for a while," said Malvegil. "But softly – these men are Lomerians after all."

As the patrol got close, Gedrun told them that they were a mercenary company in service of the chancellor – a lie that he had prepared in advance. He showed their captain a fake writ of employment emblazoned with a reasonable facsimile of the chancellor's seal. That and some friendly words and smiles put the Myrdonians at ease and they dropped their guard. A few discrete hand gestures were all it took for Gedrun to have the Myrdonians surrounded and disarmed before they knew what was happening.

A few were bruised and battered in the process, but they avoided an all-out bloodbath.

"They'll be missed erelong enough, my lord," said Gedrun. "We'll need to move you into the city quickly – with a small group, before suspicions arise. Otherwise, they may seal the city gates, fearing that whoever waylaid their patrol might be a danger to the city. You'll have to go in with only a handful of men. More than that might garner unwanted attention."

Lord Malvegil, Stoub, and a few picked men split off from the main group and rode on to Lomion City. Their garb marked them as middling merchants traveling with a group of freesword bodyguards and a wagon full of wares – a sight as common as dirt in Lomion City, the most uncommon city of all.

They crossed the Great Meadow – the picturesque swath of well-tended grassland that bounded the city on three sides and served as a vast parkland for city residents. The grassy portion of the meadow was reserved for recreation and foot traffic only; horses, wagons, and livestock were strictly sequestered to gravel paths (wide enough for at least two large wagons to pass) that crisscrossed through the meadow. Those roads had clear signage and were laid out in a thoughtful pattern so as to get horse and wagon traffic to their destinations efficiently, without infringing any more than necessary on the tranquility of the meadow.

A wide, water-filled channel that connected

to Grand Hudsar Bay was cut around the entirety of the city perimeter, save where it fronted the bay on its eastern and southern sides. Some 150 feet wide and thirty feet deep, the channel served as a moat, eliminating the possibility of any enemy pushing siege engines to the walls and threatening the city. The meadow, the channel, and the bay had their own guard force tasked with protecting them. They policed access and prevented dumping and pollution upon penalty of arrest, hefty fines, and/or imprisonment. Their tasks were challenging given the city's vast population and its large, busy port. But the guards performed their jobs diligently, and consequently, the bay and the channel were clean enough to drink from and were popular fishing and swimming spots when weather permitted.

The great stone walls of the city rose up behind the channel – and looked more like natural stone formations that had grown out of the soil than manmade structures. The city walls were immense – the tallest and widest walls known to exist anywhere in Midgaard. Despite their great height, behind them, many tall buildings of impressive and varied design and appearance were visible from the meadow, in large part due to the contours of the land as it rose up toward its highest point near the city center.

Malvegil and his squad made certain to stick to the gravel road so as not to draw the attention of the meadow guards. They blended in with the crowd, and it was a crowd. Throngs of people of every age, shape, size, creed, and color made their way in and out of the city all day and much of the night, going about their business, traveling to and from nearby and far-off villages, towns, and cities. Merchants, sometimes alone or in small groups, sometimes in vast caravans, came and went continuously. Lomion City, you see, was a city nourished by wagons and ships. The trade they brought was its lifeblood.

Besides merchants, those who traveled to and from the city by land were mostly volsungs, the native folk of the kingdom as well as many parts of the continent beyond Lomion's borders. A slim majority of the crowd they walked amongst were volsungs of northron stock, like the Malvegils themselves: fair skin, dark, straight hair, gray or blue eyes. Not as tall and broad as true northerners like the Eotrus, but solidly built all the same.

Most anyone in Lomion who wasn't a volsung was labeled a "foreigner," regardless of residency or actual birthplace. Nonresidents of Lomion City or its surrounds typically arrived via ship, docking at one of the wharfs in Lomion City's huge port.

Though outnumbered by the volsungs, foreigners of every stripe and ethnicity were found in Lomion City, some types common, others exceedingly rare. Some were permanent residents, others diplomats or merchants, and some were sightseers on holiday or out for adventure.

Some foreigners identified themselves by their country or region of origin (or that of their ancestors), others, by their religion, such as the Thothians, while still others maintained a tribal or racial identity, such as the dwarves and the gnomes, who in truth, physically differed no more from volsungs than did most foreigners.

The variations between and amongst the foreigners and the volsungs were relatively minor: hair, facial features, skin hue, height, and build. The foreigners spoke myriad languages and dialects; though near everyone also spoke Lomerian. The foreigners maintained their own customs: dress, food, religion, and whatever else was important to their respective traditions. First or second-generation immigrants often chose to live in enclaves of their fellows. They built and decorated their buildings and neighborhoods in their own style, wore their traditional garb, and cooked their traditional food. All this lent a cosmopolitan feel to Lomion City and made it a more diverse mix of peoples and cultures than was found in any other city in the kingdom, and perhaps in all of Midgaard.

The road to the main gate was congested when the Malvegils arrived. A large caravan was departing for Dyvers, another great Lomerian city, a goodly ways to the west. Their horses and wagons plodded along, grinding traffic to a halt at one of the arch bridges that spanned the channel. The next closest bridge was a long walk away. Malvegil decided to wait to cross at the first bridge, in part, because the thronging crowd made it less likely that anyone might recognize them, since only those very close to them would be able to get a good look at them.

The Malvegils gathered close together and waited their turn to get onto the bridge. Some folks in line were polite in their ways, but many foreigners stood too close to the Malvegillians, leaning against them, or inadvertently pushing them as they all shuffled slowly along like penned sheep. Any many in the crowd stunk. Apparently, bathing was not on the priority list of certain of the foreigners. That drove the Malvegillians mad. They were not big city dwellers, and their concept of personal space was violated by the crowd. They could tolerate some stench, but not getting shoved. Any number of them seemed ready to draw their weapons and hack down the crowd around them. But none of them did.

After more than half an hour, they finally made it onto the span; another half hour put them through the gate. The south gatehouse as it was called, was a massive structure of stone and steel that rose eighty feet or more, with great stone towers that straddled the entry. The gates themselves were massive wooden doors at least two feet thick and tightly banded with thick steel plates. Multiple steel portcullises loomed over the entry, ready to be dropped into place at a moment's notice. Passing through the gate gave some sense of the massive scale of the walls. Malvegil estimated that they were no less than fifty feet thick, all stone. The bridge deck as well as the city entry and the streets beyond were paved in cobblestones.

While still very close to the gate, as they made their way through the crowd, a tall man passing by them dropped a parcel he carried and bent to pick it up. Just as he stood up, a crossbow bolt blasted through the side of his head – a bolt in clear line to have struck Lord Malvegil had the man not gotten in the way at just that moment.

"The Hand!" cried Stoub. He drew his sword, as did the others. The men huddled close to their lord, trying to shield him with their own bodies from any further attack. Those few people nearby that noticed what happened, which wasn't many given the general din and close quarters, yelled, screamed, or gasped. The crowd began to part, trying to understand what had happened.

"Run," shouted Stoub. "Knock them out of the way." The Malvegillians barreled through the crowd. They'd gone but five steps when Stoub shoved Malvegil and put his hand up (which held a small shield) and deflected another bolt aimed at his lord. Ten strides later, the soldier next to Malvegil took a bolt in the shoulder. He pulled it out himself and kept moving.

The bolts stopped. They must have passed out of range of the assassin, but they kept up their pace, and zigzagged through crowds of local city dwellers, farmers, merchants, noblemen, commoners, and thugs, on streets that were havens for merchants' shops, stalls, and street hawkers that collectively sold every ware imaginable.

For the first two blocks, they bowled over anyone in their way. After that, they grew more cautious and tried to make their passing go unnoticed, especially as watchmen's whistles began to sound behind them. The last thing they needed was to be detained by the watch. Then their enemies would know exactly where they were and lay an ambush from which they would never escape.

Once the Malvegillians passed beyond the mercantile district, the crowds thinned, the going got easier, and their pace quickened. They headed to Dor Lomion, Lord Harringgold's majestic fortress, which stood near the city center. They traveled via the most direct route available, looking warily over their shoulders as they went, but there was no sign of pursuit. At least, none visible to them.

As they made their way down an alley, a sewer cover burst open several yards ahead of them. Out of it scampered a gnome, covered in grime.

"Found them," yelled the gnome. Behind him came more of his ilk.

"Back," shouted Stoub as he grabbed his lord's arm again and turned back the way they came. Their weapons were out again.

"Wait. Stop," yelled the gnome, but they ignored him. "He kept calling after them, but they didn't make out his words. Just as they reached the end of the alley, four gnomes raced around the corner and barreled into them. The gnomes and two Malvegillian soldiers went down in a heap, blocking easy passage out of the alley. Stoub looked back. At least a half dozen of the sewer gnomes were right behind them.

"Take them," shouted Stoub as he lifted his sword to attack position.

"Stop!" yelled one the gnomes in front. "Stop! We're not the enemy." The gnome pulled himself to his feet. The soldier he'd collided with had one hand on the gnome's collar and a dagger against his chest. The gnomes beside him had their arms around the soldier's, trying to hold him back. "Easy man," said the gnome spokesman to the soldier. "I'm no enemy of the Malvegils. Stand down."

"Grim? Is that you?" said Lord Malvegil.

"Aye, my lord," said the gnome. "Grim

Fischer at your service," he said, a broad smile on his face. "It's good to see you."

"Good old Grim," said Malvegil warmly. "Stand down men. Grim is a Harringgold man and an old friend. It's been a while."

"Too long," said the gnome as he moved forward and shook Malvegil's hand. Sorry I missed you last trip, especially seeing as what happened, but the Duke had me otherwise occupied."

"You didn't happen upon us just now," said Stoub.

"My boys have been tracking you since you passed the gate. For big folk, you people move fast."

"We had some encouragement," said Malvegil. "We could have used your help back there."

"You had it," said Grim as he pulled out two cloth insignias from his pocket, hastily cut from some garment. Each cloth had the pattern of a black hand sewn onto a red background. "Those two with the crossbows won't be bothering you again, but I expect that there will be more. There always are with The Hand. It's best that we get off the streets afore any more of their brethren show up. I have standing orders to escort you to the Duke upon your arrival at the city. You caught me by surprise, though. We didn't expect you for two months at least. What brings you here early?"

"Two months?" said Malvegil. "The Duke's missive said to come at once."

"Not the one that I know of," said Grim. "And I'm sure that the Duke would've told me if things changed, so that I could handle your security

189

properly. Something don't smell right about this."

"Agreed," said Malvegil.

"Then this whole excursion may have been a trap," said Stoub.

"To lure me here or to lure me away from the Dor?"

"To lure you here, it had to be," said Stoub. "Let's get you to the Duke quickly.

X
THE BEARDLESS DWARF

A troop of cavalry trotted up the road, two abreast – a mixture of medium and heavy horse. The smaller horses bore soldiers clad in chainmail or leathers and equipped with bows, short swords, and other battle gear. The huge destriers that rode beside them wore barding of steel mail and plate, draped with colorful caparison. Upon them rode knights fully accoutered for war. And these were no common knights – they were Northmen. They were knights of Dor Eotrus, stalwart and proud. Most were large and imposing. All of them were battle born, bred, and ready. They wore sculpted and polished plate armor of exquisite detail yet pragmatic design that retained the dents and gouges of long use. They carried shields adorned with their family crests; blue capes; helmets topped with multi-hued feathers or ribbons; and tabards adorned with the colors and sigil of House Eotrus.

Near the front of the column rode the officers: Sir Ector Eotrus, third son of Lord Aradon (recently passed), the acting Lord of the House in his brothers' absence; Sir Sarbek, acting Castellan – a grizzled veteran and Dor Eotrus's most senior knight; Indigo Eldswroth – handsome, heavily muscled, and exceptionally tall – the very stereotype of the Northman; Sir Wyndham the Bold of Weeping Hollow, the rugged young knight captain of the cavalry squadron amongst which they rode, and the lieutenant, the squadron's second-in-command, another veteran, almost as old as Sarbek, but as spry and agile as a recruit.

"Sir Ector," said Captain Wyndham as he looked back at the men that rode just behind him, "shall we ride on into the night, or would you prefer to set a camp afore dark?"

"Can we make it to Mindletown tomorrow?" said Ector.

"If we ride for a few more hours tonight, we should arrive around nightfall tomorrow. If we camp now, we'll arrive late in the night tomorrow, or early the next morning, if we set another camp tomorrow night."

"Let's push on," said Ector. "I want to get there tomorrow, and the earlier the better."

They rode very late into the night; oil lanterns providing the only light that guided their way; they finally set camp near midnight. The men put up their tents and then gathered around several hastily built fires. They drank hot tea, but ate only cold food, dried fruits, nuts, and jerky before bedding down for the night.

"Four men per watch, three shifts of two hours each," said Captain Wyndham to the lieutenant, as he sat at the officers' fire, a mug of steaming tea in hand. "Have the men ready to move out at dawn."

"Eight men per watch," said Ector. "And remain at strict combat footing."

The other men turned an eye toward him.

"Sir?" said Wyndham.

"Eight per watch, strict combat footing," said Ector. "Make it so."

"Aye, sir," he said. He nodded to the

lieutenant who set off at once.

"You expect trouble?" said Wyndham. "So close to the Dor?"

"Something is kidnapping or killing folks from Mindletown. That's why we're out here, isn't it?"

"We're still many miles out from Mindletown, sir," said Wyndham. "Unlikely anyone causing mischief there would be out this far."

"It's not anyone that he's worried about," said Sarbek.

"Then I don't understand," said Wyndham.

"The thing that attacked my brother (Claradon) in the citadel," said Ector. "There may be another."

"I know that we're not to speak of such things, but seeing as it's just us . . ." said Wyndham.

"Speak freely, lad," said Sarbek. "As you said, it's just us here . . . "

"Didn't that thing – what was it called?"

"A reskalan," said Indigo.

"Didn't the reskalan come from the Vermion Forest – conjured up from Nifleheim?"

"So we believe," said Ector.

"There's a lot of ground betwixt the Vermion and Mindletown. It seems odd that it would have hiked all the way up there."

"Maybe," said Ector.

"Who knows what goes on in the mind of an animal," said Indigo. "Or a monster – if it really hails from Nifleheim."

"No disrespect, sirs," said Wyndham, "but I heard that farmer's report about howling in the night and people going missing and such. It sounds like a wolf pack to me – gone hungry and come down from the mountains. Maybe the pack took someone, and developed a taste for human flesh. If it's not that, it could be a big mountain lion, or a panther, or a bear. This far out into the wild, people get killed by animals every year. What makes you think it's one of the reskalans?"

Sarbek looked as if he had just scored a major victory and looked at Ector as he spoke. "Exactly what I've been saying. We're wasting our time out here. With Lomion in troubled times and your brothers away, your place is at the Dor, not out here in the deep woods."

"You said that at least five times afore we left," said Ector.

"Seven times, by my count," said Indigo.

"And I'll keep telling you until you listen," said Sarbek.

"Well, I'm not going to listen. The people of Mindletown need help and I'm to help them, whether it's against wolves, a bear, a reskalan, or whatever."

"Of course we're going to help them," said Sarbek. "That's our duty, our responsibility, but Wyndham and his squadron can do that. They don't need you."

"The town has a constable," said Indigo, "and he has at least three or four deputies."

"I don't doubt the capabilities of the good captain or his men; that's not the issue," said Ector. "And if the constable knew what was going on and could handle it, they wouldn't have sent for help. The folk out here are fiercely independent. Father told us many times that they never ask for anything of the Dor. Never. They must be desperate. If it was just some rogue animal, they'd be done with it in no time, and we'd never even hear about it. It has to be something truly dangerous that's after them. Something that has got them scared. Whatever that is, I want to see it for myself."

"Mindletown also has Captain Pellan," said Indigo.

"The beardless dwarf?" said Sarbek. "In Mindletown? I thought that she retired to Wortsford?"

"Nope, Mindletown," said Indigo. "She's even on the town council."

"I'd forgotten that," said Sarbek. "All the more reason that this is a waste of our time. Pellan is an old pro. With Wyndham backing her up, she can handle most anything, including a reskalan."

Ector made no further comment.

"You're needed more at the Dor now than ever before in your life," said Sarbek."

"Nine," muttered Indigo.

Ector's voice took on an irritated tone. "Then you should have stayed to watch over things. That's your primary responsibility, isn't it? With Ob away, you're the castellan."

"My primary responsibility is to see that you don't get yourself killed, which is why I'm here."

"Fine, keep me from getting killed," said Ector chuckling. "I've no interest in getting dead. We've had far too much of that of late. But I'm still going to see this through."

"There's no convincing you, is there?" said Sarbek.

"No," said Ector. "Dead gods, we're most of

the way there already. It's a bit late to go back now anyway, don't you think? Let's get done whatever needs doing up Mindletown way, then we'll head back straightaway. The Dor will survive without us for a few more days."

"Fine," said Sarbek.

"Good," said Ector.

Indigo took out his journal and started writing.

"Nothing has even happened yet," said Sarbek, "What are you writing?"

"He never stops scribbling," said Ector. "It's like an addiction."

"Unless there are pretty girls around, then he stops," said Sarbek.

Reading from the journal, Indigo said, "On the way to Mindletown, on the fifth day of the twelfth month in the common year 853 by Lomerian reckoning, Sir Sarbek du Martegran gave up an argument." He looked up at the others and smiled. "That's a first, and worth recording."

The night passed uneventfully. They woke up tired and sore from their travels and from sleeping on the ground, but they managed to set out soon after dawn. They rode at a strong pace all day, stopping only briefly as needed to care for the horses.

"Sir, we should reach Berrill's Bridge within two hours," said Captain Wyndham to Ector. "The bridge marks the border of Mindletown Township."

Howls sounded in the distance, from the north.

The lieutenant rode at the van and his hand came up halting the column. The men went quiet.

More howls came from the north; from the direction they were going.

"That's no wolf pack," said Sarbek. "Indigo?"

"It's not anything that I've heard afore," said Indigo. "Whatever it is, it's not native to these woods."

"Well, lad," said Sarbek to Ector. "It looks like we were right to join this patrol. Maybe it is a stinking reskalan."

"I hear at least two different calls, maybe more," said Ector.

"Three," said Indigo. "There are three up ahead, and more far off in the distance – I can barely hear them, but they're there."

"Let's get moving," said Sarbek. "We're losing light. Wyndham – have them ready their bows; helmets on, and all weapons ready. Keep them in tight formation."

"Aye, Castellan," said Wyndham.

The set off at a trot up the road, went around a bend and the road opened up in a long straight run. A couple of hundred yards in the distance they saw a group of monstrous creatures loping down the road in their direction.

"Charge," shouted the lieutenant of his own accord. The whole company did so.

Pellan braced her makeshift spear with her foot and angled it toward the trolls as they leaped. The first vaulted over the top of the spear, but the second came in lower. Pellan adjusted the angle of the spear in expert fashion and the troll landed atop it, screeching – impaled through the center of its chest. Pellan tried to dive out of the way as it crashed down, but an explosion of splintering wood, slashing claws, and flying troll caught her and knocked her to the ground. She rolled and scrambled to her feet, dagger in one hand, a fist sized rock that she had picked up in the other.

The alchemist dodged the troll that leaped at him, using the tree for cover.

The impaled troll thrashed on the ground, roaring and howling. Pellan wanted to rush in and slice its throat to finish it, but its thrashings were too wild – she dared not chance the claws.

The second troll stalked her, and the third circled the alchemist.

The second lunged toward her. She flung the stone as hard as she could. Luck was with her. It struck the troll dead on. It crushed its nose and battered an eye. It staggered back bleeding and dropped to its rump. Pellan leaped into the air. She came down atop the troll's chest, and in the same motion, she thrust her dagger under the troll's chin. It sank to the hilt: up into the troll's brain.

With barely a pause, Pellan pulled the dagger out and spun around. The impaled troll had pulled the spear fragment from its chest and was holding it in one hand, while the other hand strove to staunch the geyser of yellow blood that gushed from its chest. Blood pooled on the ground around it. It wasn't getting up any time soon.

The third troll rolled over and over on the ground with the alchemist. The alchemist's hands were locked around the troll's throat in a death grip. The troll punched and slashed, tearing into the alchemist, but his grip did not loosen. Pellan ran to them. She waited until the troll rolled to the top, then slammed her dagger's blade through the back of its neck. The blow was so powerful that it severed the troll's spinal cord and shattered the dagger. The troll went limp. Pellan bounced up. But now she was unarmed.

She saw the impaled troll trying to rise. How it still lived at all, considering its vast blood loss, was hard to fathom. Pellan frantically scanned the ground. She spied a large rock, ran to it. She hefted it up over her head – a seventy pounder. She moved to where the troll struggled and flung the rock down at its head. The troll blocked it with its arms, but the impact shattered one of them. Pellan scooped up another rock, and threw it at the troll. It rolled to the side, but the stone hit it in the shoulder. Pellan picked up the first stone again. She slammed it down on the troll, smashing its arm and head. She lifted it again and battered the troll's head. Then again. Then again, and again, until its skull was no more than mush and bits of bone. Even then, the troll's legs quivered and spasmed, but it would never rise again.

The troll that she had stabbed up under the chin was on its feet, blood streaming down its chest, growling a distorted, wet-sounding growl from the blood that clogged its throat. It charged at Pellan. She sidestepped, and tripped it. The troll fell to the ground, face first. Pellan was on its back in an instant and repeated her stone attack – this time with a fist-sized rock (the largest within reach). She hit the troll over and over as it struggled to rise and knock her off. It was too strong for her; she couldn't hold it down, and the smaller stone did it too little damage even in her powerful grip. Pellan clung to its back and continued to smash the back and top of its head with the rock, and she pummeled its claws each time they tried to grab or slash her.

An arrow struck the troll's chest. Pellan saw it hit. She looked up and saw horses charging toward her. She was shocked that she hadn't heard them. Two more arrows slammed into the troll's chest, to seemingly little effect. The troll growled and began to move toward the horsemen, ignoring Pellan who still clung to its back.

A destrier galloped toward them, lance lowered, bearing Eotrus colors. Pellan slid off the troll's back but a moment before the lance impacted its abdomen and shattered. The rider thundered by as the troll stumbled back, the broken end of the lance protruding from its belly. Pellan stuck her leg out and tripped the troll. It fell and lay on the ground stunned and bleeding.

Other knights pulled up their horses all around. Pellan went to the nearest horse and snatched a hammer from its sheath. She dashed back to the troll who had already pulled the lance tip out and was sitting up, snarling. She raised the hammer and smashed it down, but the troll blocked the blow with its hands and arms, though the impact made a sickening crunch as its bones shattered. Pellan tried to wrench the hammer free, but somehow the troll clung to it. Pellan dropkicked it in the face, knocking it flat to the ground. She scrambled up, hammer again in hand and swung it in a wide arc. This time, the troll wasn't fast enough. The hammer caught it full on against its jaw, teeth and blood spurting across the ground. The troll tried to roar, but the sound came out more as a whimper. It tried to rise. Pellan struck it in the head with the hammer. Then again. Then again. Then it moved no more.

Pellan was covered in yellow trolls' blood and gore. Red streaks of her own blood dripped down her forehead, her arms, and one of her legs.

"You see," said Sarbek, "I told you the beardless dwarf could handle the trouble. A waste of our time coming up here."

"Beardless dwarf," shouted Indigo as he raised his hand high in salute.

"Beardless dwarf, beardless dwarf," chanted the soldiers, all holding up their hands in salute.

Pellan pushed through the press of horses and men and hurried to where the alchemist lay. The flesh was flayed from his arms. His face was deeply cut and torn down to the bone. His chest wounds were ripped open. Blood pooled around him. Somehow, he still breathed and his eyes were open.

She knelt down beside him and eyed his wounds. There was nothing she or anyone could do – he should already be dead.

"Did we get them?" he said weakly.

"All three," said Pellan. "Killed them good and proper."

"Good work, but get gone now and warn the Eotrus," said the alchemist.

"They're here – the Eotrus. They answered our call."

He nodded. "Dwarf, I will toast you in Odin's hall tonight. The gods will know your name."

Pellan couldn't say anything; she could only nod, her eyes wet.

"You look like crap," he said, and then closed his eyes for the last time.

"What are these things?" said Indigo. "Some kind of ogres?"

"Wendigo," said the lieutenant. "My grandmother told me of them."

"You're both wrong," said Sarbek. "They're mountain trolls. I saw one when I was a lad of ten. It came down from the high mountains. Your grandfather," he said pointing to Ector, "went after it with a full brigade. They were out in the wild for weeks as I remember, and came back a dozen men short, but they killed the thing, and brought its body back for all to see. Best as I can remember, it looked much as these do."

"And Captain Pellan took out three of them by herself," said Ector.

"No armor, no sword," said Indigo. "Who let her retire?"

"I remember it being a lot bigger than these," said Sarbek. "I guess things always seem bigger when you're ten. Get the dwarf cleaned up, and give her some fresh clothes. Wrap up two of the troll bodies – we're taking them with us."

"There're more of them," said Pellan

"We heard their howls, Captain," said Sarbek. "How many? And where are they? And how fares Mindletown?"

"There are enough that they wiped out all of Mindletown in a single night. Four hundred folk. The trolls may still be there."

"Dead gods," said Sarbek.

"The whole town?" said Ector.

"Some other folk might have gotten away," said Pellan. "I'm not sure. But they sacked the whole town. Broke into every building; killed everyone they found."

"Nothing like this has happened in generations," said Sarbek. "Wyndham, send two riders to the Dor at top speed; give them each three horses and have them ride all night. They are to deliver the troll bodies to Leren Sverdes for examination. More importantly, they're to tell Malcolm to deploy a full brigade to support us. We'll expect them here within four days. Under no circumstances is Malcolm to ride with the brigade. He's to remain at the Dor until we return."

"And have Malcolm raise the Dor to combat footing," said Ector.

"Hold on, lad, that means pulling in all the folk from the farms and villages," said Sarbek. "That will impact the final harvest of the season, and cause a major uproar. That's just not warranted based on what we know now."

"What if there are a hundred of those things all headed south, and we can't hold them here?" said Ector. "We've had one town wiped out already."

"We'll hold them, but your point is well taken," said Sarbek. "Combat footing it is, Wyndham. And have the Dor send ravens to all within Eotrus demesne warning of the threat."

"Aye, Castellan," said Wyndham.

More howls sounded in the distance and repeated every few minutes thereafter.

"If you want to try to hold them, we've got to get to Berrill's Bridge afore they do," said Pellan. "Keeping them on the other side of the river is our only chance to contain them."

"Agreed," said Sarbek.

"For Odin's sake," said Pellan, "can somebody give me a sword, a dagger, and a shield? I'm about done fighting with sticks and stones. I don't suppose you've got any armor my size?"

"No, but we've got the rest," said the lieutenant.

"Mount up," shouted Ector.

In moments, the squadron was ready to move, Pellan on a spare horse. They tied the alchemist's body to the back of another horse – for they hoped to give him a proper burial near his home. The soldiers poured oil on the remaining troll corpse and set it aflame.

The squadron made it to the bridge without incident. It looked clear, but it was hard to tell for certain. There was a partial moon that night, but visibility was sorely limited.

Berrill's Bridge was no rickety footbridge; it was wide, strong, and spanned two hundred feet over the water below, making it one of the longest bridges in the entire kingdom. It was the most northerly of the few safe crossings over the Ottowhile River during much of the year. That made it a gateway to the northeastern mountains and parts foreign beyond. The path had little traffic beyond local townsfolk, farmers, and woodsmen, for the mountain paths that led to other lands were long and dangerous, but what traffic did pass that way was important, especially to the Eotrus. Certain foreign merchants friendly to the Eotrus knew the secret paths through northeastern mountains, and used them, the long road through the forest, and ultimately, Berrill's

Bridge to introduce valuable trade goods to the region. That made it worth the investment to the Eotrus to commission the bridge, which was built almost entirely by gnome masons brought up from Portland Vale. The bridge's presence spawned four towns, including Mindletown, and half a dozen little villages, and scores of farms and homesteads in what was previously uninhabited forest. The bridge had no permanent garrison, but was manned in shifts by guardsmen and civilian volunteers based in Mindletown.

The bridge was entirely constructed of stone. It had four arches, each supported by a great stone pier set deep into the rock below. Small stone guard posts stood empty on each end.

"Was there any sign of the watchmen when you passed through?" said Sarbek to Pellan.

"Trolls must have got them before we arrived. They jumped us midspan. You should check underneath. They came up on us over the sides."

"We'll watch for that," said Wyndham.

The lieutenant and two soldiers moved on foot down the hill toward the water, torches in hand, to get a view of the bridge's underside.

"We should set a strong force at the far end and try to hold there," said Ector. "We can retreat back along the span if needed, keeping some of our number on this side as reserves, and to make sure we don't get boxed in, in case any of them are on this side already."

"Smart thinking, lad," said Sarbek. "Captain," he said to Wyndham, "make it so."

Wyndham started moving the troops over.

"Hold up, Captain," shouted Pellan. "Wait

until your man gets back. Let's make sure it's clear first."

Wyndham stared at her skeptically and looked toward Sarbek. The Castellan gave him a signal to hold up.

Not a minute later, the lieutenant ran back up the hill just as a group of trolls – ten or twelve of them in all – pulled themselves up and over the side rails of the bridge.

"The scum were clinging onto the underside of the arches like beetles," shouted the lieutenant. "Without the torches, we'd have never seen them."

"Good work, dwarf," said Sarbek to Pellan. "If they'd come over on us as we were crossing, it would have gotten messy."

"It's going to get messy, anyway," said Pellan. "There are too many of them."

"You took out three by yourself," said Indigo. "We've a whole squadron."

"Dwarf, if we were out in the open, I might agree with you – maybe," said Sarbek. "But confined to the bridge, we can run them down. We'll make them pay a weighty toll if they try to cross here. Let's give them hell, boys," he shouted. "Give them a taste of Eotrus steel!"

The men cheered.

The trolls stood still and steady on the bridge, near midspan, waiting. The presence of some thirty horse soldiers seemed no deterrent to them at all.

"Is that all of them, lieutenant?" said Wyndham. "Are you sure no more are hanging on down below?"

The lieutenant traded hand signals with two

of his men that were positioned partway down the slope, to the north and the south sides of the bridge.

"We can't see any others, sir," said the lieutenant.

"Captain Wyndham," said Ector. "Prepare for a charge. Have the supply train remain here with the reserves."

The lieutenant sounded his horn directing the men to make ready.

"Go for their heads and necks only," shouted Pellan. "Cut off the heads or smash them to mush. Nothing else will stop them. Stab them in the heart and they'll just get up again, if they even go down at all. Do you hear me?" she shouted turning all about, making certain that she had the men's attention. "Destroy their heads – it's the only way to kill them. That and fire."

"You heard the Beardless Dwarf, men," shouted Sarbek. "Do as she said. Sound the charge."

The lieutenant did so.

As one, the squadron charged, four abreast, taking up the entire width of the bridge. The stones of the bridge deck thundered with their passing. The lead riders held lances; the soldiers in the row behind stood tall in their saddles and aimed bows.

A charge of armored horse put fear in the hearts of any enemy. The Eotrus expected the trolls to turn tail and flee, or to brace for the impact, or perhaps to just stand there stupidly, not knowing what to do. But they did none of that. Instead, they charged directly at the horsemen, racing at them in their apelike gait, arms flailing as they got close. The archers let loose, skewering the lead trolls, but the arrows had little or no effect.

At the last moment, the trolls at the fore leaped high, with greater agility than any man could muster, and lunged at the riders, trying to sail above the horses and knock the knights from their saddles. The trolls behind dived toward the horses' legs. Both charges broke with the terrible impact: lances shattered, trolls were trampled, horses went down, men and trolls went flying and smashed into the deck, some battered and broken, some dead – some few were even thrown over the side. It was chaos.

Ector tried to rise, but a man was atop him, not moving. Ector's foot was trapped under his horse. He pulled himself free, surprised that he wasn't injured, only winded, and disoriented. There was a blur of motion around him. Trolls pounced on men, his men. Yells, screams, roaring. There was too much destruction around him – he realized he had to have been unconscious for some seconds at least.

He pulled his sword; then Indigo was at his side, red blood on his face, yellow on his sword. "A close fight," he shouted. "We've got to get you clear of here."

Ector stepped on and stumbled over bodies of horses, trolls, and men, as Indigo pulled him to the side of the bridge by the parapet. They ran down the span back toward the supply train. There would be help there. Six or eight soldiers watched the horses. Ector tried to see what was happening, but his head was foggy. A lot of horses were down. The fighting was thick and frenzied.

Ector saw the lieutenant fall beneath the claws of two trolls. He stabbed and sliced them, and would have killed them both three times over if they were normal creatures, but his cuts had little effect, for they healed nearly as quickly as he struck.

Ector saw two horses crash into a troll just past the west end of the bridge, for the fighting extended that far. The riders' lances pinned it to the ground. Its claws broke through both lances in no time. Sarbek appeared, sword in hand, and took a mighty swing. His weapon cut deep into the back of the creature's head and it fell limp to the ground. Another soldier crushed the thing's head with a battle hammer. It would not rise again.

Indigo pulled Ector along as the soldiers from the supply train rode up, crossbows in hand. They loosed their bolts and jumped from their mounts, drawing swords, and ran into the fray. Ector marveled at their bravery. These were the support troops, lightly armored, and mostly older men and boys, yet in they charged where great knights fell.

"We've got to get back in there," said Ector as he pulled his arm free from Indigo.

"You're hurt."

"I'm fine. Let's go."

Indigo looked him up and down and apparently was convinced. He looked back, the fighting just behind them. "Odin knows they could use us." They waded back into the fray. The fighting was thick and bloody and continued so for some time.

A troll leaped at them. They dived to each side. It barely clipped their armor with its claws, though that was enough to rend the metal. Indigo was on his feet in a flash. His sword arced down as the troll scrambled up, and severed the creature's arm just below the elbow. The thing screamed and kicked. Indigo took the impact on his shield, though it knocked him back several steps. Ector found himself swinging his sword. The troll reflexively tried to block the blow with his claws (which lay on the ground along with the rest of its severed limb), so Ector's slash got through and opened a deep cut in the troll's chest. Yellow blood that smelled like sulphur shot from its stump and splashed over Ector's tabard. Ector pulled his sword back and thrust it through the center of the troll's chest. He regretted the blow as soon as it landed. He knew he needed to go for its head, but it was hard to change one's fighting style on the fly. The creature roared and reached out to him with both arms. The one that still had claws grabbed hold of Ector's shoulder and tried to pull him closer.

Indigo yelled, "Duck." Ector did. Indigo's sword passed over his head and hit the troll at about ear level. The sword cut through half the troll's head before it stuck. Somehow, the thing did not fall. Instead, it hefted Ector aloft by his shoulder, his toes barely touching the ground. Ector pulled out his dagger and stabbed at the troll's wrist. Indigo stepped in close and stabbed and cut the troll in the neck, over and again. After several strikes, the troll dropped to its knees. Ector cut through enough of its wrist that it finally released him. Before their eyes, the troll's wounds began to close, to heal of their own accord. Indigo picked up a fallen battle hammer and slammed the troll in the back of the head. It fell face down to the deck. He smashed it two more times until the head was destroyed.

"Burn the bodies," shouted Sarbek from some ways away. "Throw oil on them and burn them."

"Bash their heads in," yelled Pellan from the center of the bridge span, "or cut them off. If you don't they'll keep getting up."

The battle was over, but the killing continued. Men followed Pellan's and Sarbek's advice and hacked at fallen trolls on all sides of the small battlefield. Smoke and fire rose from two or three spots where they set the trolls aflame. Mostly they finished them off by smashing their heads to pulp.

Even as they pounded the life out of the last quivering trolls, they heard more howls, and from not far off.

"Another group comes," said Wyndham whose face was bloody, one arm hanging limp at his side.

Ector looked around. Half their squadron had fallen, but there were more men standing than horses. Eight of twelve knights, six of sixteen men-at-arms, and four of the eight support troops still lived. Two of the men-at-arms were badly wounded; the rest of the squadron was mobile and could fight, though some, like Wyndham were hurt. The lieutenant was amongst the dead. Pellan, they said, killed three more trolls in that battle, though Ector saw none of it.

Were it not for the spare mounts that they had brought, there would have been too few horses for those who remained.

"Mount up," shouted Sarbek. "Strap the wounded to horses and let's move now. We're off in two minutes." There would be no discussion this time. They were heading back to the Dor with all the speed that they could muster.

They moved at a gallop for a half mile or so and then slowed as more and more horses began to straggle behind, either they or their riders too fatigued to keep up. Ector's head was spinning. He still felt disoriented. He couldn't believe what had happened. So many men dead – all under his charge.

Ector had never seen a cavalry charge broken by unarmed troops on foot. He had never heard of such a thing. If he hadn't seen it himself, he may not have believed it. And he was angry that he didn't know the lieutenant's name. He'd seen him countless times at the Dor over the years, and had spoken to him on many occasions, but "lieutenant" was all he ever seemed to be called by anyone. Ector was frustrated and angry that he had to leave his body behind. He had to leave the bodies of all his fallen men in the road – right there, where they fell. Would the trolls eat them? Would they desecrate their corpses? Those men deserved a proper burial by their families. They deserved dignity.

As he rode along, Ector looked at the men around him. Sarbek breathed heavily and looked exhausted though he seemed otherwise unhurt. At times like these, the old soldier's years caught up with him. Pellan had a big bruise across the right side of her face. Indigo appeared unhurt, but his face was grim.

For a goodly time, there was very little said. The howls continued in the distance. At one point, there was a great uproar: screeching, howling, and bellowing, much louder than before, and from more throats.

"They've reached the bridge and found the battlefield," said Sarbek. "And they're not happy."

"Will they pause and lick their wounds, or slink back whence they came, or come straight after us, out for blood?" said Pellan.

No one knew at that moment, but within a half hour, they all knew. The troll calls grew louder and closer. The squadron was being followed, stalked, hunted.

"Sounds like a lot of them," said Indigo. "Dozens, maybe. And they're gaining ground on us."

"We have to move faster," said Sarbek. "If we can make it to Rhentford, we have a chance."

"A handful of men-at-arms and a bunch of farmers and merchants will do us little good," said Indigo. "We'll just bring the trolls down on them. Get them all killed."

"If we head off the road, they'll catch us the faster," said Wyndham. "Like Sarbek said, Rhentford is our only chance. If there's time, we can fortify the old church and try to hold out until our brigade arrives."

"We stay on the road," said Ector. "It's our fastest route and best chance. Hopefully our men get to Rhentford far enough ahead of us, so they have a bit of time to prepare."

Within an hour, the trolls had moved to

within a mile of the squadron. Their howls were so loud that even at that distance it seemed as if they were on top of them. Some of the trolls growled in angry voices, others, hooted and hollered as if they were laughing, as if they were having fun. In the dark of the night, those sounds were terrifying. The men kept looking back over their shoulders, wondering when the trolls would bound into view just behind them.

"Some of the horses are falling behind," said Wyndham. "What do we do?"

"Keep going," said Sarbek.

"They'll get picked off," said Wyndham. "We could turn and fight. Make a stand."

"If we stop now, we're dead," said Sarbek. "We can't fight them in the open and certainly not in the dark. So we're not stopping."

The trolls drew closer and the horses ran faster, frothing and breathing heavily. One of the horses went lame. Its rider jumped off, and a comrade picked him up and they rode on together. The trolls went wild when they came upon the lame horse and tore it to pieces. That occupied several of them, but the rest continued the hunt.

Sarbek moved his horse next to Ector's. "They're going to catch us," he said quietly so that no one else heard. "I want to call every man for himself. Then every man can move at his own pace, or scatter off into the woods if he wants. At least a few of us will get away. If we hold together as a group, we're only as fast as our slowest horse. And that's too slow. They'll catch us and we'll all die. We've got the split up. But me and Indigo will stay with you, come what may."

"No," said Ector. "We're close to Rhentford. We push through together. That's what my father would do, isn't it?"

"Aye, he'd keep the squadron together even if Loki himself and a corps of storm giants were on his tail, howling for blood and souls, but just because he would do it that way, doesn't mean it's the right way. You've got to make your own decisions now, and not just do what you think he would do."

"I just told you my decision."

Sarbek nodded. "So you did. On to Rhentford, come what may."

As they drew close to the village, a troll leaped out of a tree and tackled one of the knights at the very back of the troop, taking down the horse as well as the rider. Moments later, a second troll did the same, this time to the two soldiers that shared a horse. The main troop of trolls was close. They couldn't stop to help their men.

"Did they get ahead of us somehow?" said Ector.

"Don't think so," said Sarbek. "More likely an advance party, watching the town. These things got some brains to them. Sound the horn," he shouted. "Warn the town."

And they did – over and over again they blew their horn as they approached the village. When they rode into town, the people were armed and assembled in and around the two stoutest buildings in the village: the Odinhome, an impressive stone structure of some thirty feet in height; and the mercantile, a general store of thick masonry construction across the street from the Odinhome.

They pulled up their horses before the Odinhome. Several of the horses immediately collapsed; others refused to go any farther.

The Eotrus guardsmen stationed in the village stood outside the Odinhome, by their horses, armed and ready for action. Several armed townsfolk ran out from the Odinhome to see what was what.

"Is it trolls?" said one guard.

"You're going to stay to protect the village, aren't you?" said one civilian, probably the village elder or councilman. "You can't abandon us here."

"Trolls," shouted Wyndham so that all could hear. "A whole pack of them – they'll be here in moments. Barricade the windows and doors. Distribute arms to everyone – women and boys included."

"Dismount," shouted Sarbek. "You men," he said pointing to the town guards, "bring me those horses – Master Ector needs them."

"What?" said Ector.

"Indigo," said Sarbek, "get Ector on one of the fresh horses. I want him and you and the dwarf moving within one minute. Get back to the Dor double time. And don't look back."

"Aye," said Indigo.

"I've got plenty of fight left in me, old man," said Pellan. "You don't need to send me packing."

"That's why you're going with Ector," said Sarbek. "Keep him safe. That's your job now."

"Castellan – you should go with them," said Wyndham. "I don't need you. One more sword won't make a difference here, but your presence will matter at the Dor."

Sarbek seemed conflicted. Pellan hopped up on the biggest of the horses and made the decision for Sarbek. She grabbed him by the collar and hefted him off his feet one-handed, and started moving, Sarbek dangling off the side cursing.

"I'm not leaving my men," said Ector. There would be no debating it.

Indigo punched him in the side of the head, knocking him senseless. He scooped Ector up, lifted him over the back of a horse, and looped a rope around him a few times to keep him from falling off. Indigo vaulted onto another horse and grabbed the reins of the fourth (which they put Sarbek on once they got well away). They sped off with all the speed they could muster, considering.

As they passed out of sight, Wyndham shouted orders, organizing the defense. He was the only man still mounted. As a cavalry unit, the squadron was finished. The horses were completely spent and would be of no use anytime soon. He ordered two thirds of the soldiers and knights into the Odinhome and the other third into the mercantile, splitting the archers between them. A few men were still busy pulling the last of the packs and supplies from the horses.

A troll leaped out of nowhere. With a single swipe of its claws, it tore through the steel barding of Wyndham's horse and cut deep into its flesh. The horse screamed, reared, and went down. Wyndham jumped off, rolled, and made his feet, wincing with pain. He pulled his sword. He had no shield, his left arm still hung limp at his side. The troll that felled his horse took a bite out of its side as the horse screamed and thrashed its legs. Wyndham stepped up and hacked at the troll's neck, but the troll dodged the blow. It paused, and stared at Wyndham, looking him up and down. Then it laughed – a wide toothy cackle that caused the hairs on the back of Wyndham's neck to stand up. It lunged at his chest, but Wyndham was too fast. He was young, but he'd had years of training, including many lessons under Sir Gabriel's tutelage. Wyndham brought the sword's pommel down on the back of the troll's head, stunning it. Then he spun around and swung the sword in a wide arc. The powerful strike caught the troll in the neck and severed its head with that single blow. Other trolls were in the town square by then, attacking the horses, but here and there they fought against what men remained outdoors.

"Get inside," shouted Wyndham to his men. "We can't hold them out here–"

His words cut off when a troll barreled into him from behind. Vigilant as he was, he never saw the thing coming. Wyndham went down face first to the dirt, his sword knocked from his hand. The troll bit down on the back of his neck – an attack that likely would have killed him instantly but for his armor. Like that of all the Eotrus knights, Wyndham's armor had a tall steel neck guard that protected the back of his neck and a portion of his head from ear to ear. The neck plate itself was concealed by the manner in which his cape was fastened.

The troll's jaws bit down on the neck guard without restraint. Wyndham heard and felt the metal bend and rend as the troll's teeth bit through the metal. How many of the troll's teeth broke off or were torn out wasn't clear, save to say it was some, for yellow blood spurted from its mouth. It spit out more blood, along with fragments of teeth and metal.

The troll, though a good deal shorter than Wyndham, was very heavy. Wyndham couldn't shake it off and the troll's weight drove him to his knees. He pulled a dagger from his waist pack and thrust it over his shoulder at the troll's head, hoping to get the eyes.

He did.

The troll screamed and backed off.

Wyndham scooped up his sword from where it lay a few feet away, spun, and prepared to swing. But this time the troll was too fast. It lunged in close and its claws raked across Wyndham's chest, once, and then again. Those claws tore through his steel armor, with sparks flying and a terrible grating sound, as if the armor was naught but cotton. Wyndham staggered back. A second troll pounced on him, and knocked him to the ground as if he weighed no more than a babe. Before he could rise, both trolls jumped atop him. The weight was crushing, as if they each weighed as much as two or three big men. Wyndham buried his dagger in one of their throats – a blow that would have killed a normal creature, but not a troll. It barely fazed it. They had him pinned down. He had no chance.

"Odin," he shouted. "Odin!"

The last two of his men still outside fought their way toward him, but they died for it. The men inside saw the trolls tear their young captain to pieces, and there was nothing that they could do to save him.

Inside the Odinhome, some of the men moved heavy pieces of wood over the windows and frantically hammered them in place, as others piled every scrap of furniture in front of the doors. The folks too young or too old to fight hid in the back of the hall. Their relatives, men, women, and older children stood before them, holding whatever weapons they had, ready to defend themselves and those they loved until victory was theirs or death took them. The soldiers and some of the men braced themselves against the doors and windows to hold back any attempted incursion by the trolls. They even lit torches to fend them off. It was all they could to keep the trolls out.

It wasn't enough.

Indigo stopped the horses about half a mile south of town. Ector and Sarbek were both cursing. Threats were flying. The only things they couldn't agree on were whether they'd kill Pellan first or Indigo, and in what creative way.

"I'm not leaving my men," shouted Ector. "I'm not going to run. I'm going back."

"It's too late, lad," said Sarbek. "They're locked up tight in the Odinhome by now. If we go back, we'd be stuck on our own in the streets. All that we'd do is to get dead. We're heading home as fast as these horses can carry us. There's no other option left to us."

They resumed their cantor down the road. No other town lay between them and Dor Eotrus. They'd pass a few farms, but nothing more, and they had no way to even warn the farmers, save to stop at each door.

They made good speed since their new horses were well rested, yet after a few hours they heard the troll calls again.

"Those things never give up," said Pellan. "Do we really look that tasty?"

"Maybe they have a taste for hairless dwarves," said Sarbek.

"Then they should like you too," said Pellan, "you withered old fart."

"A little respect, captain," said Sarbek sharply.

"I'm retired," said Pellan. "Kiss my butt."

"No, you're not," said Sarbek. "In times of war, the House in dominion can reinstate the commission of all retired troops and can conscript new ones, as the need arises. You're hereby reinstated, dwarf."

"Kiss my butt," she said again.

"Thanks for the advice about smashing their heads," said Ector to Pellan. "By the time that we figured that out, we would have lost a lot more men."

"We'd have lost the whole squadron on the bridge," said Indigo.

"You're welcome," said Pellan. "But you can kiss my butt too, because I'm retired."

They pushed through all night without stopping, relying on the moon's light to keep them on the road. Twice, a single troll, faster or more determined than their kin, came at them. The first one came up from the rear. It breathed so heavily from the long chase, that they heard it while it was still a ways off. As soon as it drew close enough, Indigo turned in his saddle and put a crossbow bolt through its forehead. It dropped into the darkness beside the road.

The second troll attacked two hours later. This one jumped from the trees on their eastern flank. It too made enough noise that the men were ready for it, but both Indigo's and Sarbek's crossbow bolts missed. They dismounted to fight it, for fear that it would injure or kill some of the horses and strand them on foot. Four together, they made short work of it, though Sarbek took a blow to the shoulder that set him to cursing and laid him on his back for some minutes.

The pursuit continued. How many trolls hunted them, they didn't know. They didn't want to know. All they cared about was staying ahead of them so that they could make it back to the Dor. They pushed their horses and themselves to their limits, yet the trolls drew closer with every mile.

Finally, they reached the edge of the wood where the forest path opened to the great, wide meadows that surrounded Dor Eotrus and the Outer Dor, even as the trolls came into sight behind them. They howled ever louder as they drew closer to their prey.

A small contingent of soldiers guarded the road at the edge of the wood. Ector and the others slowed as they approached the guards.

"Get back to the Dor, double time," shouted Sarbek. "There are trolls on our heels! Move!"

"Run for it," shouted Pellan. "All of you."

"Back to the Dor, now," shouted Ector.

The soldiers looked confused, but heeded the

warnings.

They'd gone about 100 yards toward the Dor when the trolls reached the edge of the wood. There they stood at the tree line. No hooting or hollering, no roaring or howling. They looked upon a city of men, perhaps for the first time. Hundreds of buildings. Tall walls of stone. Thousands of people and animals. They stood there watching for some time.

Through their spyglasses the Eotrus saw them conversing with each other, speaking in their guttural language. How many there were was uncertain. Several score at the least, but perhaps more. The Eotrus never knew what they said. Their best guess was that the trolls were in awe of the great buildings and size of Dor Eotrus and the town that surrounded it. It put a fear in them that held them back; that kept them rooted to the tree line.

But if any of the Eotrus understood trollspeak and had been able to read their lips through one of the spyglasses, they would know that what they said was altogether different. The trolls debated two subjects: how they'd divide up the spoils, and how long this new food source would last.

XI
EVERMERE

"Three days of nothing but bluster and black," said Ob as he stood at *The Falcon*'s bow, the wind blowing so hard he had to grip the railing with both hands to keep his footing sure. "Sailing near blind on faith and fortune, the wind pushing us who knows where, and now we happen upon an island not on any chart or in any man's memory. It don't feel right to me; I don't care for it one bit."

"It looks like a nice enough place to me," said Dolan standing beside him. He spoke loudly to be heard over the wind. "What little I can see of it."

Ob shook his head. "The rest of us can't see nothing from here, Mr. Hawk Eyes. It's too dark and too far. What see you? Tell us true."

"Docks, wooden buildings, lights in windows, smoke from a big chimney. Can't tell if there are any folks about though."

"Who would be dumb enough to be out in a storm like this? No sir, I don't expect we'll see a living soul; not until we go a knocking. Assuming that we go ashore at all."

"We have to," said Theta as he stepped up next to the others, his long, midnight blue cloak pulled close about him. He loomed beside the gnome, standing more than twice his height. "We need to resupply; there's not enough drinking water to get us to where we're going. They're getting one of the longboats ready now," he said, pointing toward the stern. "I'll be in it."

"Are we sure that Bertha checked all the barrels?" said Ob as he turned astern. The group of seamen that rigged up one of *The Falcon*'s longboats struggled against the howling wind and lashing rain as they did their work.

"She says she did," said Theta. "All tainted, except for the ones in the hold below the Captain's Den."

"That damn navigator fixed us up good and proper," said Ob. "Conjuring up a demon and setting it on us wasn't enough for him. He had to go poison our stores too." Ob spit over the rail in disgust.

"We don't know for certain that it was him," said Theta.

"We questioned all and everybody right good, from the cabin boys to the captain, and all our own men too. They seemed alright, best I can tell, and I'm as good a judge of men as most anybody."

"Except for the first mate," said Dolan. "He's a sour one."

"Yep, except for him," said Ob. "I don't trust that bugger one bit, but the boys are keeping a close eye on him. I don't think Slaayde even trusts him. But your ankh thingy came up clean. How do explain that?"

"It's not infallible," said Theta. "There may be more traitors amongst us. We must be vigilant."

"Mr. Fancy Pants, I think you're a bit paranoid, and touched in the head, but that doesn't necessarily mean you're wrong. We'll keep our eyes open, don't you worry."

"You do that," said Theta.

Captain Slaayde walked across the deck, leaning heavily on a cane, Guj and Little Tug beside him. The captain shouted orders to several seamen that huddled here and there in whatever meager refuge from the wind they could find.

"He doesn't even show his face anymore without those two bruisers shadowing him," said Ob.

"Can't blame him for that," said Dolan. "This voyage has been harder on him than any of us what's still breathing."

"Aye," said Ob. "He barely looks the same man as him we met when we strolled aboard in Lomion City. Poor bugger. He's had one bad break after another."

"Some would say he's been lucky," said Theta. "He's survived where most men wouldn't have."

"Fair point, though I doubt he sees it that way," said Ob. "It looks like he's fixing to put more longboats in the water." When Ob turned, Theta was already headed down the ship's ladder to the main deck. He strode directly up to Slaayde.

"One longboat only," said Theta in a tone that made clear it was not up for discussion.

Slaayde sighed and shook his head. "The men deserve a break after all we've been through. There's a town over there, across the bay," he said pointing. "I saw it through the spyglass. Well-ordered houses; cheery smoke from each; well-kept piers. A seaman couldn't hope for a more kindly sight in a storm. It means a hot meal with fresh bread, and if we're lucky, warm beds on dry land. My men deserve that."

"Did you see the rocks, and the reefs?" said

226

Theta.

Slaayde took a death breath before replying. "*The Falcon* can't pass safely through the bay in this storm," said Slaayde, "but we can make it in the longboats if we're slow and steady. I know my business, Theta, just as you know yours. I'll stick to seamanship and you stick to steel. Got it?"

"It might not be a friendly port," said Theta. "We can't chance more than one boat."

"I can't see too much from this distance in the dark," said Slaayde, "but I can see enough to know that that is no pirate's den; it's just a town. What's there to be afraid of? Lomion is not at war with anybody, you know. The whole world isn't out to get us."

"Laddie," said Ob, stepping up beside them, "best we check things out all cautious and smart afore we go taking up residence or pitching our tents on some old uncharted island, don't you think?"

"We don't even know that it's uncharted," said Slaayde. "My guess is we're far off our course, but we haven't been able to make a good star reading or even a moon reading through these clouds for over seven full days — so we don't know where the heck we are. And Ravel can't find half the charts. Darg was a slob, the traitorous scum; he kept the map room a mess. Even so, I think some of the charts are missing — more of his sabotage. Maybe we can pick up some new ones ashore. But whether the island is charted or not, it's an unknown port to me — so I want a strong shore party at my side, just in case."

"That would leave the ship vulnerable," said

Theta. "Do you want to find it boarded and bested if we need to fall back?"

"My lads will keep it clear, don't you worry, but there's wisdom to your words that I won't ignore. Let's say this — we send one boat now with some of our best, but if the port is friendly, we stay over for a full day of rest at the least. I'll bring the crew ashore in shifts."

Theta nodded.

"Agreed," said Ob, "but we stay one day only, no more."

Theta, Dolan, Artol, Glimador, and several soldiers stepped aboard the longboat, fully armed and armored, and bundled against the weather. Ob followed them aboard.

"Where is the wizard?" said Theta.

"Bundled up in blankets, hat, and scarf at Claradon's bedside," said Ob. "He says this is no weather for a goodly man to be out and about in. That fellow has always been a lazy bugger, and it gets worse every year."

"It will be the quieter without him," said Dolan.

Theta leaned toward Artol. "We need the wizard."

"Aye," said Artol. He stepped off the longboat and headed below deck.

Ob rolled his eyes. "Now we've got to suffer Magic Boy's whining the whole time. Why?"

"He has proved useful time and again," said Theta. "Don't underestimate him."

"I'm going," shrieked Bertha as she, Slaayde, Ravel, Guj, and Tug approached the longboat.

"No, you're not," said Slaayde. "This could be

dangerous; we don't know what's out there, or whose town that is. Fighting men only are going."

"Ravel is no fighter," said Bertha.

"We need new charts," said Slaayde. "I need him to read them and select them, or else I have to do it. I'm getting a bit tired of doing everything, so I'm taking him along."

"If he's going, I'm going. And what do you mean, 'you do everything yourself?' I think I take pretty good care of you, Mr. Captain, sir. Do you need me to start wiping your behind now too?"

Slaayde sighed and his face flushed. "I can have Tug carry you to your cabin and lock you in."

"I would scratch his eyes out if he tried."

Slaayde shook his head. "No doubt, you would try. If I let you go, will you promise to keep quiet and behave?"

She smiled a fake smile. "I'll be a good girl, Mr. Captain, sir, don't you worry."

Slaayde rolled his eyes and then he and Guj helped her onto the longboat. When she was safely aboard, she stepped close to Slaayde, put an arm around him, and kissed him on the cheek.

A few minutes later, Artol appeared, carrying Tanch over his shoulder, and deposited him into the longboat, his hands tied, a gag in his mouth.

"Maybe it will be quiet after all," said Dolan.

"Did you have to do that?" said Ob to Artol.

"He threatened to turn me into a toad," said Artol looking offended. "Had to clam him up for safety's sake. I've got a passel of children, you know; they don't need a toad for a father."

"A toad or a bear, what's the difference?" muttered Ob as he undid the wizard's bonds and Tanch pulled the gag free. The wizard glared at

Artol, but said nothing.

"No hard feelings, Tanch old boy?" said Artol.

"A blind rat," said Tanch.

Artol's face went pale. "What say you?"

Tanch's face was harsh; his eyebrows arched, his voice low, slow, but sharp. "Not a toad; a blind rat. That's what I'll make you. When you least expect it."

Artol's mouth hung open. He looked as if he were about to faint.

Try as he might to hold it in, Ob began to laugh; a second later, Tanch burst out laughing, and then the others followed, including Artol.

The long row into port was bitterly cold, the wind howling in their ears, the icy spray assailing their skin, the turbulent water testing their skills at tiller and oars. Though it was midday, the storm clouds made it as dark as twilight. Fog hung over the deep bay and the town, further obscuring their vision.

After they entered the sheltered, semicircular bay, the wind calmed a good deal, though the water was still rough. Slaayde's sailing skills kept them off the jagged rocks that loomed up out of the water seemingly at random.

"Another rock coming up," said Ob. "A big one."

"That's no rock," said Dolan.

"It's a wreck," said Slaayde. "An old one."

The rotting remnants of a big merchant vessel loomed before them, impaled on the rocks and split in two, most of the ship submerged.

"There are two more to our right, off a ways," said Dolan, "and at least one to the left."

"Dear gods, this is a deathtrap," said Tanch. "What have you gotten us into now?" said Tanch as he looked accusingly at Theta. "We need to turn back afore it's too late."

Slaayde peered all around and turned behind, as if to check how hard it would be to turn the longboat about.

"We need the water," said Theta. "Slaayde, find us a path through."

"Guj, give us some light," said Slaayde. Guj made to light a lantern, to hang from the longboat's pole.

"Don't light it," said Theta. "Let's not give away our position and numbers just yet."

Guj turned toward Slaayde looking for direction.

"I need to see to get past the rocks," said Slaayde.

"They've probably seen the ship already," said Tanch from under his bundled hood.

"The water is calming," said Theta. "You can do this; we'll take her in slow."

"Hard astern," shouted Tug at the bow. "There's a reef!

Slaayde leaned on the tiller and the men rowed hard. The longboat scraped the reef or the rocks.

"Oars out!" said Slaayde. "Push us off."

Several of the men used the oars as poles to push off the reef, while the others rowed on the other side. After several moments, they were in the clear.

"We leaking?" said Slaayde.

"We're sound up here," said Tug.

"And here," said Guj from amidships.

After nearly an hour of exhausting and stressful rowing, they finally pulled alongside the longest of the harbor's wooden piers, which looked sound and reasonably well maintained. They tied off the boat and climbed up a wooden ladder onto the pier's deck, which stood barren and deserted.

"What ho, a lookeyloo," said Ob of the dark-cloaked, silent and still sentinel that stood at the inland end of the pier. "So much for stealth and surprise."

"That fellow has been standing there since we were in the middle of the bay, at least," said Dolan. "He never moved, as far as I can tell."

"A scarecrow then?" said Ob.

A heavy patch of fog crossed the pier, blocking the group's view inland for several seconds. When it cleared, the scarecrow was gone.

"The bugger slinked off," said Ob. "No doubt he recognized Old Mister Fancy Pants, and dashed off to rouse an army of devils and whatnot to swoop down on us. They're probably taking up a tune even now; their dreams come true, the old harbinger of doom dropped into their laps."

"Dolan," said Theta. "When is the last time we had gnome?"

"You mean, in a stew, or raw on the bone?" said Dolan matter-of-factly.

"Stewed."

Dolan scratched his head. "Quite a spell, Lord Angle. I never developed much of a taste for it," he said, his expression serious.

Theta nodded. "Tends toward dry and chewy."

"Aye, best to stew it low and slow, until it drips off the bone," said Dolan, "but that takes a goodly time. Hardly worth it, considering."

Ob looked horrified during the whole exchange, turning back and forth between their faces, hoping they were joking, but he couldn't see their expressions clearly in the dark. He just couldn't tell if they were kidding.

"I'm taking my men with me," said Slaayde to Theta. "One or two of yours should stay with the boat."

"If it's a friendly port, guards won't be needed," said Theta. "If it's not, one or two won't be enough. Best we stay together and be on our guard."

"There's only one other boat docked in the whole port," said Artol pointing to a mid-sized schooner docked at the far pier. "Besides that one, not even a dinghy; not on any of the piers as far as I can see."

"You'd think there would be fishing boats at least," said Glimador.

"They may have put the bigger ships out to sea when they saw the storm coming," said Slaayde. "And pulled the small ones out of the water."

"Or they may have parked them up the coast in some better protected harbor," said Tug.

"Maybe so," said Ob, still warily eyeing Theta and Dolan. "But it don't smell right to me."

"It's downright suspicious," said Tanch. "We probably should head back. No doubt, we can find better places to replenish our stores. Let's go."

The others ignored Tanch and proceeded down the pier two or three abreast. Tanch followed. Soon they heard music, such as you would expect from a tavern or an inn. At the end of the pier, they found themselves on a wide wooden boardwalk that spanned between all the piers and ran in both directions, beyond the limits of their sight. Narrow streets paved with wood planks led up from the docks. The streets were lined with wood-planked buildings of one or two stories, a few, three. Some of the buildings were old, others new, but all were generally in a decent state of repair.

"You see them?" whispered Dolan.

"Aye," replied Theta.

"See what?" said Ob. "There's nobody about."

"A dark figure in a doorway here, another in a window there," said Dolan.

"We're being watched and they don't want us to know it," said Theta.

"Now look here, Dolan may be farsighted like a stinking hawk, but up close, my eyes are as good as anyone's and I don't see any stinking lurkers."

"Dolan sees better than you, up close and far off," said Theta. "And so do I."

"Of course you do," said Ob. "You do everything better than everybody else, don't you? You stinking tin can! And which is it this time that's watching us — ruddy townsfolk or demons out of hell?" he said.

"Can't tell yet," said Theta, his tone matter-of-fact.

Ob stared, again not knowing if he meant to be serious.

"Which way?" said Glimador as he walked at

the van.

"Follow the music," said Theta.

The Dancing Turtle was a large inn of stained wood plank and paneled walls. Trestle tables and benches dominated the public room; a long bar lined one wall, a large mirror behind it. The place was unusually clean; the floor wasn't sticky, and it didn't even smell bad. In all, it was as fancy a place as some of the best inns in Lomion City.

Numerous patrons lounged at the tables, eating and speaking in quiet voices while being served by modest waitresses that ambled from one table to the next. More than a few patrons dozed at their seats, several snoring away; a few sat at the bar doing much the same. By and large, the patrons looked like dandies — fancy surcoats, clean cut faces, well-coifed hair, silken shirts and pantaloons. As a people, they were fair of skin, their hair typically black, though some few were red or blonde. Most were in their twenties, the rest in their thirties or forties, and nearly all were tall, lean, and muscled. Not a stitch of armor to be seen, though more than several but less than most wore swords at their hips. Three men and a woman sang soft ballads off in one corner as they played their lutes. Most everyone awake looked over the group with interest, but didn't pause their doings.

"Thank the gods," said Tanch. "Civilization at last." He pulled back his hood, pushed past the others, and headed straight for the bar.

"Not what I was expecting in a little port in the middle of nowhere," said Artol.

"Not a soldier's bar," said Ob. "That's for certain."

"Nor a seaman's," said Slaayde. "But that won't stop me from ordering an ale and sitting a spell."

A demure serving girl shuffled over to the group, all smiles and fluttering lashes. She sat them at two large tables near the back of the inn and took their drink orders.

"Are you men here for the festival?" she asked.

"Why of course," said Slaayde with a smile. Bertha scowled at him as he stared at the waitress, but she held her tongue. "When do things get started?"

"Luncheon is at three, of course, but the party doesn't really get going until midnight. You've arrived in good time. Last night was the first night and things were a bit crowded and disorganized. Tonight should be better."

"I guess that explains why everyone looks so tired," said Slaayde.

She nodded. "We party until dawn, seven days straight during the Winter Festival. It's my favorite time of the year. No one misses it."

"Mine too," said Slaayde smiling.

Bertha kicked him under the table.

"As travelers, you will be our honored guests."

"That sounds wonderful," said Slaayde. "We're looking forward to it. Tell me, is that fellow what sells maps still around?"

"You mean, Old Harry? He's closed up tight in the afternoon. You folks lost?"

"No, of course not," said Slaayde. "We're just looking to update our charts."

"Half the folks what show up here are lost.

Old Harry's shop is one block west, and one north. He'll take care of you, but you will have to wait until tonight when he opens. I'll be right back with your drinks." And she was off.

"What port town has a big festival with no ships docked?" said Artol.

"Odd, that," said Ob.

"And what shopkeeper is closed during the day and opens up at night?" said Dolan.

Tanch hurried to the table, a broad smile on his face. He held up a tumbler of amber colored liquid. "They have hundred year old brandy," he said. "And not the cheap stuff — it's Dover Gold. Lomerian merchants must pass through here." He sat back in his chair, his face content for the first time since before they set out from Dor Eotrus. "Now this is the kind of place I like to drink," he said. "Sit in style and comfort sipping an exotic vintage, served by a pretty girl. Things are looking up."

The inn's door opened and several figures stepped in, each heavily bundled against the weather.

"Your scarecrow from the pier," said Artol to Ob. "And he's brought some friends."

Scarecrow looked around, spotted the group, and headed straight towards them, his cohorts following.

"Be ready, boys," whispered Ob.

"Afternoon," said the scarecrow when he halted before the group's tables. The man was short, and stooped, with a badly broken nose and scraggly teeth. "The Duchess invites you to luncheon at her villa."

"I don't believe that we're acquainted with

the Duchess," said Slaayde.

"Or you for that matter," said Artol.

"I expect that's why she wants to meet you," said the man. "My name is Slint. The Duchess runs Evermere, so you best come as she asks. Anyone can give you directions to the villa; it's just up the hill anyways — hard to miss. Her food is better than here." With no more than that, Slint turned and left the inn, all but one of his shadows followings. The one who remained took a seat at the bar and pretended that he wasn't watching the group.

"What do you make of that?" said Artol.

"It's not a big town," said Slaayde. "They may just want to size up a bunch of rough looking strangers — to make certain that we're not trouble."

"Or they plan to jump us and rob us, or kill us dead," said Ob. "Do we go or do we grab some water barrels and hightail it?"

"If they mean us harm, we will not have time to procure all the supplies we need," said Theta. "So we might as well go."

The joy now gone from Tanch's face, he said, "At least the brandy is good."

The Duchess's villa was large and built of wood plank, similar to, but more ornate than the other buildings in town. A nondescript elderly servant woman ushered Theta, Ob, Slaayde, Bertha, Tanch, and Dolan, into a large dining hall, set for many. The balance of the shore party was off attempting to procure the needed supplies and maps.

A smartly dressed, thin man of whited pallor

soon marched into the room. His eyes widened as he looked the group over. Then he turned about, as if he were searching for someone. His eyes probed the corners of the anteroom and the halls beyond before he returned his attention to the dining hall. "I was advised to expect fifteen," he said in a sharp, nasally voice. "Where are the rest? I see only six."

"I chose not to bring the lowliest of my servants," said Par Tanch.

In response, the man-made a clucking sound with his mouth. "The invitation was for all, and all were to come," he said sharply.

"That was not at all clear," said Tanch. "Mayhap you should have a dispatched a more reliable messenger to extend the invitation. Run along now, like a good man, and tell the Duchess that Par Sinch Malaban and his retinue have arrived and await her pleasure." Tanch made a shoeing motion with his hand and turned away, the conversation over.

The man stood with mouth agape for some seconds. "Most irregular," he muttered as he marched out huffing.

"You're full of surprises, wizard," said Slaayde. "I thought I was going to have to do all the talking."

"He does this whenever he gets the chance," said Ob. "A born actor — or liar, not sure which."

"After what happened with Prior Finch, mayhap it's best that you all leave the talking to me," said Tanch.

Slaayde squirmed, his hand reaching to the old wound on his leg.

The wizard took a seat at the far end of the

table, opposite from where he expected the Duchess to sit. He directed Slaayde to sit next to him, and then Bertha beyond. The others were to stand as guards. Theta went along with it all without voicing a word.

A majestic woman dressed in festival finery swept into room, the heavy footsteps of her bodyguards announcing her arrival well before she came into view. She was past young, but by no means old, stunningly beautiful, with long flowing hair, fair skin, and curves where they should be. Her arms were bare save for black silken gloves that reached to her elbows. She had piercing green eyes, the pupils unusually large; her lips were thick and full and unusually red — no doubt colored by some makeup of exotic type. Her bodyguards stood tall, broad, and muscled, their golden armor near as fancy as Theta's.

"Ah, Par Sinch," she said, beaming, "I trust I have not kept you waiting too long?"

Tanch waited until she was halfway across the room before he rose and stepped forward. "The wait was worth it, dear lady," he said, extending his hand, but only after she had extended hers, "to meet with a vision of grace and beauty such as you."

She smiled, nodded, and looked him up and down. "I am the Duchess Morgovia of House Falstad. Welcome to Evermere," she said, not releasing his hand.

Tanch's voice was strong and confident. "Par Sinch Malaban of the Blue Tower — the High Seat of Wizardom in Lomion City."

"It's rare that one of your olden profession visits our little island, Par Sinch," she said, still

240

firmly gripping his hand. "Tell me, what brings you here?"

"A grand voyage of discovery, my lady," said Tanch, now looking a bit uncomfortable. He gently pulled back his hand, but she held him fast, her smile never wavering. She was in charge.

"Once in every archwizard's life," said Tanch, "he must set out to explore the world — to see and learn what there is to see and learn, for wisdom's sake. It makes one more worldly — as a wizard should be, as I'm sure that you'll agree. And by chance, my humble travels have brought me here."

She nodded, finally releasing her grip.

"Allow me to introduce the good captain Slaayde, whose valiant ship has brought me to these fine shores, and his lovely companion, the Lady Bertha."

Slaayde bowed and kissed the Duchess's hand, though she looked at him dismissively. Bertha she didn't seem to see at all.

"You must tell me all about your travels, Par Sinch. I fear we are rather isolated here, and news of the events of the world is often late in arriving. Tell me what news there is. Please," she said, gesturing to indicate that they should sit.

Servants brought out large platters of food and fine red wine. Mutton was the featured dish, prepared in many varieties and with considerable skill. During the meal, Tanch spun a grand tale of travel about the world, describing sights, deeds, and common news of the last year; Slaayde jumped in here and there to supplement his telling. After a half hour or so of discussion, Tanch mentioned that his servants were likely hungry as well, and this granted the others seats at the table. To Tanch's surprise, they were served the same choice dishes and wine as he and the Duchess. The Duchess had many questions and the conversation stretched out over more than three hours before her interest was sated.

"I'm so pleased that you arrived during the Winter Festival," said the Duchess. "It is our grandest time of year. Tonight will feature the annual running of the bulls."

"And what is that, if I may ask?" said Tanch.

"One of our eldest and most exciting traditions. During the Winter Festival, the ranchers bring their choicest cattle and sheep to Evermere Town. On the first day of the festival, the sheep are slaughtered and we serve mutton each day thereafter for supper. Our chefs prepare the most delightful assortment of dishes. Each chef has their own specialties and the people travel from inn to inn, and manor house to manor house sampling the offered fares. Just after midnight on the festival's second day, we release the bulls. They run wild through the streets and our men hunt them down, if you can believe it. On the third night, we do the same with the cows, though only the women hunt them. I know that it sounds an odd thing, but that is our tradition, and we revel in it. We feast on beef each dinner for rest of the festival. I hope that doesn't sound overly barbaric to you, Par Sinch, but the element of danger during the bulls' run is mayhap the most exciting event of the year for us here on our little island. It's a long tradition on Evermere, going back to our earliest days."

"Sounds most exhilarating, dear Lady," said

Tanch.

She smiled ear to ear. "I'm so happy that you feel that way since our tradition requires all our guests, the male ones at least, to participate in the bulls' run."

"I'm not a warrior, my Lady," said Tanch, his face filled with concern.

"Ah, but the men with you are," she said, gesturing toward the group. "Let them do the fighting. All you need do is run alongside them for a short ways, just to honor our tradition. And then, tomorrow, we will dine together again. My chef prepares beef even more skillfully than he does lamb, and from the look of your plates, I see that you enjoyed chef's lamb."

Tanch nodded. "That sounds delightful, and I shall be honored."

"The honor is mine," said the Duchess. "I trust that you've secured rooms at The Dancing Turtle for the evening?"

"Not yet, but such was my plan."

"Then I must delay you no longer. The Turtle is our finest inn and, as such, will fill up fast; the nobles from the outlying farms will soon arrive and they'll scoop up all the best rooms in town. I wouldn't want to see you left out in the cold."

"Then we must be off at once," said Tanch.

As they prepared to leave, the Duchess placed a firm hand on Tanch's arm. "If by chance, not enough rooms remain at The Turtle, I would be happy to make appropriate accommodations available here for you, Par Sinch," she said with a coy smile, her hand never leaving his arm, her eyes locked on his.

"How gracious of you, dear lady," said Tanch.

He bowed and kissed her hand.

When he looked up, he found her eyes focused on an ornate display case a few feet away. It held several books of leather binding. "I wonder," she said. "Can you read any of the olden languages?"

"Several, my Lady."

"I thought that might be part of your wizardly training." She stepped over to the display case, opened it, and removed one of the books. It was the smallest and least ornate of the collection. "This book has been in my possession for a good many years and try as I might, I've never been able to find anyone who can read it. I've often wondered if it's written in some long-dead language, or even some esoteric code, or mayhap, in some language known only to the members of your profession. Would you have a look at it for me?"

She handed it to him and he opened it, studied the first page, and then flipped through a few more.

"Can you read it?" she said, a hopeful smile on her face.

"A dead language, indeed. It's written in Throng Baz. I'm not fluent in it, but I can read it with some difficulty. It seems to be a journal."

"Wonderful," she said, giddy. She firmly grabbed both his hands. "Translate it for me and I will be forever in your debt."

"I would be happy to, but such an endeavor would take a good deal of time."

"Of course, but please, I beseech you, read as much as you can this evening. I've been dying to know what it says for years. I will drop by The

244

Turtle before the Bulls' Run starts and you can tell me whatever wonders you've learned from the book by then."

"I can't promise that I'll have gotten far, my Lady, but I'll relate to you whatever I find."

"Oh, that would be wonderful. I'm so happy that you're here, visiting us. Your presence is certain to make the festival even grander than it would have been. I so look forward to continuing our discussions." Her face was filled with delight, her smile, ear to ear. "An Archwizard of the fabled Tower of the Arcane, here, in Evermere. It's quite unbelievable."

"That went well enough," said Slaayde after they'd left the villa. "Well done, wizard."

"She was quite enchanting," said Tanch. "Don't you think?"

"She's a bitch," blurted Bertha.

Slaayde rolled his eyes.

"You were staring at her, and not just at her face," said Bertha. "You're all animals; all of you. Fancy knights and officers, but put a pretty thing in front of you, and you're no better than old sea dogs. You disgust me."

"Don't be silly; I have eyes only for you, my dear," Slaayde said. He pulled her close as they walked along and kissed her cheek.

"What do you think, Theta?" said Ob.

"In three hours she never asked how long we planned to stay or where we're headed after we leave here."

"You're right," said Ob. "She would want to know how long we were staying; any Duchess would. Especially, if she had an interest in old

Tanch, as she seemed to."

"Maybe she just forgot to ask," said Dolan.

"She said we'd talk more later," said Tanch. "This initial meeting was just to get acquainted; business talk comes later. Besides, she seemed a bit nervous to me. Maybe she didn't feel comfortable delving into our business just yet."

"She didn't seem nervous to me," said Ob. "Confident, at least in her own charms, I would say."

"That woman," said Bertha. "She was not nervous at all. She had you eating right out of her hands and she knew it. She was toying with you. I don't know why, but she was."

"Her guards were sizing us up, studying our weapons and armor," said Theta.

Ob nodded. "I saw that too, from the first, but that's not such an odd thing for a fighting man to do. I looked their armor over, I did. Fancy stuff."

"Tourney armor," said Theta. "Flimsy; all for show."

"She didn't ask about trade," said Slaayde. "A place like this survives on it. If I were her, I would have asked for a full ship's manifest and started bargaining for whatever they need. She didn't bring it up at all."

"As I said, I'm sure she's just leaving that business for the next meeting," said Tanch. "Or mayhap she has people to handle such matters and will be having them contact us."

"There's an awful lot of ships' wood used on this boardwalk and all the buildings," said Dolan. "Where you figure they get all the wood from?"

"Must have a lot of wrecks hereabouts," said

Ob.

"We're being followed," said Dolan. "Two of them; been on us since we left the villa."

"When we turn down the next street," said Theta to Dolan, "slip into the alley and let them pass you by. Then track down our men and find out the status of the resupplying. Meet us back at the inn."

"I'll go along too," said Ob. "To keep old Hawk Eyes out of trouble."

Ob and Dolan caught up to Artol, Glimador, Tug, and their men down by the piers. They had rented several carts and were hauling a load of water barrels to the longboat. The storm had subsided over the previous hours and they had already transported two full loads of water and other supplies back to the ship.

"Is it enough?" said Ob.

"This load will put us at about half of what we wanted," said Artol. "But it was all they were willing to sell. They bring water down from springs farther inland. They won't have more available afore late tomorrow at the earliest, so if we want more water, we'll be stuck here for a bit."

"Any luck with the charts?" said Ob.

Artol shook his head. "Ravel wasn't able to rouse the mapmaker. Seems he has odd hours this week because of the festival. If we don't catch him tonight, we may have to wait until tomorrow night to see him, and then shove off the following morning."

"I figured as much," said Ob. "Me and Mr. Hawk Eyes are going to do a bit of reconnoitering. Let Theta know, so he don't get all worried and such. We'll see you back at the inn sometime afore midnight. Keep your eyes open and stick together; I still have a bad feeling about this place."

Just as the Duchess had warned, The Dancing Turtle was much busier upon the group's return. A few rooms were still available, which Tanch rented on behalf of the others to keep up his charade as leader. They all rested for a bit and then gathered again in the inn's public room. Many more tables and chairs had been squeezed into the space, made all the tighter because they left a generous area open for a dance floor. The group managed to secure the same two large tables in the back since most of the patrons wanted seats closer to the bar and the dance floor.

The public room bustled with activity, though it was strangely quiet and subdued. Haughty patrons made their entrances wearing ball gowns and fancy dress; many wore wigs and eye masks. Musicians played dignified music and the guests danced the waltz and other fancy steps practiced by the nobility. The room was cold despite the burning hearths and the growing crowd. A haze of pipe smoke hung about, but the smell of roast mutton wafting from the kitchen dominated the room. Patrons milled about the bar and around the tables, drinks in hand, the merry-making well under way.

Slaayde, Bertha, Ravel, and Guj sat at one table, talking and drinking. Theta and Tanch sat in relative silence at the other. Theta scanned the room, discretely looking from person to person, no particular expression on his face. Tanch had his nose buried in the book the Duchess loaned him.

An hour and half before midnight, the atmosphere of the taproom gradually began to change. The demure serving girls were replaced by scantily clad barmaids that carried trays one-handed and danced between the tables, accepting with a smile, as often as dodging, gropes from various patrons, both male and female alike.

Glimador and Artol returned from their toils about an hour before midnight, the music, loud; the laughter, raucous; and the dancing, wild. They sat at Theta's table and ordered wine.

"Tug and our troopers are making one last run to the ship with some foodstuffs and miscellaneous supplies," said Artol. "We'll need to pick up more water tomorrow, but other than that, and the maps, we've got everything on our must-have list."

"Good," said Slaayde. "I'm just glad that this turned out to be a friendly port."

"If anything is going to happen," said Theta to Artol and Glimador. "It will happen during the running of the bulls. They'll use the confusion and the crowd to split us up and try to capture or kill us."

"You think that they're planning that?" said Artol. "They're an odd lot, but they haven't done us wrong yet that I know of. Has something happened?"

"No, nothing has happened," said Theta. "Some things just don't add up. Just be ready. Keep your armor on, your weapons close, and stick together, no matter what happens. Understood?"

"Aye," said Glimador and Artol.

"And don't get drunk."

"Theta, you're not a lot of fun at a party," said Artol.

"So I've been told."

"Did Ob and Dolan get back yet?" said Glimador looking around for them.

"No, they're still skulking," said Theta.

"If both you and Ob smell something off," said Artol, "then there must be something to it. I'll keep my head clear."

"Me too," said Glimador.

As midnight approached, the party grew even livelier. Beer and red wine flowed freely. More women, mostly young, attractive, and scantily clad, showed up and joined in the merry making. The aristocratic patrons were mostly drunk and disheveled by then, some having removed various articles of clothing, putting all modesty aside. Nearly half the patrons bunched up on the dance floor and danced to a fast tune that none of the men had heard before.

Theta's mood grew darker and his face more grim, even as most everyone else's grew the happier.

"You see something?" said Artol to Theta.

"They're looking at us too often," said Theta. "Too much interest. At first, I thought it was because we're strangers, but it's something more than that."

"I noticed that too," said Artol. "But I thought it was just my pretty face winning over the locals," he said with a smile and a laugh.

250

Bertha and Slaayde joined in the dancing. Women came over to the other men and asked them to dance as well. Ravel and Guj joined in, but Theta, Artol, Tanch, and Glimador kept their seats.

"They even like the lugron," said Artol to Theta. "And he's got the ugliest mug on the whole ship. You were right. Something is off here."

One young blonde grabbed Theta by the hand and tried to pull him to the dance floor, all smiles and lashes and curves. He didn't budge. He merely shook his head and she moved away, pouting. Others did the same to Glimador and Artol. Glimador ended up dancing beside their table with two girls. Artol, red-faced and looking very uncomfortable, managed to resist their charms. Tanch merely told them he was doing something for the Duchess, and they left him alone. Tanch scanned the room for the first time in nearly an hour and was shocked to see just how much of their clothes many of the patrons had removed. Some walked about and danced topless becoming intimate with those around them; others had their shirts and dresses hanging off them in tatters.

Then Tanch saw the raucous crowd part to let the Duchess and her bodyguards pass through. She walked toward his table in a tight dress that showed a bit more skin and curves than a proper woman ever would, hips swaying, a broad smile on her face. The book slipped from Tanch's hand.

She squeezed past Artol and slipped into the chair next to Tanch. "I'm so happy to see that you're reading my book." She reached out and put her hand on his. "Pray tell me, what is it about? Have you gotten far? What secrets does it hold?"

"I'm sorry to say, dear lady, that it's not a journal at all."

The smile dropped from the Duchess's face. "Then what is it?"

"A book of fiction — fairy tales, and adventure. An interesting story, rather frightening actually and quite original, but I'm afraid, it's not very well written. Probably meant for children."

The Duchess looked deflated. "That's quite disappointing," she said, studying his eyes as he spoke, as if weighing the truth of his words. "And quite surprising," she said. "Oh well, let's waste no more time with it then."

Tanch made to hand it back to her, but she waved it away. "You may keep it. I've no interest in fairy stories, but mayhap you will find it entertaining."

The door to the inn slammed open loud enough to be heard even over the din. A man stepped in and jumped atop the table nearest the door. The crowd quieted. "Festival!" he yelled at the top of his lungs, laughing and slavering between the words. "Festival! Festival!"

He jumped down and ran out the door. The music stopped and the crowd started quickly making for the door.

The Duchess turned back toward Tanch, her smile renewed. "The running of the bulls is about to start. Let's go, we must get to our places, quickly. You don't want to miss the start and I've got a speech to give." She took Tanch by the hand, her grip firm, and nearly pulled him to his feet. "Let's go, men," she said to Artol and Theta, seeming to notice them for the first time. "Believe me, you don't want to miss the start. It's the best part."

The girls with Glimador pulled him along. By that time, Slaayde and the others were lost in the throng. Theta made eye contact with Artol, as if to say, "See, they're splitting us up." Theta and Artol were the last two out of the inn, save for two of the Duchess's guards – hulking men near as big as Theta. Theta tried to usher them out before him, but they didn't budge, so he reluctantly gave them his back.

The crowd outside numbered in the many hundreds, perhaps the thousands of citizens, laughing and cheering. The whole population of the island must have gathered. The crowd extended to the street beyond, and perhaps to even a third street beyond that – the revelers apparently having spilled out of other bars and homes. Many were gathered just north of The Dancing Turtle. The front door of The Turtle lay at the very front edge of the crowd. Shouts of "Festival! Festival!" came from all around. "Release the bulls! Release the bulls!" began the chant.

Duchess Morgovia stepped atop a chair placed in the middle of the street in front of the crowd. Several men near her pounded on metal pots to get the crowd's attention.

"Beloved citizens of Evermere, honored guests (her eyes found Tanch and she winked)," said the Duchess after all had gone quiet. "Welcome to the second night of the grand Winter

Festival!"

"Festival! Festival!" roared the crowd.

"The night of the running of the bulls!"

"Release the bulls!" roared the crowd.

"Tonight marks the 300th year of the founding of our community and the 300th anniversary of our first Winter Festival. I believe tonight's bulls' run will prove one of the most exciting in memory. The rules are the same as always. Once the bulls are released, all our men, and any women so inclined (several women cheered), will chase them down. Let no bull escape, but please beware their horns and their hooves, for they are sharp and deadly. We don't want anyone hurt."

Cheers all around.

"Now, men of Evermere, take your places and get ready."

The men, hundreds strong, formed a line facing south (toward the docks). More than a few had swords in hand, though no armor did they wear, but most were barehanded — completely unarmed. All eyes faced south, past The Turtle. Once everyone was in position, someone handed the Duchess a large swatch of cloth that she held up high with one hand, anticipation growing in the crowd. "Is everyone ready?" she said looking around.

"Aye," yelled back many amongst the throng.

With a dramatic flourish, the Duchess swung her arm down, and yelled, "Release the bulls."

Seconds went by, the crowd silent, but no sound or sight of the bulls appeared; the men of Evermere poised on the balls of their feet to begin their run, their breathing heavy in anticipation.

The Duchess looked to the west side of the street, confused. "Release the bulls," she yelled louder this time. Again, nothing happened.

"What's the trouble?" yelled someone in the crowd. "Open the pen. We don't have all night; there's drinking to do."

"Is the pen door stuck again?" said the Duchess. "Not again this year; I thought that we had that fixed?"

A rattling of metal came from the west side of the street. It sounded as if someone was fumbling with a heavy metal latch.

"Release the bulls," yelled several in the crowd."

"Get the pen opened!" yelled others. The anticipation and frustration growing, people starting booing and yelling. "Release the bulls!" Release the bulls!" chanted the crowd.

"Where are my bulls?" shouted the Duchess. "Where are my bulls? Oh, wait," she said turning toward The Dancing Turtle.

"There they are!" she said, pointing. At that precise moment, every one of the gathered citizens of Evermere went silent and turned toward front of The Dancing Turtle. The Duchess's hand and all their eyes were affixed on the doorway where stood Tanch, Theta, Artol, Slaayde, Guj, Ravel, Bertha, and Glimador. Wide leers formed on the Evermerians' thin and ever so pale faces. Even as their lips parted, their upper canine teeth grew from normal proportions to more than three inches in length, their mouths hanging open, hungry: hungry for blood.

"Oh, shit," said Theta.

"Oh, shit," said Artol.

"Oh, shit," said Slaayde.

"Darn, I thought she liked me," said Tanch.

"Told you she was a bitch," said Bertha.

"Run bulls, run," shouted the crowd.

END

Thanks for reading *Blood, Fire, and Thorn*. I hope that you enjoyed it, and that you will consider taking a few moments to return to where you purchased it
(http://www.glenngthater.com/thank-you.html)
to leave a brief review. Reviews help my work gain visibility and provide me with valuable feedback about what my readers enjoyed and didn't enjoy about the story.

To be notified about my new book releases and any special offers or discounts regarding my books, please join my mailing list here: http://eepurl.com/vwubH

Thank you again, and please check out the other books in the Harbinger of Doom series.

BOOKS BY GLENN G. THATER

<u>THE HARBINGER OF DOOM SAGA</u>
GATEWAY TO NIFLEHEIM
THE FALLEN ANGLE
KNIGHT ETERNAL
DWELLERS OF THE DEEP
BLOOD, FIRE, AND THORN
GODS OF THE SWORD
THE SHAMBLING DEAD
MASTER OF THE DEAD
SHADOW OF DOOM
WIZARD'S TOLL
VOLUME 11+ (forthcoming)

HARBINGER OF DOOM
(Combines *Gateway to Nifleheim* and *The Fallen Angle* into a single volume)

THE HERO AND THE FIEND
(A novelette set in the Harbinger of Doom universe)

THE GATEWAY
(A novella length version of *Gateway to Nifleheim*)

THE DEMON KING OF BERGHER
(A short story set in the Harbinger of Doom universe)

Visit Glenn G. Thater's website at http://www.glenngthater.com for the most current list of my published books.

Join Glenn G. Thater's mailing list (for notifications of new book releases and special discounts): http://eepurl.com/vwubH

GLOSSARY

PLACES

THE REALMS

Asgard: legendary home of the gods
–**Bifrost**: mystical bridge between Asgard and Midgaard
–**Valhalla**: a realm of the gods where great warriors go after death
Helheim: one of the nine worlds; the realm of the dead
Midgaard: the world of man
–**Lomion**: a great kingdom of Midgaard
Nether Realms: realms of demons and devils
Nine Worlds, The: the nine worlds of creation
Nifleheim: the realm of the Lords of Nifleheim / Chaos Lords
Vaeden: paradise, lost
Yggdrasill: sacred tree that supports and/or connects the Nine Worlds

PLACES WITHIN THE KINGDOM OF LOMION

Dallassian Hills: large area of rocky hills; home to a large enclave of dwarves
Dor Caladrill:
Dor Eotrus: fortress and lands ruled by House Eotrus, north of Lomion City
––**Berrill's Bridge**: a large bridge over the Ottowhile River, northeast of Dor Eotrus, on the West Road
––**Markett**: a village east of Dor Eotrus, within

Eotrus demesne

--**Mindletown**: a town of 400 hundred folk, a few days northeast of Dor Eotrus, in Eotrus demesne

--**Odinhome, The**: temple to Odin located in Dor Eotrus; also used as a generic terms for temple/church of Odin.

--**Ottowhile River**: a large river northeast of Dor Eotrus, passable only via bridges for much of the year.

—**Outer Dor, The**: the town surrounding the fortress of Dor Eotrus. Also used generically as the name for any town surrounding a fortress.

-- **Rhentford**: small village on the road between Dor Eotrus and Mindletown.

—**Riker's Crossroads**: village at the southern border of Eotrus lands, at the crossroads that leads to Lomion City and Kern.

-- **Stebin Pass**: a pass through the foothills of the Kronar Mountains, northwest of Dor Eotrus.

-- **Trikan Point Village**: village east-northeast of Mindletown, in Eotrus demesne

—**Vermion Forest**: foreboding wood west of Dor Eotrus

— **Temple of Guymaog**: where the gateway was opened in the Vermion Forest

-- **Wortsford**: a northern town within Eotrus demesne

Dor Linden: fortress and lands ruled by House Mirtise, in the Linden Forest, southeast of Lomion City

Dor Lomion: fortress within Lomion City ruled by House Harringgold

Dor Malvegil: fortress and lands ruled by House Malvegil, southeast of Lomion City on the west bank of the Grand Hudsar River

Dor Valadon: fortress outside the City of Dover

Doriath Forest: woodland north of Lomion City

Dover, City of: large city situated at Lomion's southeastern border

Dyvers, City of: Lomerian city known for its quality metalworking

Grommel: a town known for southern gnomes

Kern, City of: Lomerian city to the northeast of Lomion City.

Kronar Mountains: a vast mountain range that marks the northern border of the Kingdom of Lomion

Lindenwood: a forest to the south of Lomion City, within which live the Lindonaire Elves

LOMION CITY (aka Lomion): capital city of the Kingdom of Lomion

–-**Dor Lomion**: fortress within Lomion City ruled by House Harringgold

–- **Channel, The**: moat around Lomion City, 150 ft wide by 30 ft deep; connected to Grand Hudsar Bay

–- **Grand Hudsar Bay**: the portion of the Grand Hudsar River that meets Lomion City's south and east borders.

–- **Great Meadow, The**: picturesque swath of grassland outside the city gates

—**Tammanian Hall**: high seat of government in Lomion; home of the High Council and the Council of Lords

—**Tower of the Arcane**: high seat of wizardom; in Lomion City

—**The Heights**: seedy section of Lomion City

—**Southeast**: dangerous section of Lomion City
Portland Vale: a town known for southern gnomes that are particularly skilled bridge building masons
Tarrows Hold: known for dwarves

PARTS FOREIGN

Azure Sea: vast ocean to the south of the Lomerian continent
Black Rock Tower: Glus Thorn's stronghold
Bourntown:
Darendor: dwarven realm of Clan Darendon
Dwarkendeep: a renowned dwarven stronghold
Dead Fens, The: mix of fen, bog, and swampland on the east bank of the Hudsar River, south of Dor Malvegil
Grand Hudsar River: south of Lomion City, it marks the eastern border of the kingdom
Emerald River: large river that branches off from the Hudsar at Dover
Ferd: Far-off city known for its fine goods
Jutenheim: island far to the south of the Lomerian continent.
Karthune Gorge: site of a famed battle involving the Eotrus
Kirth: Par Keld is from there
Kronar Mountains: foreboding mountain range that marks the northern border of the Kingdom of Lomion.
Lent
Minoc-by-the-Sea: coastal city
R'lyeh: a bastion for evil creatures; Sir Gabriel and Theta fought a great battle there in times

past.

Saridden, City of
Shandelon: famed gnomish city
Southron Isles: islands in the Azure Sea
Thoonbarrow: capital city of the Svarts
Tragoss Krell: city ruled by Thothian Monks
Tragoss Mor: large city far to the south of Lomion, at the mouth of the Hudsar River where it meets the Azure Sea. Ruled by Thothian Monks.

PEOPLE

PEOPLES OF MIDGAARD

Emerald elves
Lindonaire elves (from Linden Forest)
Doriath elves (from Doriath Forest)
Dallassian dwarves (from the Dallassian Hills). Typically four feet tall, plus or minus one foot.
Gnomes (northern and southern), typically three feet tall, plus or minus one foot.
Humans/Men: generic term for people. (In usage, sometimes includes gnomes, dwarves, and elves)
Lugron: a barbaric people from the northern mountains, on average, shorter and stockier than volsungs, and with higher voices.
Picts: a barbarian people
Stowron: pale, stooped people of feeble vision who've dwell in lightless caverns beneath the Kronar Mountains
Svarts (black elves), gray skin, large eyes, spindly limbs, three feet tall or so.
Vanyar Elves: legendary elven people

Volsungs: a generic term for the primary people/tribes populating the Kingdom of Lomion

HIGH COUNCIL OF LOMION

Selrach Rothtonn Tenzivel III: His Royal Majesty: King of Lomion
Aldros, Lord: Councilor
Aramere, Lady: Councilor representing the City of Dyvers
Balfor, Field Marshal: Councilor representing the Lomerian armed forces; Commander of the Lomerian army
Barusa of Alder, Lord: Chancellor of Lomion; eldest son of Mother Alder
Cartagian Tenzivel, Prince: Selrach's son, insane; Councilor representing the Royal House.
Dahlia, Lady: Councilor representing the City of Kern
Glenfinnen, Lord: Councilor representing the City of Dover
Harper Harringgold, Lord: Councilor representing Lomion City; Arch-Duke of Lomion City
Jhensezil, Lord Garet: Councilor representing the Churchmen; Preceptor of the Odion Knights
Morfin, Baron: Councilor (reportedly dead)
Slyman, Guildmaster: Councilor representing the guilds; Master of Guilds
Tobin Carthigast, Bishop: Councilor representing the Churchmen
Vizier, The (Grandmaster Rabrack Philistine): The Royal Wizard; Grandmaster and Councilor representing the Tower of the Arcane

NOBLE HOUSES

HOUSE ALDER (Pronounced All-der)

A leading, noble family of Lomion City. Their principal manor house is within the city's borders

Batholomew Alder: youngest son of Mother Alder

Bartol Alder: younger brother of Barusa, Myrdonian Knight

Barusa Alder, Lord: Chancellor of Lomion, eldest son of Mother Alder.

Blain Alder: younger brother of Barusa

Edith Alder: daughter of Blain; a child

Edwin Alder: son of Blain

Mother Alder: matriarch of the House; an Archseer of the Orchallian Order

Rom Alder: brother of Mother Alder

HOUSE EOTRUS (pronounced Eee-oh-tro`-sss)

The Eotrus rule the fortress of Dor Eotrus, the Outer Dor (a town outside the fortress walls) and the surrounding lands for many leagues.

Aradon Eotrus, Lord: Patriarch of the House (presumed dead)

Adolphus: a servant

Claradon Eotrus, Brother: (Clara-don) eldest son of Aradon, Caradonian Knight; Patriarch of the House; Lord of Dor Eotrus

Donnelin, Brother: House Cleric for the Eotrus (presumed dead)

Ector Eotrus, Sir: Third son of Aradon

Eleanor Malvegil Eotrus: (deceased) Wife of

Aradon Eotrus; sister of Torbin Malvegil.

Gabriel Garn, Sir: House Weapons Master (presumed dead, body possessed by Korrgonn)

Humphrey (Humph): Claradon's manservant

Jude Eotrus, Sir: Second son of Aradon (prisoner of the Shadow League)

Knights & Soldiers of the House:

– **Sergeant Artol**: 7 foot tall veteran warrior.

– **Sir Paldor Cragsmere**: a young knight; formerly, Sir Gabriel's squire

– **Sir Glimador Malvegil**: son of Lord Torbin Malvegil; can throw spells

– **Sir Indigo Eldswroth**: handsome, heavily muscled, and exceptionally tall knight

– **Sir Kelbor**

– **Sir Ganton**: called "the bull" or "bull"

– **Sir Trelman**

– **Sir Marzdan** (captain of the gate, deceased)

– **Sir Sarbek du Martegran** (acting Castellan of Dor Eotrus)

– **Sir Wyndham the Bold of Weeping Hollo**w: knight captain

– **Lieutenant, The**: veteran cavalry officer

– **Sergeant Vid**

– **Sergeant Lant**

– **Sergeant Baret**

– **Trooper Graham**

– Trooper Harsnip (deceased), Sergeant Balfin (deceased), Sir Miden (deceased), Sergeant Jerem (deceased), Sir Conrad (deceased), Sir Martin (deceased), Sir Bilson (deceased), Sir Glimron (deceased), Sir Talbot (deceased), Sir Dalken (deceased)

Malcolm Eotrus: Fourth son of Aradon

Ob A. Faz III: (Ahb A. Fahzz) Castellan and

Master Scout of Dor Eotrus; a gnome

Sirear Eotrus, Lady: daughter of August Eotrus (deceased)

Stern of Doriath: Master Ranger for the Eotrus (presumed dead)

Talbon of Montrose, Par: Former House Wizard for the Eotrus (presumed dead), son of Grandmaster (Par) Mardack

Tanch Trinagal, Par: (Trin-ah-ghaal) of the Blue Tower; Son of Sinch; House Wizard for the Eotrus. Aliases: Par Sinch; Par Sinch Malaban.

Sverdes, Leren: House physician

HOUSE HARRINGGOLD

Harper Harringgold, Lord: Arch-Duke of Lomion City; Lord of Dor Lomion, Patriarch of the House

Grim Fischer: agent of Harper, a gnome

Marissa Harringgold: daughter of Harper, former love interest of Claradon Eotrus.

Seran Harringgold, Sir: nephew of Harper

HOUSE MALVEGIL

Torbin Malvegil, Lord: Patriarch of the House; Lord of Dor Malvegil.

Landolyn, Lady: of House Adonael; Torbin's consort. Of part elven blood.

Eleanor Malvegil Eotrus: (deceased) Wife of Aradon Eotrus; sister of Torbin Malvegil.

Gedrun, Captain: a knight commander in service to Lord Malvegil

Glimador Malvegil, Sir: son of Torbin and Landolyn; working in the service of House Eotrus.
Gravemare, Hubert: Castellan of Dor Malvegil
Hogart: harbormaster of Dor Malvegil's port.
Karktan of Rivenwood, Master: Weapons Master for the Malvegils
Stoub of Rivenwood: Lord Malvegil's chief bodyguard; brother of Karktan
Torgrist, Brother: Dor Malvegil's high cleric.
Troopers Bern, Brant, Conger: Malvegillian soldiers

HOUSE TENZIVEL (the Royal House)

King Selrach Rothtonn Tenzivel III: His Royal Majesty: King of Lomion
Cartagian Tenzivel, Prince: Selrach's son; insane.
Dramadeens: royal bodyguards for House Tenzivel
--Korvalan of Courwood, Captain: Commander of the Dramadeens.

OTHER NOBLE HOUSES OF LOMION

House Tavermain
House Grondeer
House Dantrel
House Forndin
A minor House loyal to and located within Eotrus lands. Their major holding is known as Forndin Manor.
Alana Forndin, Lady: matriarch of the House
Sir Erendin of Forndin Manor: eldest son of

the House (deceased)

Sir Miden of Forndin Manor: younger brother of Erendin (deceased)

Sir Talbot of Forndin Manor: younger brother of Erendin (deceased)

House Hanok

A minor House loyal to and located within Eotrus lands. Their major holding is known as Hanok Keep.

Sir Bareddal of Hanok Keep: in service to the Eotrus (deceased)

OTHER HOUSES AND GROUPS

CLAN DARENDON OF DARENDOR
Royal clan from the dwarven kingdom

Bornyth Trollsbane, High King of Clan Darendon.

Galibar the Great: the prince of Darendor, first son to Bornyth and heir to Clan Darendon

Jarn Yarspitter: councilor to Bornyth

THE BLACK HAND
A brotherhood of Assassins

Brethren, The: term the assassins use for fellow members of The Hand.

Grandmistress, The: the leader of The Hand

Mallick Fern: an assassin; The Hand's second ranking agent

Weater the Mouse: a Hand leader

BROOD TET MONTU OF SVARTLEHEIM
The royal house of the svarts

Diresvarts: svart wizard-priests

Guyphoon Garumptuss tet Montu: high king of Thoonbarrow, Patriarch of Brood tet Montu, Master of the Seven Stratems, and Lord of all Svartleheim, offspring of Guyphoon Pintalia of the Windy Ways, Traymoor Garumptuss the Bold, and Trantmain lin Backus tet Montu, great king of the undermountains
Cardakeen rack Mortha: a svart seer
Orator, The: the spokesman for the svart king

THE LORDS OF NIFLEHEIM AND THEIR MINIONS
Azathoth: god worshipped by the Lords of Nifleheim and The Shadow League/The League ofLight; his followers call him the 'one true god.'.
Arioch: a Lord of Nifleheim
Bhaal: a Lord of Nifleheim; came through the gateway in the Vermion but was banished back by Angle Theta
Hecate: a Lord of Nifleheim.
Korrgonn, Lord Gallis: son of Azathoth
Mortach: (aka Mikel): a Lord of Nifleheim; killed by Angle Theta
—**Reskalan**: demonic foot soldiers in service to the Lords of Nifleheim
—**Zymog**: a reskalan
--**Brigandir**: supernatural warrior(s) of Nifleheim
--**Einheriar**: supernatural warriors of Nifleheim

THE ASGARDIAN GODS
Odin (the All-father)
Thor, Tyr, Frey, Freya, Heimdall, Loki
--**Valkyries**: sword maidens of the gods. They choose worthy heroes slain in battle and conduct

them to Valhalla.

OTHER GODS
Dagon of the Deep: appears as a giant lizard; lives in caverns beneath an uncharted island deep in the Azure Sea.
-- **Dwellers of the Deep**: very large, bipedal sea creatures that worship Dagon.
Thoth:

GREAT BEASTS, MONSTERS, CREATURES, ANIMALS
Barrow Wight
Blood Lord: legendary fiends that drink blood
Dire Wolves: extremely large breed of wolves
Duergar: mythical undead creatures
Dwellers of the Deep: worshippers of Dagon; huge, bipedal fishlike creatures
Fire Wyrm or "Wyrms": dragons
Giants (aka Jotuns):
Ogres:
Leviathan: a huge sea creature
Saber-cat: saber toothed tiger
Tranteers: the lithe, speedy horses bred in Dover
Trolls, Mountain: mythical creatures of the high mountains
Wendigo: monster of legend

THE EOTRUS EXPEDITION

THE CREW OF *THE BLACK FALCON*
Slaayde, Dylan: Captain of *The Black Falcon*
Bertha Smallbutt: ship's quartermaster
Bire Cabinboy: ship's cabin boy
Chert: a young seaman
Darg Tran, son of Karn, of old House Elowine: ship's navigator
Eolge: a crewman (deceased)
Fizdar Firstbar "the corsair": former first mate (presumed dead)
Guj: boatswain. A half-lugron.
N'Paag: First Mate
Old Mock: a crewman (deceased)
Ravel: ship's trader and medic
Tug, Little: Near 7-foot tall part-lugron seaman; Old Fogey — Tug's battle hammer

THE PASSENGERS OF THE BLACK FALCON
Sergeant Artol: 7 foot tall veteran warrior.
Claradon Eotrus, Brother: (Clara-don) eldest son of Aradon, Caradonian Knight; Patriarch of the House; Lord of Dor Eotrus
Dolan Silk: Theta's manservant
Ganton, Sir (the Bull): a knight of House Eotrus
Kayla Kazeran: part Lindonaire elf, rescued from slavery in Tragoss Mor
Kelbor, Sir: a knight of House Eotrus
Lant, Sergeant: a soldier of House Eotrus
Lomerian Soldiers: a squadron of soldiers of House Harringgold, assigned to assist House Eotrus.
Malvegil, Sir Glimador: first cousin to

273

Claradon; son of Lord Malvegil

Malvegillian Archers: a squad of soldiers assigned to assist House Eotrus by Lord Malvegil

Ob A. Faz III: (Ahb A. Fahzz) Castellan and Master Scout of Dor Eotrus; a gnome

Paldor Cragsmere, Sir: a young knight of House Eotrus, formerly, Sir Gabriel's squire

Seran Harringgold, Sir: nephew of Arch-Duke Harper Harringgold — assigned to assist House Eotrus

Tanch Trinagal, Par: (Trin-ah-ghaal) of the Blue Tower; Son of Sinch; House Wizard for the Eotrus. Aliases: Par Sinch; Par Sinch Malaban.

Theta, Lord Angle (aka Thetan): a knight errant from a far-off land across the sea. Sometimes called the Harbinger of Doom

Trelman, Sir: a knight of House Eotrus

Vid, Sergeant: a soldier of House Eotrus

THE ALDER EXPEDITION

THE CREW/PASSENGERS OF THE GRAY TALON

Alder Marines: squadrons of soldiers from House Alder

Bartol Alder: younger brother of Barusa; a Myrdonian Knight

Blain Alder: younger brother of Barusa

DeBoors, Milton: (The Duelist of Dyvers). A mercenary

Edwin Alder: son of Blain

Kaledon of the Gray Waste: a Pict mercenary

Kleig: Captain of The Grey Talon

Knights of Kalathen: elite mercenaries that work for DeBoors

Myrdonian Knights: squadron of knights assigned to House Alder

THE LEAGUE OF LIGHT EXPEDITION

THE CREW/PASSENGERS OF *THE WHITE ROSE*

Brackta Finbal, Par: an archmage of The League of Light

Ezerhauten, Lord: Commander of Sithian Mercenary Company

Frem Sorlons: captain of the Sithian's Pointmen Squadron

Ginalli, Father: High Priest of Azathoth, Arkon of The League of Light.

Glus Thorn, Par: an archmage of the League of Light

Hablock, Par: an archmage of the League of Light (deceased)

Keld, Par of Kerth: a middle-aged wizard of the League of Light, short, stocky, balding, and nervous.

Lugron: a barbaric people from the northern mountains, on average, shorter and stockier than volsungs, and with higher voices.

Mason: a stone golem created by The Keeper of Tragoss Mor; companion to Stev Keevis.

Morsmun, Par: an archmage of the League of Light (deceased)

Mort Zag: a red-hued giant

Oris, Par: an elderly wizard of the League of

Light; former mentor of Par Keld.

Ot, Par: an archmage of the League of Light (deceased)

Pointmen, The: an elite squadron of the Sithian Mercenary Company

Rascelon, Captain Rastinfan: Captain of *The White Rose*

Rhund, Par: a wizard of the League of Light

Sevare Zendrack, Par: Squadron wizard for the Pointmen

Sithians: mercenaries under the command of Ezerhauten; some are soldiers, some are knights

Stev Keevis Arkguardt: an elven archwizard from the Emerald Forest allied with The League of Light; former apprentice of The Keeper

Teek: lugron guard/jailor

Weldin, Par: a wizard of the League of Light

Thorn, Par (Master) Glus: an archwizard of the League of Light; a sorcerer

–-**Lasifer, Par**: Glus Thorn's gnome assistant/apprentice.

–-**Nord**: a stowron in Thorn's employ

Tribik: lugron guard/jailor

Varak du Mace: First Mate of *The White Rose*

SITHIAN MERCENARY COMPANY

Ezerhauten, Lord: Commander

Frem Sorlons: Captain, Pointmen Squadron

Landru, Par: a squadron wizard (deceased)

Miles de Gant: a knight; son of Count de Gant

Rewes of Ravenhollow, Sir: a knight (deceased)

Tremont of Wyndum: a knight captain

THE POINTMEN (an elite squadron of the Sithian Mercenary Company)
Frem Sorlons: captain, Pointmen Squadron
Sevare Zendrack, Par: squadron wizard for the Pointmen
Putnam, Sergeant: Pointmen,1st Squad
Boatman: Pointmen (deceased)
Borrel: Pointmen; a lugron
Bryton: Pointmen (deceased)
Carroll, Sir: Pointmen; a knight
Clard: Pointmen; a lugron
Dirnel: Pointmen; a lugron (deceased)
Held: Pointmen (deceased)
Jorna: Pointmen (deceased)
Lex: Pointmen
Little Storrl: Pointmen,1st Squad; a young lugron
Maldin, Sergeant: Pointmen,2nd Squad, (Badly wounded, spear through chest)
Moag: Pointmen,1st squad; a lugron
Roard, Sir: Pointmen,1st Squad; a knight (deceased)
Royce, Sir: Pointmen; a knight
Torak: Pointmen; a lugron
Ward: Pointmen
Wikkle: Pointmen; a lugron

MILITANT AND MYSTIC ORDERS
Caradonian Knights: priestly order; patron— Odin
Churchmen: a generic term for the diverse group of priests and knights of various orders.
Freedom Guardsmen: soldiery of Tragoss Mor
Grontor's Bonebreakers: a mercenary

company. The Iugron, Teek and Tribik belonged to it.

Halsbad's Freeswords: a mercenary company that Pellan once worked for.

Kalathen, Knights of: mercenary knights that work for Milton DeBoors

Myrdonians: Royal Lomerian Knights

Odions, The: patron—Odin; Preceptor—Lord Jhensezil; Chapterhouse: in Lomion City

Orchallian Order, The: an Order of Seers; Mother Alder is one of them.

Order of the Arcane: the wizard members of the Tower of the Arcane

Rangers Guild, The: Chapterhouse – Doriath Hall in Lomion City; Preceptor: Sir Samwise Sluug; loyal to House Harringgold.

Sithian Knights, The: Preceptor—Lord Ezerhauten

Sundarian Knights: patron: Thor; Preceptor: Sir Hithron du Maris; Chapterhouse: hidden in Tragoss Mor

Tyr, Knights of (aka Tyrians): patron—Tyr

THE EVERMERIANS
Duchess Morgovia of House Falstad: ruler of Evermere

Slint: aka the "scarecrow"

PEOPLE OF MINDLETOWN
A town of several hundred folks within Eotrus demesne. The Odinhall is their most secure building.

Alchemist: town council member of Mindletown

Baker, The and sons: townsfolk of Mindletown

Butcher: town council member of Mindletown

Cobbler: townsman of Mindletown; lives across the street from the alchemist
Constable Granger: constable of Mindletown
Farmer Smythe: a townsman of Mindletown (deceased)
Iceman: an ice merchant that sells his ice to Mindletown; hails from the northwest.
Innman: an innkeeper in Mindletown
Mikar Trapper: a trapper that sells his wares in Mindletown
Miller and his sons: townsmen of Mindletown
Old Cern: town elder of Mindletown
Old Marvik: a Mindletown merchant that lived across from the alchemist
Pellan: the "beardless dwarf"; a town council member of Mindletown and former Captain in Dor Eotrus's guard
Tanner, Mileson: a townsman of Mindletown
Thom Prichard: a townsman of Mindletown (deceased)
Wheelwright and his wife: townsfolk of Mindletown (both deceased)

OTHERS OF NOTE

Azura du Marnian, the Seer: Seer based in Tragoss Mor
Gorb: Azura's bodyguard (deceased)
Rimel Stark: Azura's bodyguard and famed Freesword
Dirkben: Azura's bodyguard (deceased)
Brondel Cragsmere, Sire: father of Sir Paldor of Dor Eotrus
Coriana Sorlons: daughter of Frem Sorlons
Dark Sendarth: famed assassin in league with

House Harringgold and House Tenzivel

Du Maris, Sir Hithron: Preceptor of the Sundarian Chapterhouse in Tragoss Mor; from Dor Caladrill

Halsbad: a mercenary leader

Harbinger of Doom, The: legendary, perhaps mythical being that led a rebellion against Azathoth

Jaros, the Blood Lord: foe of Sir Gabriel Garn

Keeper, The: elven "keeper" of the Orb of Wizard beneath Tragoss Mor

Krisona, Demon-Queen: foe of Sir Gabriel Garn

Kroth, Garon: newly appointed High Magister

Sluug, Sir Samwise: Preceptor of the Rangers Guild; Lord of Doriath Hall

Mardack, Grandmaster (Par) of Montrose: famed wizard; father of Par Talbon of Montrose

McDuff the Mighty: a dwarf of many talents

Pipkorn, Grandmaster: (aka Rascatlan) former Grand Master of the Tower of the Arcane. A wizard.

Prior Finch: a prior of Thoth in Tragoss Mor (deceased)

Sarq: a Thothian Monk. Known as the Champion of Tragoss Mor

Shadow League, The (aka The League of Shadows; aka The League of Light): alliance of individuals and groups collectively seeking to bring about the return of Azathoth to Midgaard

Sluug, Sir (Lord) Samwise: Preceptor of the Rangers Guild; Master of Doriath Hall

Snor Slipnet: Patriarch of Clan Rumbottle; a gnome

Talidousen: Former Grand Master of the Tower

of the Arcane; created the fabled Rings of the Magi.

Thothian monks: monks that rule Tragoss Mor and worship Thoth

Throng-Baz : an ancient people that used runic script

Valas Tearn: an assassin said to have slain a thousand men; foe of Sir Gabriel Garn

Valkyries: sword maidens of the gods. They choose worthy heroes slain in battle and conduct them to Valhalla.

Vanyar Elves: legendary elven people

TITLES

Archmage / Archwizard: honorific title for a highly skilled wizard

Archseer: honorific title for a highly skilled seer

Arkon: a leader/general in service to certain gods and religious organizations

Freesword: an independent soldier or mercenary

Grandmaster: honorific title for a senior wizard of the Tower of the Arcane.

Hedge Wizard: a wizard specializing in potions and herbalism, and/or minor magics

High Magister: a member of Lomion's Tribunal.

Leren: (pronounced Lee-rhen) generic title for a physician

Magling: a young or inexperienced wizard; also, a derogatory term for a wizard

Master Oracle: a highly skilled seer

Par: honorific title for a wizard

Seer (sometimes, "Seeress"): women with supernatural powers to see past/present/future

events.
Wizard (aka Mage, Sorcerer, etc.): practitioners of magic

THINGS

<u>MISCELLANY</u>

Alder Stone, The: a Seer Stone held by House Alder

Amulet of Escandell: a magical device that detects the presence of danger; gifted to Claradon by Pipkorn

Articles of the Republic: the Lomerian constitution

Asgardian Daggers: legendary weapons created in the first age of Midgaard. They can harm creatures of Nifleheim.

Axe of Bigby the Bold: made of Mithril; gifted to Ob by Pipkorn

Book of the Nobility: treatise containing the traditional Lomerian laws with respect to the nobility.

Chapterhouse: base/manor/fortress of a knightly order

Dargus Dal: Asgardian dagger, previously Gabriel's, now Theta's

Dor: a generic Lomerian word meaning "fortress"

du Marnian Stone, The: a Seer Stone held by Azura du Marnian

Dyvers Blades: finely crafted steel swords

Ether, The: invisible medium that exists everywhere and within which the weave of magic travels/exists.

Ghost Ship Box: calls forth an illusory ship; created by Pipkorn and gifted to Claradon.

Granite Throne, The: the name of the king's throne in Lomion City. To "sit the granite throne" means to be the king.

Mages and Monsters: a popular, tactical war game that uses miniatures

Mearn: comes in a jar

Mithril: precious metal of great strength and relative lightness

Essence of Nightshade: a lethal, fast-acting poison; carried by Black Hand agents as suicide pills to thwart capture

Orb of Wisdom: mystical crystal spheres that can be used to open portals between worlds.

Ragnarok: prophesied battle between the Aesir and the Nifleites.

Ranal: a black metal, hard as steel and half as heavy, weapons made of it can affect creatures of chaos

Rings of the Magi: amplify a wizard's power; twenty created by Talidousen

Seer Stones: magical "crystal balls" that can see far-off events.

Shards of Darkness: the remnants of the destroyed Orb of Wisdom from the Temple of Guymaog.

Spottle: a dice game that uses a live frog

Sventeran Stone, The: a Seer Stone loaned to the Malvegils by the Svarts.

Tribunal: the highest-ranking judiciary body in the Kingdom of Lomion; members of the tribunal are called "High Magisters."

Valusian steel: famed for its quality

Weave of Magic; aka the Magical Weave: the source of magic
Worfin Dal: "Lord's Dagger," Claradon's Asgardian dagger
Wotan Dal: "Odin's Dagger"; gifted to Theta by Pipkorn.
Yggdrasill: sacred tree that supports and/or connects the Nine Worlds

LANGUAGES OF MIDGAARD
Lomerian: the common tongue of Lomion and much of the known world
Magus Mysterious: olden language of sorcery
Militus Mysterious: olden language of sorcery used by certain orders of knights
Old High Lomerian: an olden dialect of Lomerian
Throng Baz: a dead language
Svartish: language of the svarts
Trollspeak: language of the mountain trolls

COMBAT MANEUVERS, TECHNIQUES, AND STYLES
Dyvers' thrusting maneuvers
Dwarvish overhand strikes
Cernian technique
Sarnack maneuvers
Lengian cut and thrust style
Valusian thrust

MILITARY UNITS OF LOMION
Squad: a unit of soldiers typically composed of 3 to 8 soldiers, but it can be as few as 2 or as many as 15 soldiers.
Squadron: a unit of soldiers typically composed

of two to four squads, totaling about 30 soldiers.

Cavalry Squadron or Troop: same as "squadron" but often has additional support troops to tend to the horses and supplies.

Company: a military unit composed of 4 squadrons, totaling about 120 - 150 soldiers. Mercenary Companies can be of any size, the word "company" in their title, notwithstanding.

Brigade: a military unit composed of 8 companies, totaling about 1,000 soldiers

Regiment: a military unit composed of 4 brigades, totaling about 4,000 – 5,000 soldiers

Corps or Army: a military unit composed of 4 regiments and support troops, totaling about 20,000 – 25,000 soldiers

MILITARY RANKS OF LOMION

(from junior to senior)

Trooper

Corporal

Sergeant

Lieutenant (a knight is considered equivalent in rank to a Lieutenant)

Captain

Knight Captain (for units with Knights)

Commander

Knight Commander (for units with Knights)

Lord Commander (if a noble)

General (for Regiment sized units or larger)

ABOUT GLENN G. THATER

For more than twenty-five years, Glenn G. Thater has written works of fiction and historical fiction that focus on the genres of epic fantasy and sword and sorcery. His published works of fiction include the first ten volumes of the *Harbinger of Doom* saga: *Gateway to Nifleheim*; *The Fallen Angle*; *Knight Eternal*; *Dwellers of the Deep*; *Blood, Fire, and Thorn*; *Gods of the Sword*; *The Shambling Dead*; *Master of the Dead*; *Shadow of Doom*; *Wizard's Toll*; the novella, *The Gateway*; and the novelette, *The Hero and the Fiend*.

Mr. Thater holds a Bachelor of Science degree in Physics with concentrations in Astronomy and Religious Studies, and a Master of Science degree in Civil Engineering, specializing in Structural Engineering. He has undertaken advanced graduate study in Classical Physics, Quantum Mechanics, Statistical Mechanics, and Astrophysics, and is a practicing licensed professional engineer specializing in the multidisciplinary alteration and remediation of buildings, and the forensic investigation of building failures and other disasters.

Mr. Thater has investigated failures and collapses of numerous structures around the

United States and internationally. Since 1998, he has served on the American Society of Civil Engineers' Forensic Engineering Divison (FED), is a Past Chairman of that Division's Executive Committee and FED's Committee on Practices to Reduce Failures. Mr. Thater is a LEED (Leadership in Energy and Environmental Design) Accredited Professional and has testified as an expert witness in the field of structural engineering before the Supreme Court of the State of New York.

Mr. Thater is an author of numerous scientific papers, magazine articles, engineering textbook chapters, and countless engineering reports. He has lectured across the United States and internationally on such topics as the World Trade Center collapses, bridge collapses, and on the construction and analysis of the dome of the United States Capitol in Washington D.C.

CONNECT WITH ME ONLINE

My Website:
http://www.glenngthater.com

To be notified about my new book releases and any special offers or discounts regarding my books, please join my mailing list here: http://eepurl.com/vwubH

My Twitter Page:
http://twitter.com/GlennGThater

BOOKS BY GLENN G. THATER

THE HARBINGER OF DOOM SAGA
GATEWAY TO NIFLEHEIM
THE FALLEN ANGLE
KNIGHT ETERNAL
DWELLERS OF THE DEEP
BLOOD, FIRE, AND THORN
GODS OF THE SWORD
THE SHAMBLING DEAD
MASTER OF THE DEAD
SHADOW OF DOOM
WIZARD'S TOLL
VOLUME 11+ *forthcoming*

THE HERO AND THE FIEND
(A novelette set in the Harbinger of Doom universe)

THE GATEWAY
(A novella length version of *Gateway to Nifleheim*)

HARBINGER OF DOOM
(Combines *Gateway to Nifleheim* and *The Fallen Angle* into a single volume)

THE DEMON KING OF BERGHER
(A short story set in the Harbinger of Doom universe)

Visit Glenn G. Thater's website at http://www.glenngthater.com for the most current list of my published books.

Printed in Great Britain
by Amazon

62214653R00173